# RISKING IT ALL

# RISKING IT ALL

## SM KOZ

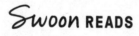

Swoon READS

New York

A Swoon Reads Book

An imprint of Feiwel and Friends and Macmillan Publishing Group, LLC
175 Fifth Avenue, New York, NY 10010

Our books may be purchased in bulk for promotional, educational, or
business use. Please contact your local bookseller or the Macmillan
Corporate and Premium Sales Department at (800) 221-7945 ext. 5442 or by
email at MacmillanSpecialMarkets@macmillan.com.

Library of Congress Control Number: 2018955581
ISBN 978-1-250-31366-9 (hardcover) / ISBN 978-1-250-31367-6 (ebook)

Book design by Liz Dresner

First edition, 2019

10  9  8  7  6  5  4  3  2  1

swoonreads.com

To my dad, who taught me
"What doesn't kill you makes you stronger"

# RISKING IT ALL

# CHAPTER 1
## PAIGE

**"Fired up!"**

"Fired up!"

"Feeling good!"

"Feeling good!"

"Motivated!"

"Motivated!"

"Ded—"

Alex, the commander of Alpha Battalion, stops our jogging cadence abruptly as Commander Anderson, the dean of students, approaches him.

"Commander Jernigan!" the dean yells, motioning for Alex to join him.

Alex jogs over to the dean and a guy who has stepped out from behind him. This new guy clearly doesn't belong here. He's wearing jeans, a long-sleeved red T-shirt, and stylish sneakers that won't last for a single run during PT—physical training. The most obvious sign he's not a Wallingford student, though, is his full head of blond hair hanging over his eyes and ears.

Alex makes eye contact with me and motions for me to take over. "Lieutenant Commander Durant is in charge," he says to our battalion before continuing with the dean and the new guy.

I step out of line to put myself next to the ten rows of cadets and continue with the cadence.

"Dedicated!" I yell, getting us back to where we were.

"Dedicated!" the cadets reply, their heavy footsteps keeping time as we pound out our five miles.

"All right!"

"All right!"

This added responsibility puts more pep in my step than usual. As lieutenant commander, I don't get this job as often as I'd like, though I do have plenty of other responsibilities.

"Everybody!" I yell as we pass under an arch and onto the gravel path that circles our campus. I take a deep breath and smile at the nice view of the mountains. The trees are a little barer than they were yesterday, the ground is littered with a few more red and gold leaves, and mist rises from the valleys, despite it being the middle of the afternoon. If it were up to me, there would only be one season and it'd be fall.

"Everybody!" the cadets reply.

"Fired up!"

"Fired up!"

When we start on our second lap around campus, Alex and the new guy join us. I drop back into line, but Alex motions for me to fall out of formation to stand next to the new guy. I do as he orders and try to get a better look at the guy while staring straight ahead.

He's shuffling his feet, slumping his shoulders, and huffing and puffing despite just starting to jog at what is really a leisurely pace. Then he stops. He literally stops on the gravel, causing three cadets to run into him, knocking him to the ground.

"What the hell?!" he barks, sending them a glare as they sidestep him and return to their places in line.

"Get up," I say as the rest of our battalion pulls away.

"No," he replies, brushing dirt from his sleeve.

"It wasn't a request; it was an order. Get up."

"Make me."

My jaw almost drops at his display of disrespect, but I quickly catch myself. I can't let him think he's got the upper hand.

"Get up now or you'll be disciplined."

"Fine. I'll get up," he says, standing with a smirk.

I nod, happy he came to his senses. "We'll need to sprint to catch up to them. Commander Jernigan doesn't tolerate cadets who fall behind," I reply, looking at the group now far away. "I hope those shoes are more comfortable than they loo—" Where'd he go?

Turning around, I see him sauntering along the path to a bench. Then he sits down. On the bench. During PT.

"Cadet!" I yell. "Your behavior is completely unacceptable!"

"My name's Logan," he grumbles before raising his fist into the air and then jutting his middle finger out. This time, my jaw does drop.

It's clear by this guy's attitude he's not here by choice. Wallingford Academy has split admission: half of the cadets, like me, apply and have dreams of a military academy after graduation, and half are sent here by their parents or the court when all other attempts at correcting their behavior have failed. Most of these delinquents, or DQs as we call them, come at the start of a semester, though, not four weeks in. And they aren't nearly as disrespectful. The drill sergeant usually gets that out of them during their two-week boot camp.

As I begin marching toward the new cadet, Alex comes racing back at us. "What's the problem, Paige?"

"No problem," I reply, shaking my head and smoothing back my black hair, making sure none of it has come free from my braid. I don't want Alex to think I can't handle the new guy. I've never had a problem with DQs before, and I'm not about to start now.

"Why's Evans sitting down?"

"He's being petulant. I've got it, though."

"Move your ass now!" Alex yells, ignoring me and causing my jaw to tense and my blood pressure to rise higher than it's been throughout our run. Later, once we're alone, I'll call him out on this. I'm a great cadet and even better officer. Given two more minutes, I would've gotten the new guy—Logan Evans, apparently—in line. Alex should know that. Besides being my commander, he's one of my best friends.

The new guy gives Alex the finger, and suddenly my annoyance disappears. I cringe, waiting for the punishment that's coming. Poor Evans doesn't stand a chance.

Alex stalks over to the bench with narrowed eyes and slow, confident steps. "You will never do that to me again. Understand?"

"I'll do whatever the hell I want," Evans mutters, meeting Alex's eyes briefly before dropping his gaze to the ground.

"The correct answer is 'Yes, sir, Commander Jernigan.'" He rests his hands on his knees and bends down until he's eye level with Evans. "This cocky attitude of yours might have worked where you're from, but it's not going to work here. You will spend your personal time tonight cleaning all the whiteboards in the classrooms."

"Screw you," Evans says, standing and trying to push his way past Alex. Except Alex has at least fifty pounds more muscle, so he doesn't budge, and Evans has to squeeze past him.

"Make that two nights of personal time. Want to try for three? I have no problem standing here the entire afternoon and taking away all your free time for the rest of the semester. In fact, I'd enjoy it."

Evans pauses, his back to Alex, and his shoulders fall.

"It's your choice," Alex says.

Evans slowly turns around and starts jogging at what really is more of a walking pace along the gravel path. Alex nods. "Good decision, cadet." Then he speeds up to join the rest of our battalion while I accompany Evans. At this pace, we'll never catch the others, but at least he's trying and will eventually get the miles in.

I consider starting a new cadence song with him, but he's already out of breath and red-faced. There's no way he can yell on top of running.

Unfortunately, our crawling pace is going to make me miss the rest of PT. I'll need to figure out a time to get my push-ups and pull-ups in, although I doubt I'll have a chance until late tonight since right after PT, I have cross-country practice, then it's dinner, followed by study hall, and then two hours of personal time, most of which will be spent at debate club. If I'm quick, I can probably fit in my workout after debate club and before lights-out at 10:00 P.M.

Other than debate club and my second round of PT thanks to Evans, it's an exact replica of yesterday. That's one of the nice things about Wallingford—you always know what to expect. There are never any surprises.

Without warning, he turns right onto the lawn, and then sprints between two buildings. Well, it's a sprint for him. I could easily catch up, but I stand staring at his back instead.

So much for no surprises. Where did he find that spurt of energy? And where in the world is he going? The only thing behind those buildings is the staff parking lot and then forest leading up the mountain. Unless he plans on committing grand theft auto or living in the wild, there's nothing for him back there.

With a sigh, I pick up my pace and follow in his footsteps, twice as quickly as he went. It takes a few minutes, but I find him sitting on a yellow cement parking block with his elbows on his knees and his head in his hands.

"You have to finish PT," I say, stepping in front of him.

"Nope."

"Yes."

"Look," he says, raising his head, "you'd have better luck convincing me to jump off a cliff than you will getting me to run five miles. It's not going to happen. There's no way in hell I'm doing all this military shit."

He doesn't have a choice. The only way to avoid the strict routine is to leave Wallingford, which I imagine isn't an option for him. But maybe it is. Only one person knows the answer to that. "You can take it up with the dean. Let's go to his office."

With a nod, he says, "I'll head over there in a minute," before stretching out his legs and leaning back on his arms, as though he's enjoying a causal summer afternoon lounging around a pool.

Except it's not summer, there's nothing casual about Wallingford, and our pool is only used for swimming laps, not floating on a raft and soaking up the sun. "I've got to get back to PT. We need to go now."

"I don't need a chaperone."

"I'm sure you understand why I don't trust you to go on your own."

He remains silent, so I continue. "You are free to mess up your life all you want, but I won't have you messing up mine. I need to get back to PT, but I can't do that until you either rejoin PT or I deliver you to the dean."

He stands, but not before sending an annoyed look in my direction. "Fine, let's go to the dean's office."

We cross through the parking lot to a sidewalk and then quietly make our way to the administrative building.

"You've delivered me," he says when he reaches for the door. "You can go back to your pack of brainwashed robots."

"Excuse me?" I reply, my hands landing on my hips. His disrespect seems to have no end.

He waves his hand in the general direction of the athletic field, where my battalion should be done with their run by now. "I'd hate to mess up your life. Go back to whatever it is you're supposed to be doing."

I grit my teeth and bite my tongue. He needs a lesson on how to behave around here, but that responsibility will need to fall on his peer mentor. I can't be expected to turn him around in only a few minutes.

Hopefully whoever is paired with him will be able to do it quickly because Alex will have zero patience with him if he keeps acting like this. Fortunately, it usually doesn't take long. My last match was the beginning of my junior year, and it took less than a semester for my good behavior to rub off on her. She went from a C to an A average and from picking fights in her spare time to being a key player on the soccer team.

As far as my responsibility to Evans, it ends here. Since he refused to do PT, I brought him to the dean. Nothing more can be expected of me. I turn on my heel before sprinting back to my battalion.

Throughout the rest of PT, I can't stop thinking about the guy. He might be the worst cadet I've ever seen. Sure, all DQs have issues, but most of them respond to our threats. And want to avoid the dean at all costs, not volunteer to see him. He's an unusual one, for sure.

I have no idea what the dean's plan is for him, but boot camp really needs to be in his future. Maybe some hard-core drill-sergeant treatment will be the kick in the pants he needs.

Once we're done with our exercises, I start to head for my dorm with my roommate, Leah, who also happens to be my best friend. Suddenly, a flash of red between a cluster of pine trees catches my attention. I turn in the direction and stare.

"What's going on?" Leah asks when she notices I've stopped.

"I thought I saw something. Back there," I reply, pointing. It was the exact color of Evans's shirt, but it couldn't be Evans. The dean wouldn't allow him to wander around campus alone.

Squinting, she says, "I don't see anything. It was probably just a squirrel."

Convinced she must be right, I nod. For some reason, I've got Evans on my mind. It's ridiculous. He's just another DQ, one who may not even be here by tomorrow morning. It's time to forget about him and how he messed up my PT so I can focus on the important things I've got going on.

Like the urgent discussion I need to have with my dad.


The next morning, in the mess hall, I follow Alex from the buffet line to where Leah and some of our other friends are seated.

They're congratulating Chris on his acceptance into the Naval Academy, which he just received yesterday. I start to say something, but I'm interrupted by a voice behind me. "Lieutenant Commander Durant."

I turn around to find the dean standing there. My stomach drops and the two bites of breakfast I've taken feel like a bowling ball weighing me down. I quickly review everything I've done the past twenty-four hours, but can't come up with anything that would lead to a visit by the dean. I got As on my two tests. All the girls passed their room inspections. Lights-out was seamless. I did get frustrated at cross-country practice when I lost to a junior right in the last 100 yards, but I took out my frustration by running sprints. No one should have a problem with that.

"Sir, yes, sir," I say, sitting at attention, not letting my voice give away my nerves.

"Please come to my office after breakfast." Lowering his voice, he says, "I have something important to discuss with you regarding the new cadet."

I gulp and nod as my stomach drops even lower. Evans. Was I not imagining things in the forest yesterday? Was he somehow sneaking around? That's impossible . . . unless he never went to the dean after I dropped him off.

How could I make such a careless mistake? I should've escorted him into the office. What if he went AWOL? Will the dean hold me responsible? "Yes, sir," I say with another gulp. "I'll report to your office immediately after breakfast."

He turns around without another word and leaves the mess hall.

Leah lowers her fork and gives me a sympathetic look. "What happened?" she asks.

I crack my knuckles. "I'm not sure." I don't want to admit my mistake in front of the other officers.

"Did you sneak off campus?" Deborah, the girl to my left, asks. "No."

"Were you caught using your phone during school hours?" Alyssa, a girl seated across the table, asks.

"No."

"Are you hiding Twizzlers in your underwear drawer again?" Alex asks with a grin.

I wrinkle my nose at him. Back when I was a freshman, I thought I could keep candy in my room for a late-night snack. Turns out not even your underwear drawer is sacred. It was found within two days, and I ended up in detention for the infraction. That's also when I met Alex, who was there because he kissed a girl in the hallway between classes. Apparently, they didn't know—or didn't care—about the no-PDA-on-campus rule.

That, three years ago, was the first and last time I disobeyed a rule.

"Hey, maybe it's good news," Leah says with a hopeful smile.

I bite my lip, crack my knuckles again, and nod, although it's not. Nothing positive happened between me and Evans yesterday. I try to take a bite of sausage, but it gets stuck in my throat. Things have been going so well. My application to the Air Force Academy was going to be as strong as I could possibly make it. I had everything planned out. My dream of becoming a fighter pilot was becoming more and more real every passing day.

*Did Evans put all that at risk for me?*

# CHAPTER 2

# PAIGE

**As soon as** the bell rings, I shoot up and rush for the dean's office, unable to handle the suspense any longer. I must know what Evans did, and if my inappropriate actions are going to ruin my chances at the Air Force Academy. I need to have a spotless record. If I'm disciplined for what happened, my dream could be over.

"Sir, Lieutenant Commander Durant reports," I say when I reach his open doorway.

He says, "At ease, Lieutenant Commander Durant. Please come in and take a seat."

I enter the room but pause when I see Evans.

"I believe you've already met our new cadet, Logan Evans."

He's slouched in his chair and gives me a half wave and a smirk. My eyes grow wide at his complete lack of respect in front of the dean.

"Yes, sir." I sit down, my back rigid and my hands folded in my lap.

"Since he's joining us in the middle of the semester, he has not had the benefit of our basic training course."

"Yes, sir." That much was obvious yesterday.

"It's impossible to run the full program for one cadet in the middle of the semester, so I'd like for you to provide his training between classes and your other duties. You're the highest-ranking officer without a current match, so I feel it's the best solution to get him quickly up to speed on our customs and courtesies. Not to mention you're one of the best role models he could have."

"Thank you, sir." All my fear from a few minutes ago disappears. I'm not being disciplined at all. I'm being offered yet another leadership position, which will only improve my chances of getting into the Air Force Academy.

"Are you willing to take on this responsibility?"

"Of course, sir." It's not like there's another answer. If an administrator asks you to do something, you do it. Even if "no" were an acceptable answer, I'd never say it. I'll have to figure out how to add in the new responsibility when my days are already filled second by second, but it will be worth it. I'll make it work somehow. As my dad always says, failure is never an option.

Commander Anderson faces Evans and says, "Lieutenant Commander Durant will teach you how to survive around here, if you let her. I highly suggest you drop the attitude and embrace the opportunity to learn. Insubordination will not be tolerated. If she tells you to jump, you ask how high. Understood?"

Evans's eyes stay on his feet.

"Do I make myself clear?" Commander Anderson says with more force.

Evans nods, still focused on the ground.

"Look at me and say, 'Yes, sir.'"

He raises his eyes, glancing at me only momentarily before focusing on the dean. "Yes, sir," he says quietly, his jaw tight.

"Being respectful of others is expected at Wallingford. We will tolerate nothing less from you. Any sign of disrespect will be swiftly dealt with." He gives Evans a long, hard stare.

Evans visibly swallows and wipes his palms on the pressed creases of his black pants. If the dean's goal was to scare him, he succeeded. I've never seen a meeting between a new DQ and an administrator, so maybe this is always the approach they take. Fear is a good motivator. Maybe that's why so many of them quickly turn their behavior around.

"Evans, you are dismissed," the dean says.

He stands and walks to the door, but glances back at me for a second with a strange expression—not fear but maybe intrigue or interest. I turn around to focus on the dean once more.

"Do you have any questions about this match?" he says.

I'd love to ask why he's here, but I learned long ago information is given on a "need to know" basis. If I need to know more, they'll tell me. Until then, I'll try to ignore my curiosity. "No, sir."

"Do you have any concerns?"

"No, sir," I say, but then immediately think about his behavior yesterday. He was horrible and nothing I said helped. He did seem to listen to Alex better. And the dean. I practically groan in realization. Evans needs to learn gender means nothing here—all that matters is rank, and I'm several levels higher than him.

I'll just have to be harder on him until he understands. That's easy enough. I can be as hard as I need to be for him to listen.

The dean nods. "Good. You father wasn't thrilled with this match, but I assured him you could easily handle yourself around Evans if it ever became necessary."

His words cause my muscles to tense. My dad and the dean are best friends and go back to their own time at Wallingford and then later in the Navy SEALs, which means, unfortunately, my dad is much too involved in my life here. I never thought my dad played a role in my matches, but the dean's words leave me wondering. It's not unusual for males and females to be matched, yet all my previous matches have been female. I assumed it was coincidence, but I'm beginning to think my dad might have played a role.

Of course, I can't be too angry with him. I am his only child and, after my mom died eight years ago, I'm his entire world. He even makes the hour drive just about every other weekend to meet me for dinner. I know he does what he does out of love, even if it sometimes borders on meddling in my life.

After being dismissed, I leave the dean's office with a hall pass and a plan to rush to my calculus class, but Evans is loitering just outside the door, casually leaning on the wall even after he's seen me.

"You need to stand at attention when you see an officer, even a student officer, in an otherwise empty hallway," I say.

He rolls his eyes and blows out a breath. "I told you yesterday I'm not doing all this military shit."

"You don't have a choice. Do it or I'll assign a punishment."

"Go ahead."

He crosses his arms over his chest as he looks past me down the hallway. I follow his gaze, but nothing's there. It's just the white cinder-block walls covered with photos of all the cadets before us.

"Ten push-ups for your attitude," I say.

"What?"

"Drop and give me ten."

"No."

"Then I'll make it twenty."

"What in the hell is wrong with you people?" he says under his breath.

I narrow my eyes at him. This kind of attitude is not going to fly with our instructors. "Your options are to stand up straight or do ten push-ups. I don't care which you choose, but you need to choose right now."

Rolling his eyes, he pushes himself off the wall. "Better?" he asks with a smirk. His arms are still crossed over his chest and his heels aren't together, but I'll take what I can get at this moment. By tomorrow, he'll need to have perfect form.

"We'll sit together in the mess hall for lunch. You need to quickly learn a few basic rules around here."

He doesn't say anything, so I continue. "What's your first class?"

"Calculus."

"Really?" I reply without thinking. Most DQs are in more remedial classes. "I mean," I clear my throat, "me too. Follow me."

As we start down the hallway, I steal a sideways glance. He's about my height, maybe an inch shorter. Granted, I'm tall for a girl, so he's likely average for a guy. He's not very muscular, which makes me think I can probably do more push-ups than him.

"Whatever the dean told you about me after I left," Evans says, interrupting my thoughts, "probably isn't true."

And his story just got even more mysterious. "He didn't tell me anything."

"Oh."

I turn my head to get a better view of his face. His muscles are taut; his eyes are sad. He looks like a guy who has been beaten down by life.

After an uncomfortable silence, he adds, "I mean, you have to be a little curious . . ."

Yes. More than a little. "It's none of my business," I say, giving the response I know the dean would want me to give.

"Is that the way things work around here?"

"What do you mean?"

"Everyone keeps their shit to themselves? No gossip, no rumors?"

I wouldn't say that's entirely true. There's some gossip here, but it's not like normal high schools. Part of the issue is we don't have much time to spend gossiping. We only have a few minutes between classes, and idling in the hallway is not allowed. The other part is we're exhausted. With everything we have to do, it's hard to put much energy into spreading rumors. Unless there's something really juicy. Then it will spread like wildfire.

I have to imagine Evans's story is pretty juicy since he's joining us mid-semester, but I don't want to be the one to spread it. If it comes out, I might happen to open my ears, but I'd never fuel the flames because that'd be against our Honor Code. An Honor Code violation is one of the worst things you can be accused of.

"Gossip is kept to a minimum here," I say to answer his question.

We're only a few feet away from the door to our classroom, so I continue. "When we get inside, follow my lead. If I stand at attention, you stand. If I sit, you sit. Do not slouch in your seat. Do not talk unless spoken to. Do not do anything but listen to the instructor. Understand?"

"Yes, sir," he says with a faux salute and a sarcastic tone. "Be a mindless, brainwashed robot like everyone else. Got it."

I narrow my eyes at him.

"What noooow?" he asks, stopping and holding out his hands like I'm being unreasonable.

"One, you should refer to me as 'Lieutenant Commander Durant' or 'ma'am,'" I say, holding out my thumb. I extend my index finger and continue. "Two, you do not salute when uncovered. Three—"

His eyes roam down his body, and then he gives me a confused look.

"What?" I ask.

"From my vantage point, I seem to be fully covered. Is there something I need to know?"

I bite my lip to prevent the smile that threatens to come out. It's easy to forget how our terminology can be confusing. "A cover is your hat. Uncovered means your hat is off, which it must always be indoors."

"Oh, right. Of course. Because using the word 'hat' wouldn't make any sense." He rolls his eyes again, and I realize this is some-thing I'll need to work on with him. Senior officers do not respond kindly to eye rolls.

"Anyway, as I was saying—three, your salute was woefully inadequate should it have been a situation where you were required to salute. And four, if you mock our customs again, you'll earn yourself two laps."

"Two laps of what?"

"The track. Each lap is a quarter mile."

His eyes open wide. "You're gonna make me run half a mile for an innocent, sarcastic comment?"

"Your innocent, sarcastic comment is an affront to thousands of men and women who have dedicated their lives to preserve our freedoms. I will not tolerate it."

He closes his eyes, shakes his head, and mutters, "This place is out of control."

# CHAPTER 3
# LOGAN

**Ta-ta-ta, ta-ta-ta, ta-da.** The damn bugle blares again, making me feel like I'm at a horse race, not a penitentiary pretending to be a school.

My roommate flips on the light and rushes out of the room. I roll over and pull the wool blanket tighter around my shoulders. It's only day three, and this place is already killing me. I have fifteen minutes' "hygiene" time—which is ridiculous, who can get ready in fifteen minutes?—then it's one thing after another until the bugle signals it's time for bed. I seriously need to find where they store that thing and send it on a farewell voyage down the steep mountain cliffs I passed on my way here.

As I'm imagining the chaos I could cause with one simple act, my roommate returns. "Dude, you have five minutes," he says.

"What would happen if I just stayed in bed all day?"

"Are you sick?"

"No."

"Then they'd make your life miserable."

"It's already miserable."

"It can always be worse. Much, much worse."

I roll my eyes, but his words convince me to leave the comfort of my bed and throw on the uniform. I know he's right after what happened my first day. I thought I could disappear for a few hours, but the dean found me hiding in the woods and then wouldn't let me out of his sight, which meant I spent the first night sleeping on a cot in his office while he took the sofa. I didn't even get a blanket. It was probably the worst night I've ever had.

At least I got a bed and a blanket last night.

After a quick trip to the bathroom, I stand in the hallway waiting for inspection.

Noah is across the hall from me, next to his room. I met him during personal time last night, and we immediately hit it off because he was also forced to come here. He let me complain about this place the entire two hours without once threatening me like Lieutenant Commander Durant. Paige. Noah told me her first name when I said how ridiculous it is for me to call a girl my same age by a title and her last name.

I lift my chin in greeting to him. He does the same.

Leaning against the wall, I watch all the others. Yesterday morning, I got to skip this part since I was still on the dean's leash.

I have no intention of turning into one of these guys, standing with their shoulders back, head high, and arms straight against their sides. Why on Earth would they submit themselves to this every single morning? Besides appearing ridiculously uncomfortable, it's degrading to have someone look you up and down and decide whether they can make your life even more of a living hell.

"Cadet Evans," Commander Jernigan says when he's directly in front of me. "I know for a fact Lieutenant Commander Durant has taught you the proper way to stand at attention."

"I must've forgotten."

"I see," he says, tapping his chin with his finger. Then he turns and walks away. I can't help but smile. Score one for Logan. I knew eventually I'd win one.

I push off the wall, ready to head for the door and breakfast, but Noah shakes his head. Everyone else continues to stand perfectly still.

"What?" I ask.

Just then, Jernigan returns with a water gun. "Stand up straight," he says to me.

"Are you serious? You're threatening me with a water gun?"

He squirts it at my junk. "What are you doing?" I ask, covering the now wet spot on my pants with my hand.

"You will stand at attention or I'll have fun with this water gun. I'm sure all the girls would love to hear about the new guy who pissed his pants when his commander yelled at him."

"You're crazy," I say, shaking my head.

He squirts it again and leaves a wet mark not even a centimeter from my hand. This prick has got incredible aim.

"Stop it!" I yell.

Another wet spot.

"Seriously. What's your problem, man?"

Another spot.

"Dude! Enough!"

"Stand at attention."

I narrow my eyes at him but pull my shoulders back.

He squirts me again.

"I'm standing at attention!"

"Not correctly. Do it the right way."

I lower my arms and hold them at my sides. Then I slide my feet together.

Another wet spot.

"What now?!" I yell.

"Feet at a forty-five-degree angle. Heels together."

I do it, and he finally lowers the water gun. With a nod, he says, "That's better. Now, about your shoes."

I look down at the shiny black leather on my feet. "What?"

"They're scuffed."

"No, they're not."

He motions with his finger for me to bend down for a closer look. Then he points to a faint—very faint—white line right above the sole on the left side of my shoe.

"You've got to be kidding!"

He raises his eyebrows but remains silent.

"Seriously? No one can even see that."

"I saw it."

"You must have, like, Superman vision, then."

"Fix it. Now!" he barks, apparently not appreciating my humor. "And tuck in your shirt!"

He moves down the line to the next person while I return to my room and search through the closet until I find the black shoe polish. This guy is the biggest asshole I've met so far. The first day, he took away my very limited free time just because I can't run a marathon like him and everyone else. Today it's how I stand and my shoe. I wonder what tomorrow will be. My now-buzzed hair is an eighth of an inch too long? My socks have too much lint on them? My underwear is too tight?

I run the brush over the white line, which disappears immediately, then put the polish away. The wet spots on my pants have combined, and it does look a little like I pissed myself. I wave my hand over them to try and get them to dry, but the sound of someone clearing his throat catches my attention. Noah is motioning for me to get back in the hallway. I give up on my pants and tuck in my shirt as I take my place again.

Jernigan returns, looks me up and down, and turns away without so much as a word. I shake my head and roll my eyes.

I freaking hate that guy.

The next forty minutes are a complete waste of time. We march around for way too long, say the Pledge of Allegiance, and finally reach the cafeteria—make that mess hall—for breakfast.

My eyes scan the tables and wood-paneled walls covered with posters of ships and submarines, until I find a familiar face. I join Noah, and then we get in line for food.

"How long did it take before you didn't want to smash the bugle into a million pieces?" I ask.

He laughs and shakes his head. "Hasn't happened yet. Six weeks and counting."

"Great," I mutter as I take two strips of bacon, then add two more. I don't usually eat breakfast, but I'm starving this morning. I end up also adding three pancakes, a bowl of grits, and two cartons of chocolate milk to my tray. I consider a cinnamon roll, too, but there's no space.

"What's your plan for mandatory athletic time? A team or club sport?" Noah asks as we walk to a table.

I shrug. I haven't played organized sports since junior high. I used to be pretty good at baseball, but I can't imagine keeping up with everyone here. Being in shape is obviously a prerequisite for admission. At least for those who want to be here. If, at any time over the past four years, I'd known what I know now, I would've laid off the video games and television and spent at least a little time outside or in the gym. Now I get to totally embarrass myself in front of Paige and all the other girls who can easily kick my ass.

"Do I have to join a team?" I ask.

"Nah, but then you have to submit a workout plan and have them approve it instead. It's a big pain."

It might be worth it if I could get another couple of hours of personal time each day. I could quickly do a few push-ups, then find an isolated corner of the library to hide out. Of course, I don't have my phone—Jernigan confiscated it as soon as I got here and said I'd only get it back on weekends—and though they have Wi-Fi for our computers in the lab, they closely control which sites can be visited. So, essentially, I have no internet access. I could always read, though. I wouldn't mind two hours a day to read.

But that would only prolong the embarrassment. Although I managed to avoid PT the first day, Jernigan and Paige never let me out of their sight yesterday. And Jernigan was quick to point out how weak I am.

It was horrible. I mean, a push-up doesn't seem that hard, right? And one wasn't hard. Even two wasn't hard. I actually did okay until about fifteen. Why, for the love of God, do we have to do thirty? The girls only have to do fifteen, but a few of them, Paige included, chose—yes, chose—to do the boys' workout instead. As much as I'd like to chill during my athletic time, wanting to avoid embarrassment will likely make me bust my ass for the first time in years.

"I'm on the soccer club team now and plan to join basketball in a few weeks, if you want to do that," Noah says.

I nod. "Okay. Maybe."

"Good morning, Cadet Green and Cadet Evans."

I cringe when I hear her voice. My few minutes of freedom this morning are over. She's going to pummel me with the history of this school and all the ranks and who I salute and when I stand. It was nonstop yesterday and will probably be the same today.

"Good morning, Lieutenant Commander," I say quietly while I fight an eye roll that threatens to send my eyeballs to the other side of the room.

"Good morning. Is this seat taken?" she asks us.

"No, ma'am," Noah says. "Please join us."

"Thank you."

We eat in silence for a few moments, the easy banter between me and Noah completely gone now that she's here.

After finishing her grits and downing half her orange juice, she looks at me and says, "How were the rest of your classes yesterday?"

"Fine," I answer quietly, and then stuff the last of my bacon into my mouth.

"I was impressed by how easily you solved that volume-of-a-frustum problem in calculus."

My chewing slows, then stops. That's the first nice thing she's said to me. It's the first nice thing anyone has said to me here.

"We haven't even gotten to that yet. I think Captain Martin was testing you."

I swallow, then look at her. She smiles, the first I've seen from her, before taking a bite of toast. The smile didn't last for more than a fraction of a second, but damn if it didn't mess with the image of her I've already cemented into my brain: stick-up-the-ass, man-hating, wouldn't-know-a-good-time-if-it-smacked-her-in-the-face Lieutenant Commander Durant.

She reaches down to her bag on the floor and pulls out a small notebook. "I developed a workout schedule for you over the next month and already got it approved," she says, handing it to me. "Since I can't supervise you during athletic time, I'll be trusting you to complete these exercises on your own. If I find out you're slacking, there will be consequences."

And there's the Paige I expect. I give her a tight-lipped smile when all I want to do is flip her off.

Noah whispers, "Sorry, man."

I take the notebook from her and scan through the pages. Three-mile run today followed by three sets of fifteen push-ups and four sets of ten pull-ups. Plus about five different kinds of squats and walking lunges. I don't even know what those are.

"Am I supposed to know what all this sh—crap is?"

"Sh—crap? Is that how normal teens talk these days?"

"I assumed you'd give me two laps for saying 'shit.'" It's a reasonable thought since she assigned me two laps yesterday for referring to Wallingford as a hellhole.

She grins again and lets out a small laugh. I find myself returning the smile in spite of my annoyance. There's something about the break in her stone-cold facade that made my lips react involuntarily. Continuing to watch her, I realize she's actually kind of pretty, at least when she's not scowling. She's athletic and wears her hair like she's ready to go into battle at any moment. Those aren't necessarily what most would consider attractive characteristics, but they seem to work on her.

"Thanks for censoring yourself," she says, "but you don't need to do it for my benefit. I've heard much worse around here."

I nod, still watching her. Her skin is clear, and her cheeks are a little pink from the cold outside. Her eyes are green like mine, though much brighter. This is the first time I've truly looked at her. There's nothing remarkable about her face, yet I can't stop staring. Maybe it's remarkable in how unremarkable it is. She doesn't do anything to make any of her features stand out. They all just work together to give her a sort of natural prettiness.

"We'll eat a quick lunch today, and then I'll show you how to do the exercises," she says. "Anything less than perfect form during athletic time will be considered slacking."

Of course, natural beauty can easily be negated by her attitude.

"I've also taken the liberty of signing you up as a tutor for the first hour of personal time, seeing as you're in all the advanced classes here. It will be good for you to share your strengths with other cadets who are struggling."

"Tutor? You're joking, right?" I've always been a good student, but I like to keep it under the radar. Plus, I'm not exactly a social butterfly. I have two close friends and a semi-serious girlfriend at home, but we knew everyone at school considered our small group antisocial loners. Or losers. I guess it depended on the day. Either way, I was okay with it.

She raises her eyebrows. "Do you think I joke?"

"Nope," I say, popping the "p." "I can one hundred percent believe you have never joked in your life."

Despite it being the answer I thought she wanted to hear, she purses her lips and focuses back on her breakfast, making it clear our conversation is over.

I take a deep breath and roll my neck. Eight more months until I'm free. Well, as long as the court case goes the way it should. Otherwise, I better get used to being told what to do every minute of the day because it could be my life for many, many years.

# CHAPTER 4

# LOGAN

**"Evans, you're up,"** Jernigan says.

I grab the bat and practically crawl to home plate. I haven't played baseball in years. I had no plans of ever stepping on the diamond again, but apparently Wallingford tradition states that juniors and seniors must play against the freshman and sophomores the last Saturday in September. Every year. Rain or shine. Snow or sleet. In sickness and in health. Basically, no matter what. Other than death, there's no way out of it. I tried.

"We just need a base hit," he yells. "Don't let us down!"

I roll my eyes and shake out my arms before drawing the bat up over my shoulder. I couldn't care less if we win or lose. This is a stupid game I'm being forced to play for a stupid reason.

The first pitch is a bullet right over home plate. My reflexes are way too slow.

"Strike one!" the umpire yells.

The next pitch is an exact replica of the first. This time, I at least get a swing in, but it's way too late.

"Strike two!"

"Come on, Evans!" Jernigan yells from behind me, rattling the chain-link fence.

I grit my teeth and try to ignore him. One more pitch and I can sit my ass back in the dugout.

The ball comes at me fast and straight once more. It's like this guy is a minor league pitcher or something. I take a deep breath and swing, not expecting much.

Except the bat connects with the ball. There's a loud crack, and I have to squint to see where it goes. Deep to left field, where the outfielder misses it.

"Run! Run!" I hear from behind me.

Right.

I take off and easily get to second base. Two players come in, which puts us up by one in the middle of the second.

The next batter strikes out, ending our turn at bat. When I return to the dugout, Paige is waiting. "Nice hit," she says, smiling.

"Thanks," I mumble before sitting next to Noah.

"Dude," he says, "where'd that come from?"

"I have no idea. Lucky, I guess."

"Yeah, right. You should sign up for the team in the spring."

"I'll pass." I'm not really into organized sports anymore. Or organized anything, really.

The game continues, as well as my luck. I get another double and a single. Jernigan originally didn't have me fielding but, after my second double, decided to put me in the outfield, where I caught a couple pop flies.

The whole thing was annoying. You'd think I would've lost any skills I had after not playing for five years, but apparently not.

In the end, the upperclassmen won 11–8, and we're now at the customary celebration party in the mess hall, complete with ice cream and cake.

If they really wanted us to celebrate, they could've let us have a night in town. Or told us to sleep in tomorrow. I can think of like a million better ways to celebrate than the dessert we get after every dinner and lunch here.

Noah and I grab some ice cream and start to head toward our usual table, but Paige and another girl stop us.

"So, Evans, did you play baseball at your old school?" Paige asks, then takes a bite of cake.

"Nope."

"Were you in a league or something?" the other girl asks.

"Nope."

"He's just naturally gifted," Noah says, knocking his shoulder into mine.

I shake my head and start to scoff at him, when Jernigan waltzes over, steps between the two girls, and lays his arms on their shoulders.

"Great game tonight," he says to the group, though he doesn't specifically look at me. Which is fine. Good, actually. I'd be thrilled if we never had to look at each other again. If we never had to talk to each other, it'd be even better.

"We were just discussing how well Evans did tonight," Paige says.

He gives a half nod and what seems like a really forced smile. "I think Jones deserves the MVP, though. His pitching was on fire."

"Come on," Paige says, slipping out from under Jernigan's arm and turning to face him. "Jones walked three players."

"He struck out a lot more," Jernigan says.

"Evans hasn't practiced with us, hasn't even played baseball, and he drove in five runs and caught at least two fly balls. Was it more?" she asks, looking at me.

I shrug. I honestly don't remember.

"Three," Noah says. "And he threw out at least two more at second base."

Jernigan gives us another forced smile, this time with a clenched jaw. "Well, we'll have to see how the voting goes." Just then, someone else comes up and starts talking to him, taking his attention away from us.

"You totally deserve MVP," Paige's friend says.

I'm about to disagree, when Paige asks, "Have you met Lieutenant Commander Culver? Leah? She's my roommate and best friend."

I shake my head at the same time Leah says, "We're in the same computer programming and physics classes."

"Oh, okay," I mumble. I haven't noticed her. Then again, I don't really pay attention to other cadets during class. I'm usually staring at the clock, urging the minutes to tick by faster.

"Time to vote!" a guy yells, entering the room with a stack of paper slips. He hands one to everyone he passes, along with those tiny mini-golf pencils.

When I get my slip, I toss it in the trash. Even if I wanted to vote on any of the awards, I don't know most of the people's names. I guess I could write "Not Jernigan" for every one. Or vote for Noah for everything, though I don't get the impression he'd really care about an award. He and I seem to have a lot of similarities when it comes to Wallingford.

Noah, Paige, Leah, and I take a seat as they fill out their forms and turn them in, and I finish my chocolate ice cream. When I'm done, I stand, ready to head back to my room.

"Where are you going?" Paige asks.

"To the dorm."

"What about the awards? Don't you want to see who wins what? And if you got MVP?"

"I didn't get MVP."

"You might have. Or maybe something else."

"I don't really want an award."

"What? Why? It's an honor. Who wouldn't want an honor like this?"

"Me."

Her forehead wrinkles, and she gives me a look like I'm the strangest person she's ever met.

I shrug and turn toward the door, but she quickly stands and blocks my way. "You don't have permission to leave. The awards ceremony is mandatory for all cadets."

Of course it is.

"Quiet down, everyone!" Jernigan yells from the front of the room where there's a table lined with plaques and, for some reason, a big sombrero.

A guy next to him holds up a sheet of paper. "Who's ready for some awards?!"

Paige is still blocking my path, so I reluctantly return to my seat as the cadets around us start clapping and making noise.

Seriously.

It's like this is the highlight of their time at Wallingford. It was a freaking required baseball game.

"Before we get to the peer awards, I'm pleased to say we have a cadet who achieved an extra-special feat this year, one that hasn't been achieved in three years. This cadet managed to strike out four times in one game—which is not an easy thing to do! Cadet Redding, please come forward and accept your well-deserved Golden Sombrero!"

A guy at the table next to me stands and emphatically bows in every direction before racing to the front and donning the large hat.

It's a ridiculous award making fun of him, but he seems thrilled he was even acknowledged. I'd be hiding under the table, but whatever. Good for him, I guess.

"We've tallied the votes for the other awards," the guy at the front of the room says. "Let's start with Best Fielding Performance. Drumroll, please . . ." He pauses and looks to Jernigan, who beats on the table with his palms. "The award goes to Cadet Agarwal!"

A girl on the other side of the room stands and rushes to the front table where she accepts the plaque from Jernigan before waving and saying "thanks" to all of us. The other cadets clap and whistle and pound the tables. I lean back in my chair and cross my arms over my chest.

"And now Best Batting Performance goes to . . ."

I yawn and wonder how long this will last. We're supposed to be having personal time right now. It'd be nice to be able to do something I actually want to do, except—

"What are you waiting for?" Noah whispers, nudging me with his elbow.

"Huh?"

"Go get your plaque. You won."

I glance around the room, and everyone is staring at me.

Really? They voted for me? That makes no sense.

When it becomes clear they're not going to stop staring, I slowly stand. What am I going to do with a plaque? I can't remember the last time I won something like this. It must've been years ago.

I squeeze between tables to reach Jernigan and the other guy. Why in the world did people vote for me? And how did they even know my name? I've been here a couple of days, that's it.

Jernigan's holding the plaque, so I approach him. Unlike with the first award, where he was smiling as he handed it to the girl, he's now got a blank expression—not smiling but also not frowning. That has to be an improvement.

I take another step and reach out my hand to accept the engraved metal and wood, except my foot bumps against something. And is then dragged backward as my weight shifts uncontrollably. Before I know it, I'm face-first on the ground.

At Jernigan's feet.

With a throbbing nose. At least it's not bleeding.

I hear some quiet laughing, but nothing like I'd expect. Back at my old school, the room would've erupted. I guess there's something to be said for the self-control of Wallingford cadets.

A hand comes down to eye level, so I reach up to grab it as I search the floor. What in the hell did I trip over? There's nothing on the ground. It's just the polished speckled gray tile all around me.

When I'm back on my feet, I see who offered the helping hand: Jernigan.

And he's smiling now.

Of course he is.

It all makes sense. I didn't trip. I was tripped. That's my punishment for . . . for what? Batting well? He wanted me to get a base hit. You think he'd be happy I got a couple doubles. Apparently, in Jernigan's world, I was supposed to do just good enough so we didn't lose but not so good the other cadets would give me an award. Obviously, I'll never win with him.

"Careful there, cadet," he says with a pleased grin. "I'd hate to see you mess up your pretty face."

"Yeah, right," I scoff, yanking my hand away. "Too bad we don't have a grand dickhead of the universe award," I mutter under my breath as I grab the plaque from him.

"I heard that," he says, still smiling. "Five laps tomorrow."

I really, really should've ignored Paige and gone back to my room earlier. I could be lying in bed, staring at the ceiling, not dealing with Jernigan's shit during personal time. With a shake of my head and sigh, I head back to my table, where Paige, Leah, and Noah congratulate me.

They all ignore my epic face-plant, which I guess is nice. Much nicer than Jernigan anyway. As everyone else moves on to the other awards, I continue to watch him. He's clearly forgotten about me as he hands out more plaques with a genuine smile and pat on the back, especially when Jones gets MVP. Obviously, his issue is with me. The feeling is mutual. The only problem is, I can't dish it right back without getting laps or push-ups or him embarrassing me in front of everyone else. It's totally unfair. He can do whatever he wants, yet the moment I try to stand up for myself, he gets to make my life miserable?

I don't know anyone in their right mind who would think this is okay.

Yet here I am, thanks to my lawyer. *He* seems to think this is exactly what I need. What I need is to be at home watching a movie with Lora, then having a late night of video games with Gordy and Nate. And sleeping in until noon on Sunday. And spending the rest of the day on the beach.

But none of those things is going to happen anytime soon.

This is my life now.

# CHAPTER 5

# LOGAN

**Four days down,** two hundred fifty-three to go. The one silver lining is sixty-nine of those days are on weekends. On weekends, reveille isn't until seven.

*God*, I think, shaking my head, *now I'm starting to sound like them*. It's not reveille. It's the damn bugle alarm clock. I will never call it reveille.

At least we get an extra hour of sleep on weekends. And, after PT and mandated study hall, we have most of the rest of the day to do whatever we want. The majority of junior and senior students leave campus, but I haven't earned that right yet. Apparently I need a month of good behavior before off-campus privileges will even be considered.

I kick a pinecone off the path to the computer lab and stuff my hands into the pockets of my wool jacket, trying to ward off the chill. As I reach up to yank my beanie lower while cursing my current lack of hair, something hard collides with the back of my head, causing my teeth to rattle.

A football bounces on the ground next to my feet.

"Jesus, man," I say to myself as I lean down to retrieve the ball. Jernigan stands across the quad with his hands outstretched.

"Sorry!" he yells, though he doesn't seem at all apologetic.

I throw the ball in his direction. It's not a perfect spiral, but it does head straight for his face, which lifts my mood a little. Unfortunately, he easily catches it before it can cause any damage. Of course he does. I'm sure he's the kind of guy who automatically excels at any sport, even if he's never played it before. If we suddenly got a cricket team here, he'd probably be not only the captain but also the star player. Rugby? Same thing. God, I hate him.

He and his friends continue toward the parking lot, so I turn around and walk in the direction of the computer lab, where I can get Wi-Fi. I blow out a breath, complete with a white puff that makes me realize how freaking cold it really is. Like, it-could-snow cold. Being from southeastern Virginia, close to the beach, snow's something I'm lucky to see maybe once every couple of years, which is more than enough. And that's usually in January or February, not late September. I wonder if they'd cancel classes here if it did snow. Back home, school would be out for a week with a couple of inches, but I'm sure they're better prepared for it here. In fact, I'm sure there's not much that could alter Wallingford's perfectly designed schedule.

I pull my jacket closer, then hear a very welcome sound: the bing-bing-bing tone indicating I have a new text. That's another perk of weekends—we get our phones back.

I pull it out of my pocket and glance at the screen, excited to see who from home is writing me.

It's Lora. I start to text back, then realize I need to hear her voice after the last few days. I dial the number and wait for her to answer.

"Logan! Tell me your lawyer changed his mind and you're coming home."

I shake my head and let out a half laugh, half huff. "I wish."

"I've been texting you all week. Why have you been ignoring me?"

"I wasn't. I only got them a little while ago. We don't have access to our phones during the week."

"What?" Her confusion is clear, and I imagine her eyebrows drawn into a furrow above her pale gray eyes.

"This place is basically one step down from juvie."

"Seriously?"

"Yeah."

"You need to get out of there."

"I can't. My lawyer thinks he can get a plea bargain if I stay here until graduation. He said it's my best hope of staying out of prison."

She's silent for a moment, then says, "This sucks."

"No kidding," I reply. I'm innocent but could end up in prison. Had I realized how bad it could be, I might've put a little more thought into my decisions the night of the accident.

"I'm sorry," she says quietly. "I never expected them to—"

"It's fine," I reply, cutting her off. What's done is done. There's no changing anything now. All we can do is hope for the best at this point.

"Thank you—again—for what you're doing. It . . . it means a lot to me," she says with what almost sounds like a sniffle, but I know it can't be. She's never been the overly emotional type of girlfriend. I've never seen her cry, not even at sappy movies. I used to like it because we always avoided the typical girlfriend-boyfriend drama. We were always steady and strong. But, for some reason, it'd be nice to see her equally pissed at life right now. I mean, it is her fault I'm here.

"Yeah, I know," I reply with a sigh.

"On the bright side, it'll be easier for you to avoid your dad there."

"Yeah," I say with a small chuckle. "I guess that is one perk." She, Gordy, and Nate are the only ones who know about my war with my dad. He and I used to be best friends, but the moment I found out he cheated on my mom, everything tanked. He tried to act like life was exactly the same—showing up to my games or guitar performances, trying to play pickup with me and my friends, bringing donuts and chocolate milk over for breakfast every Sunday morning—but it wasn't.

It never could be.

Which is why I've spent the last five years devising every possible way to avoid him. It's funny that military school never crossed my mind, though Lora's right—this is probably the absolute best way to keep him away from me.

"Hey," I say, thinking I might be able to make things a little less miserable around here, "we can have visitors if you want to come up for a weekend."

"I can stay in your room?" she asks, sounding excited for the first time this call.

"Well . . ." I pause. "No, not really," I mumble. "You can't even come into my dorm. We could hang out in the rec hall."

"Where would I sleep?"

"I'd get you a motel room."

"Can you stay with me there?"

"No," I reply, my shoulders slumping. It would be nice if we could have a little alone time again. Eight months from now is going to feel like forever. "I'm not allowed off campus," I grumble.

"Hmm . . . I doubt my mom will let me go to some remote mountain town and stay in a motel by myself."

"It was just a thought," I say, trying to hide the disappointment.

After a long pause, she adds, "Maybe I could find someone to come with me. I could ask around."

"Yeah, that'd be good."

"And I'd have to find a weekend that would work."

"Yeah, sure."

It's her senior year, too. I'm sure she's got plenty of better things to do than drive all the way here to visit me. Although, to be honest, I can't for the life of me think of what those things could be. She's like me—no job, no real responsibilities, no need to study to get good grades. That's one of the reasons we got along so well—lots of time to do whatever we wanted. Add on mostly absent parents, and we had plenty of freedom to do whatever we wanted, too.

"So," she says, "That thriller I ordered a few weeks ago finally came."

"Yeah? How is it?"

"Amazing. I stayed up all night finishing it. You should read it—you'd love it."

"I'll have to—" I'm about to say "grab a copy," but that's not possible when I (1) can't leave campus and (2) can't drive even if I were allowed to leave. And I doubt online shopping sites will make it past Wallingford's firewall. "Maybe you could send it to me?" I reply with a sigh. This is what life has come to—not even being able to buy a freaking book when you want to.

"Sure."

I don't know if it's the fact that I'm exhausted from all the shit I have to do here or that I'm annoyed she gets to go on with her life like nothing has changed while I'm stuck here, but this conversation, which I had been looking forward to all morning, is suddenly making me want to crawl back into bed.

"I gotta go. Time for PT," I lie.

"Oh, okay. Text me later. I love you, babe."

"Love you, too."

As soon as I hang up, I switch hands so my frozen one can thaw out in my pocket, then start a text to Gordy, my best friend.

*I hate this place*, I type.

Not even a second later, his reply comes. *What's up man? How's the Rambo thing going?*

*I hate my life.*

I expect another immediate reply, but minutes go by with nothing. It's not until I'm inside the computer lab with my laptop booting up on the table in front of me that my phone starts ringing.

As soon as I answer, Gordy says, "How bad is it?"

"Worse than you can imagine."

"Shit."

"I'm ordered around from six in the morning until ten at night. And it's not just by adults. They've got these students with some sort of god complex who try to completely control everything I do."

"Tell them to piss off."

"I tried."

"What happened?"

"They took away my free time. Made me sleep in the dean's office. Run laps. If I don't listen to them, they could legitimately drive me insane."

"Are they allowed to do that? Maybe you need to talk to your lawyer. None of this seems legal."

"You think?"

"Yeah. Maybe your lawyer didn't realize how messed up that place is. Maybe there's another option."

Could he be right? I don't want to get my hopes up, but they rise anyway. As soon as I hang up with Gordy, I'm calling Mr. Needleham.

"You've got your computer with you, right?" Gordy asks.

"Yeah."

"Why haven't you logged in to our game? I kept checking all week. Even skipped a day of school thinking maybe you were keeping vampire hours now or something."

"I tried during personal time but got a nice warning pop-up from the ever-so-charming dean letting me know video games were prohibited."

"Damn."

"Yeah. Apparently personal time isn't actually time you can use for personal interests unless those interests are preapproved."

"What's been preapproved?"

"Oh, plenty of fun activities," I say in a mocking tone, "like working out, studying, participating in drama or some other point-less club, or taking online courses from the community college."

"Maybe you could take a course on video game design from the community college."

I smile. I can always count on Gordy to come up with interest-ing ideas. I usually support him from a distance, which is why he spends many afternoons in detention while I've been basically unknown to our principal. Well, at least I was until two weekends ago. God, has it only been two weeks since everything went down? It feels like a lifetime ago. Based on how my life has changed, it was a lifetime ago.

"Yeah, maybe I'll try that. Thanks, Gordy."

"No problem, Lo. Call whenever."

*Whenever you need me.* He doesn't say it, but that's what he means. Usually I'm the one helping him after he's gotten into trou-ble, not the other way around. In fact, two years ago, I would've put all my money on Gordy being the one sitting in military school. Yet here I am while he's still lounging on the couch in his basement.

I hang up and roll my neck. It's Sunday afternoon and instead of wasting the day with Lora or Gordy, I'm stuck in a computer lab with freshman, sophomores, and others who don't have off-campus privileges. It sucks. We're trapped here against our will. Well, at least I'm trapped against my will. I guess some of the others signed up for this knowing full well what they were getting into. I can't even imagine what would make them consider Wallingford. Things must've been really bad at home if they were willing to come here.

I take a deep breath and dial my lawyer's number. I need to convince him Wallingford is a terrible, terrible idea.

"Hello," he answers.

"Mr. Needleham, it's Logan. Logan Evans."

"Oh, hi. How are you doing? How's your military school?"

"Awful."

"What's wrong? Did something happen?"

"I can't stay here until graduation. This place is horrible," I say in a rush of words.

"Do you want the plea bargain?"

My forehead wrinkles. "Well, yeah. Of course."

"Then we need to prove it to the commonwealth's attorney. You electively choosing to go to Wallingford shows you're on the right track. It'd be a huge mistake to leave."

"Isn't there another school I could go to instead?"

"None of them would take you in the middle of the semester. If you want the plea bargain, you should stay there. I'm sorry it's difficult, but in the grand scheme of things, it's only a few months. Just do what they tell you, keep up your grades, and stay out of trouble. It'll be over before you know it."

I grit my teeth. Easy for him to say it will be over before I know it. He doesn't have to put up with this shit. Every minute here feels like an eternity. At this rate, I'll have a full head of gray hair—make that a buzzed head of gray hair—when next June rolls around.

"I know you can do it," Mr. Needleham says. "You're a good kid, Logan. A good kid who got himself into a bad situation, but you can turn this around."

I shake my head and bite down even harder. I'd love to tell him the truth—that I didn't do anything—but I can't hurt Lora. Instead, I'll stay here making myself miserable while she goes on with her life like nothing happened. When this is all over, she owes me so big.

"You there?" my lawyer asks.

"Yeah."

"Do your best. Who knows, you might even find they have something to offer you. Maybe you'll actually learn to like it there."

My jaw clenches harder yet. There's no way in hell I'd ever like it here. But if staying here is the only way to keep myself out of prison, then I have no choice. I'll have to make it work somehow.

After a terse goodbye, I open up a browser on my laptop and try to navigate to the game I was playing with Gordy before I was sent here. This is why I shouldn't have gotten my hopes up. I had a brief moment of optimism, only to be smacked back down to reality. I'm stuck here. Absolutely stuck and there's nothing I can do about it.

I sigh and wait for the site to connect, but, of course, it's blocked, just like it has been all week.

I know I should find something else—an approved activity—to do instead, but if I'm going to last here, I need to find a way to keep my sanity. It's just a video game during my personal time. It's not a big deal.

With a newfound sense of purpose, I consider how to get around the firewall. Earlier this week, I never attempted it because there was always a teacher monitoring us, but it's just students in here now. And I've got hours to figure it out, if necessary.

Without a second thought, I pull my phone back out of my pocket to turn on the hot spot, but my data connection is virtually nonexistent. Strike one. Luckily, that's not my only option. I type in the address for a proxy server I used at my old school.

Unfortunately, Wallingford seems to have a better network manager than my public high school because this site is blocked, too. I try a few others I've heard of, but none of them work. Strike two.

Off the top of my head, I know of one other possibility. If it doesn't work, then I'll need to talk to Nate. He's what you might call a recreational hacker. He does it more for the thrill and just to prove he can do it than to steal any private information. As far as I know, the worst thing he's done is removed a few black marks from Gordy's school record. I could use some help now with my police record, although that's probably a federal offense and I'm not about to drag him down with me.

I pack my computer back up and head outside into the cold again, walking around the entire quad until I finally find a place where my data connection might work. It's in the parking lot, right by the exit gate. I reach over the gate as far as I can, and the connection improves a little. It makes me wonder if Wallingford has some type of high-tech 4G blocker or if I'm just really unlucky with my carrier.

After lowering myself to the curb, I set up the hot spot and drag my laptop out of my bag again. In no time, the Tor download starts, but it's going to take forever with my weak connection. I stuff my hands in my pocket and pull my collar tighter around my neck while I wait.

With nothing else to do, I decide to catch up on texts. I have at least thirty messages from Gordy, each one getting more and more frantic and assuming the worst. The last one, dated this morning, reads, *After three days of unreturned messages, I can only conclude one thing. It's been great knowing you. You'll be missed and all that shit. RIP, Megaloser.* I smile at the nickname. He used to call me that in middle school when we first started hanging out because I had straight As, something which was totally out of the realm of possibility for him.

Glancing around, I see upperclassman continue to pour out of the dorms and into their cars before speeding down the steep road to town. It'd be nice to get away for a few hours, but it's not like town is all that great. Noah told me there's an ice-cream place, a non-chain fast-food burger place, a Piggly Wiggly grocery store, a mom-and-pop hardware store, a gas station, and a small motel. That's it.

A cold breeze whips past me, and I check the status of my download. If it doesn't finish soon, I'll be frozen solid. It's only halfway done, so I draw my knees to my chest and try to conserve body heat. A few students give me curious stares, but no one says anything. Is no one wondering why the new kid is huddled up at the edge of the parking lot, staring at his laptop? Or maybe they're just used to odd behavior from new kids.

After another ten minutes, the screen suddenly changes, which draws my attention. It's done. Thank God. I pack up my things and head back to the warmth of the computer lab, where I configure the VPN. With crossed fingers, I try the video game site again. Boom—the heavily muscled soldiers and scantily clad women slowly come into focus on my screen. I actually did it.

And I think I just gained a better appreciation for why Nate does what he does. There is a weird sense of satisfaction knowing I just outsmarted the Wallingford IT department.

Not even five minutes into my game, someone sits down right next to me, despite the many open seats throughout the room. I ignore the person but use my foot to pull my backpack on the floor closer to me.

"What are you doing?" a familiar and accusatory voice says.

"Huh?" I glance up.

Paige.

She's eyeing my computer with a frown. "Nothing," I say, closing my laptop.

"Was that a video game?"

"No, of course not."

"It sure looked like a video game."

"It was an ad for an online video game development course from the community college," I lie, thankful Gordy put that idea in my head earlier.

"Really?"

"Sure. How'd you find me anyway? Are you stalking me now?" I ask with a grin, hoping I can make her forget about the damn video game.

She purses her lips. "You were supposed to meet me in the library twenty minutes ago so we could review your plan for the afternoon."

Right. I totally forgot about that. Or maybe I was subconsciously revolting against being told what to do every freaking second of the day.

"Luckily, Cadet Floyd told me she saw you come in here. Obviously, it's a good thing she did," Paige says, waving her hand toward my computer.

"Why? You don't want me expanding my knowledge with online classes?"

"You do know lying is a violation of our Honor Code, right?"

My eyes roll, despite knowing it drives her crazy.

"Stop that," she says. "Next time you do it, I'm assigning you laps."

My eyes automatically look to the ceiling, ready to complete another spin around my skull, when I catch myself. Instead, I settle for a sigh.

"Lying is a major offense here," she says. "If you lie, I will have to report it to the dean, who will assign you detention. Do you want to change your answer?"

Shit. It's one thing to have Paige and Jernigan assign me some stupid punishment, but if the dean gets involved, then my lawyer will probably hear about it. I don't want him to know I'm getting into trouble, especially after our phone call. "Yes, it was a video game."

"It wasn't blocked?"

"Apparently there was a glitch with the firewall." I don't bother telling her I was the glitch. She doesn't need to know that detail.

"Hmmm . . . I see. You're not allowed to play video games at Wallingford. Don't do it again, or I'll have to take disciplinary action."

"Such as?"

She shrugs. "Whatever I find appropriate."

"Laps?" It might be worth a few laps to have a couple of hours of normalcy.

"Maybe. Or scraping the gum off the bottom of all the tables in here. Or cleaning the cinder-block walls with a toothbrush. Or providing IT support to fellow students during personal time since you seem to be so technologically savvy."

Shit.

She obviously realizes there's more to the story. Of course, I seriously doubt there's any gum under these tables. Everyone here is too perfect to do something like that. And the walls are spotless. And in the time I've spent in the computer lab, I've never seen a student need IT help. She really needs to put more thought into useful punishments that would actually benefit the school.

"Okay," I say, not really feeling all that dissuaded. I'll just change seats so if she comes back, I'll see her before she can plop herself next to me. "Anything else?" I ask.

"No," she says, shaking her head. "That's all. I'm headed off campus, and I expect you to be on your best behavior. Have you finished your homework yet?"

"Yes."

"Your workout?"

"No."

"Make sure you finish that. Then read a book or something. There's no reason for you to be in the computer lab if you don't have homework."

"Okay," I reply, tapping my fingers on the tabletop, waiting for her to leave so I can get back to my game. "Anything else?"

"I'll check in with you before lights-out to see what you've accomplished today. Meet me in the library at nine. Don't forget about it again."

"Aye, aye, Captain," I say with a fake salute.

"I'm not a captain," she replies with a frown. "Lieutenant Commander. And you're uncovered. Why are you saluting? You should know all this by now."

"It was a—" I'm about to say "joke," but it's not even worth it. "Right. Aye, aye, Lieutenant Commander. I'll be a good boy today. Scout's honor."

"Were you a Boy Scout?" she asks, suddenly showing more interest in me.

"Um . . . no, not really."

Her head tips ever so slightly to the right and her lips turn down. "You need to read our Honor Code today."

"I read it yesterday."

"It obviously didn't stick. Try again and focus this time." Without another word, she turns around and heads for the door.

I roll my eyes and then give her back another salute, this time with one carefully selected finger. A guy near me quietly chuckles. "That's such a bad idea," he whispers, but the wrinkles at the corners of his eyes make it clear he enjoyed the moment almost as much as I did.

## CHAPTER 6

## PAIGE

**It's Sunday afternoon,** and Leah and I are in our room, changing back into our uniforms after going off campus.

My phone rings, so I look at the screen. I blow out a long breath before answering it. "Hey, Dad."

"Hey, pumpkin. How are you?"

"Good. Leah and I just finished a hike. Can I call you back in five minutes, after I change clothes?"

"Sure. Talk to you soon."

We hang up, and Leah gives me a sideways glance as she pulls on her pants. "Have you told him about the Air Force Academy yet?"

I groan as I finish buttoning my top.

"Uh-oh. Why do I have a feeling you'll be making a call from Colorado to tell him?" she asks.

I can't wait until I start at the academy. He'd disown me for sure. "I'm waiting for the right time."

"I think the right time was when you applied."

With a shake of my head, I say, "I disagree. What if I don't get in? There's no sense getting into a major fight with him over something that might not even happen." After all, I still need to pass my CFA—candidate fitness assessment—and I worry about being able to do so.

"You'll get in," she says, not sharing my concerns. "And I think he'll be angrier the longer you take to tell him."

I groan again and sit down on my bed to lace up my black boots. She's probably right about my dad. Still, I don't want to have the confrontation unless it's necessary. She doesn't get what it's like living with him. Her parents are easy and supportive of whatever she wants to do. My dad is the opposite of hers. Maybe he feels like he needs to go overboard since he's a single parent now, like being controlling will somehow make up for not having a mom around these past eight years, but honestly, I think he had my Navy future mapped out from the moment I was born. Why else would he have me swimming laps at age three and running a 5K by age five?

"It's still the military," Leah says as she finishes braiding her hair. "He'll be proud of you whether you're a Navy pilot or an Air Force pilot." She attaches her phone to a portable speaker, and asks, "What do you want to listen to?"

"Surprise me."

She scrolls through her phone for a moment before a fairly heavy rock song starts. I've never heard it before but start humming along almost immediately. "Who is this?"

"It's a British band I like. This is their newest song."

"It's good."

She nods, then sits in her desk chair, watching me as I finish tying my laces. "You need to tell him. How about tonight? He's coming for dinner, right?"

I nod. He is coming for dinner, though I'm not ready to tell him about the Air Force. The timing still doesn't feel right. "I'll think about it," I say to end the conversation without committing to anything.

* * *

"Hey, Daddy," I say, hugging him as I meet him in the parking lot later that evening.

"Hi, pumpkin. How was your week?" he asks as he lets me go.

"Good. I aced my two tests and got third place in the cross-country meet." We start walking toward the mess hall for dinner. "And I went to the animal shelter with the community service club. We took some of the bigger dogs out for a run, then helped them assemble new cages in the cat room."

"Third place? What happened?"

I knew he was going to call me out on the race. "The competition was tough. I went out too hard and ran out of steam at the end. I'll place better this week."

"Are you doing enough sprint training? I know you love your hill and distance workouts, but I think you should replace one or two of those with speed workouts."

"Yes, sir."

"I'll talk to your coach. Make sure he's pushing you like he should."

"Yes, sir," I reply, clenching my jaw. This is one reason I want to go to the Air Force Academy. My dad won't be able to talk to my teachers and coaches as easily if I'm almost two thousand miles away.

"What about your CFA? Did you take it this week?"

My teeth clamp shut even harder. He's not going to like what I have to say about my fitness assessment, either.

"What?" he asks, stopping and looking at me. "Don't tell me you still haven't taken it!"

"I'm not ready," I reply, dropping my eyes to the ground.

"Yes, you are."

With a shake of my head, I say, "I'm too slow on the shuttle run. I need a few more weeks of practice."

"Hmpf," he grunts. "This is another reason for speed training. I really do need to talk to Coach Carroll." When we round the corner, he adds, "You're running out of time for the CFA. Your application to the Navy should be completed by now."

I gulp and nod. "I know." This would be a great opening for me to mention I'm more interested in the Air Force, but he's not in the best mood. I should wait until he's more agreeable.

Definitely.

Maybe if I do well in my cross-country meet next week I could bring it up then.

That will give me another week to figure out the best way to word it. It seems like a reasonable plan.

Or maybe in two weeks.

"You said you'd have everything submitted by the end of October," he says.

"That's still a month away," I reply quietly.

The muscles of his jaw twitch as he watches me.

"I'll have it submitted by then. I promise."

"Do I need to have Dale schedule the CFA for you?"

I shake my head. I hate when my dad abuses his friendship with the dean. I am perfectly capable of scheduling my own CFA. I'm just not ready. I can't afford to submit a less than perfect score.

"Do I need to come up here and help you train?"

With another shake of my head, I say, "I need another week or two. I'm getting better. I just want to make sure I get an acceptable score."

"You will. You're a Durant. Failure is never an option for Durants."

"Yes, sir."

I'm relieved this is the last he'll say on the topic for now, but he hasn't eased my fears at all. Even though my application is almost perfect—a 4.0 GPA, a very high rank for a cadet, as many extra-curricular activities as a cadet could be expected to fit in, and ample leadership opportunities—there's still the fitness assessment. It's a critical piece of my application. I don't want to have any doubts when I submit my score. I need to know it's in the top 10 percent.

Of course, if I do get in, I'll still have to deal with my dad and his Navy dreams for me. That might be even worse than the shuttle run.

He continues toward the mess hall, so I scramble to catch up with him while I try to think of a better topic of discussion. Something he'll actually be proud of me for. "I've got a new peer mentee," I say.

"That's right. Cadet . . . Eaves?"

"Evans."

"How's that going?" He opens the door to the mess hall, and we both enter. It's substantially quieter than during the week since many of the upperclassman are having dinner in town or at their homes if they live close. I take a deep breath, enjoying the smell of garlic bread. It's Italian night—my favorite.

"He's got issues with respecting authority, but we're working on it. He seems really bright, actually, though not very motivated."

We're quiet as we select food, then take seats at our usual table. Alex and Leah are already there, along with a couple of our other friends.

"Good evening, sir," Alex says, sitting up a little straighter. He wants to be a Navy SEAL, so he's always admired my dad and often looks to him for advice.

My dad greets him and the other students.

"It's nice to have you back at our table," Alex says, smiling in my direction. Ever since I was assigned to Evans, I've been eating all my meals with him. I glance over to his table, where he's talking with Cadet Green. They're laughing and appearing to have a much better time than when I'm with them.

"Yeah, sorry. There's just so much to teach him and so little free time."

My dad says, "Tell me more about your new mentee."

I cut a piece of chicken Parmesan and shrug. "He's a bit of a math whiz and seems to be good with computers."

Alex scoffs. "He's cocky. Thinks he's better than us or something. Thinks he can get away with whatever he wants around here."

His words cause me to frown. I don't want my dad to think I'm allowing my DQ to get away with whatever he wants.

"Is he in your battalion?" my dad asks Alex.

"Yes, sir."

"Well, I'm sure the combination of you and Paige will whip him into shape."

"We're certainly doing our best," he replies with a smile. I'm sure Alex is loving the vote of confidence from my dad.

Before I can say anything, we're interrupted by another voice. "Eric! I thought I saw you walk past my window." The dean moves behind my dad and places one hand on his shoulder. "It's nice to see you."

My dad lowers his fork and stands before shaking the dean's hand and then pulling him in for a one-armed hug. "What are you doing here on a Sunday evening?" he asks.

"Catching up on paperwork." The dean runs his palm down his face. "Every year seems to bring more and more paperwork."

"Take a break and join us for dinner," my dad says, reaching for an empty chair at a nearby table.

"Sorry," he replies, holding up his hands in front of himself. "As much as I'd love to, Claire is expecting me. I don't want to make the wife mad. Which reminds me, she's been hounding me to have you over. We should schedule something."

"That'd be nice," my dad says with a smile.

"I'll give you a call tomorrow. It was good seeing you."

They shake hands, and the dean starts to turn away, when he seems to suddenly remember something. "Lieutenant Commander Durant," he says, meeting my eyes. "May I have a word with you?"

Crap. Crappity, crap, crap, crap. Not again. A word with him is not what any cadet wants, and it's happening to me much too frequently for my liking.

"Yes, sir," I reply, standing.

We walk a few feet away for some privacy, and he says, "I'd like to speak to both you and Cadet Evans in the morning. Please come to my office after breakfast."

"Yes, sir," I reply around the lump in my throat. I can't help the small bit of uneasiness working its way into my mind. Has something happened? What could have happened? And why does the dean know about it before me? As Evans's mentor, I should always know what's going on with him.

When I return to my seat, my dad says, "I hope there's not a problem."

"I'm sure it's nothing," I reply, though even I don't believe myself. The dean doesn't schedule meetings for nothing. Of course, the last time I was worried, it turned out to be a new assignment. Maybe this is similar. Maybe he wants to commend us on how well we're doing—me at training Evans and Evans at adjusting to Wallingford.

If I hope to get any sleep tonight, I have to believe that's what it is.


"Thanks for joining me," the dean says the next morning while Evans and I sit in his office. I stifle a yawn. As hard as I tried to convince myself this meeting would be positive, I failed. Which means I got virtually no sleep, just like I anticipated.

"Yes, sir," we say in unison.

The dean focuses on Evans, who is currently sitting up straight, reported to the meeting almost correctly, and hasn't been overly disrespectful since entering the office. He's not behaving perfectly, but it's a big improvement over last week. "I'm pleased to see the progress you've made," he says.

Evans remains quiet, and I cringe at his silence. "Thank you, sir" would have been much better than saying nothing.

The dean then looks at me. "You've done a good job in a short amount of time."

"Thank you, sir," I say, before breathing out a sigh of relief. He just wants to commend us.

"However . . ."

No. No, no, no, no.

"Captain Bell brought to my attention an issue in the computer lab over the weekend. Would you care to tell me what happened?"

I glance between the dean and Evans. Is he talking about the video game? That seems like such a minor issue. Why would he call us in here for that? As soon as I saw the problem, I corrected it. As a student officer, we're given significant latitude in how we deal with issues. The dean is usually only brought in for major offenses.

"Well," I start, focusing on the dean, "Evans was able to exploit a glitch in our firewall and access a video game. I noticed and told him it was inappropriate and, if he were to do it again, he would be disciplined."

"Is there a reason you didn't discipline him immediately when you found him playing the game?"

"At that point, I had not yet specifically told him it was not allowed. I had to go with the assumption he simply didn't know and not that he was purposely being insubordinate."

The dean looks at Evans. "Did you know?"

He shrugs.

I expect the dean to demand an answer, but he just asks another question. "After her warning, did you stop playing the game?"

Evans stares at a spot behind the dean's head for a long moment.

"I should remind you I know the full story from Captain Bell and by reviewing video footage of the computer lab."

Evans blows out a breath. "The punishments she mentioned didn't seem so bad, so I kept playing."

"Then what?"

"Some of the other cadets saw me and decided they wanted to play, too. I helped them join the game."

"How many did you help?"

He shrugs again. "I don't know. Nine or ten maybe."

I spin to face him. Not only did he not listen to me, he helped ten other cadets break the rules?

"It was eleven actually. How long did you all play?" the dean asks.

"Until we were forced to leave by Captain Bell."

"At ten thirty—well past lights-out, right?"

He nods.

Logan met me in the library at nine like we had planned and claimed he had spent the whole afternoon doing his workout, reviewing the Honor Code, and then reading. It was all lies. Nothing he told me was true.

My fists clench in my lap.

"Are you aware four of the cadets missed important obligations?" the dean asks.

He shakes his head.

"One cadet missed his court-mandated group session. His probation is now at risk."

"I didn't realize," Evans mumbles.

The dean nods and steeples his fingers on his desk, as he pulls on his lower lip with his teeth while making clicking sounds. After a few moments, he says, "This puts us in an interesting situation. Evans, you will certainly receive disciplinary action for playing video games, missing lights-out, and helping others do the same, not to mention your one-finger salute to Lieutenant Commander Durant as she was exiting the room."

My head snaps in Evans's direction. He did not give me the finger again.

He's wearing a smug expression.

"Thi—" I start to say.

The dean holds up his hand to silence me. I cannot believe Evans. I'm a good mentor—one of the best—and my mentees always show it. Evans, acting like this, is beyond inappropriate. It's . . . it's making me look bad. I narrow my eyes at him.

"Ms. Durant," the dean says, focusing on me. "Did you have a plan in place to assure Mr. Evans followed your orders?"

"I—I . . . well, no, I guess not." I grind my teeth as I say, "I didn't, sir, because Evans had been doing better the day before. I assumed he would listen to me. I recognize my mishandling of this situation. I should have escorted him from the computer room the moment I knew he had no homework and then supervised him throughout the afternoon to ensure he didn't get into any more trouble with his free time."

"Good," he says with a nod. "I agree Evans needs supervision for a few weeks, which is why the two of you will wax the entire gym floor by hand during your personal time."

"Yes, sir," I reply, my back stiffening. Evans just stole *my* personal time.

"You'll finish within three weeks. It needs to be ready for basketball season."

"We'll start tonight and have it done in two weeks," I state. Besides getting my personal time back, I have to prove to the dean I'm a good mentor. When the Air Force calls, he needs to tell them I'm among the best leaders in my class, not someone who got duped by a lowly DQ.

I will not have *Evans* bringing me down.

The dean's expression softens, and he's suddenly the proud man in photos of my preschool graduation and elementary school plays. In this brief moment, he's my dad's best friend and practically an uncle to me, not the strict dean. "I'm sure you will."

He dismisses us, and we silently leave the office, but as soon as we're in the hallway, I turn on Evans. He's about to get a quick lesson on how things work around here.

"I can't believe you made me look inept," I say, jabbing my finger into his chest.

He scowls.

Just then, an instructor turns the corner and sees us. I stand up straight. "Good morning, Rear Admiral," I say. He nods at me, then eyes Evans, who is now standing with his arms crossed over his chest. I knock him with my elbow hard enough to make him flinch. His scowl grows, but he drops his arms and greets the instructor.

When the instructor disappears through a doorway, I glare at Evans again. "I gave you a tiny bit of freedom and you made me look bad." I lower my voice as I say, "Your days here just got a whole lot worse."

"Bite me," he says, before storming off down the hallway.

I stare after him with my jaw practically touching the ground. He did not just say that to me.

# CHAPTER 7

# LOGAN

**"It's gonna take** two coats," Earl, the janitor, says while scratching the white whiskers on his chin.

"Okay, so what do I do?" I ask, ready to get started. Paige, in all her ass-kissing glory, lost us an entire week to finish this. I have no idea how long it will take, but since we only have two hours of personal time each weekday and sixteen hours on the weekend, I have a feeling we'll be cutting it close.

And I can't get into any more trouble with the dean. Not even an hour after being reamed out by him, I got the dreaded request to go to the main office. I assumed it was round two with him, but it turned out to be Mr. Needleham on the phone. Needless to say, he was not happy about being contacted by the dean with what he called "bad news." In no uncertain terms, he made it clear I needed to stay out of the dean's office or I could kiss any sort of decent plea bargain goodbye, meaning another incident with the dean equals jail time for me.

His call was what made me realize there will be no more video games. I can't even imagine what I'll do around here during my personal time now. Stare at a wall and go insane, probably. At least I won't have to worry about that for a couple of weeks with the dean's punishment.

"Scoop up a little of the wax like this," Earl says, wrapping a cloth around his hand and sticking it into the tub.

Just then, the door to the gym opens and Paige marches in with her typical uptight attitude. She sees me sitting on the floor next to the janitor and says, "You're early."

"No, you're late," I counter.

She glimpses at her watch, then turns her wrist in my direction. "We said we'd meet here at twenty-hundred hours. That's in ten seconds."

I blow out a loud breath and roll my eyes.

"Stop doing that!" she says as she settles onto the floor next to Earl. "Drop and give me ten."

"Seriously?"

"Yes, *seriously*. I told you I didn't want to see any more eye rolls."

This is the fifth . . . maybe sixth time today she's given me push-ups or laps. The first time was for telling her to "bite me." I figured that would earn me something, so no biggie. The next was for forgetting to salute someone outside. I honestly didn't even realize I had to salute her. Learning the stupid rank insignias isn't as easy as you'd think. Two days ago, she would've let that slide and just quizzed me on the ranks again until I had it down. The new, I-will-make-your-life-miserable Paige apparently has other plans. As far as the rest of today's push-ups, I don't remember what they were for, which means it must've been stupid shit.

I shake my head as I roll into push-up position and complete ten in what I think is perfect form. On a positive note, it's a little easier than it was last week, so all the PT and mandatory athletic time and punishments must be having some effect.

"Next time," she says, "drop lower. Your elbows were at a hundred-degree angle, not ninety."

"Yes, *ma'am*." I don't even try to hide my annoyance. As much as I disliked her last week, she's taken it to a whole new level since our meeting with the dean this morning. And for the first time, I get the impression she feels the same about me. I'm beginning to wonder how this "mentoring" thing is supposed to work with two people who can't stand each other.

Earl clearing his throat stops our arguing. "Should we get started?" he asks, smiling at me, then her.

"Yes," both Paige and I reply together.

"You need to rub the wax in the direction of the planks like this," he says, showing us how to do it. "Work on about a two-foot section at a time. You want a light, even coat. When it dries, it'll be a little cloudy, but we'll buff that out after you finish the first coat."

"Okay," I say with a nod. It looks easy enough. Tedious and boring, but not hard.

Paige picks up a rag of her own, and we both get started while Earl watches. It's quiet, other than the sound of our boots squeaking on the floor whenever we move to a new section.

After a few minutes, Earl says, "You both seem to have the hang of it. I've got to do some painting behind the bleachers. Holler if you need anything."

We both thank him and then continue to work while he disappears.

"You're using too much wax," Paige says. I look up to find her watching me.

"No, I'm not."

"Yes, you are. The floor is white."

"It'll buff out."

"Earl said it should be a little cloudy—not white."

"God, you are annoying," I say, scraping some of the wax off my rag and back into the tub, though it's probably still got too much on it.

"I'm annoying? Have you looked in a mirror recently?"

I turn my back on her, ignoring her comment.

"Do not turn away when I'm talking to you, Evans."

"What do you want from me? I'm here, doing this shitty job at this awful school, yet you're still not happy."

I'm facing away from her so I can't see her reaction, but her silence is deafening. She's never silent. "Look," I finally say, turning around. "I'll do a good job, okay? I can't afford to let the dean down again. I have too much riding on this."

"You have too much riding on this?" she says, suddenly finding her voice again. "My entire future depends on me graduating from Wallingford with top honors. I can't have you undermining my leadership skills."

It takes all my willpower not to roll my eyes. I'm sure her future is *so* much more dependent on doing well at Wallingford than mine is. She might only get into a top-100 school instead of an Ivy League one. Or maybe she'll only be able to join ROTC as a lowly non-ranked cadet. I can absolutely guarantee she's not headed to prison if things don't go well.

"Is everything a competition to you?" I ask with annoyance as I grab a new rag from the pile and wrap it around my hand. "Because I promise I've got you beat on this one."

Her lips press into a thin line, and I expect some remark about my disrespect, but she just stares at me until it's uncomfortable. I force my eyes back to the floor.

We begin to work again, silently this time as each of us moves farther and farther away from the other with our progress. What I wouldn't give to have Lora here right now. We can talk about anything for hours and hours. Even after a year of dating, time together speeds by. Instead, I'm stuck here with Paige and every minute feels like an eternity. It's going to makes for a very long and mundane personal time, but then again, I'd rather have silence than Paige's nasty attitude.

She must agree.

The next day, I'm perusing the library shelves since I'm not allowed to go back to my room until study hall is over, but I'm already done with all my homework. I wander down the aisle, looking for something published in this millennium as I enjoy my first real break from Paige all day. And man, do I need it. She's out of control. She's an overzealous dictator drunk on the power juice.

I turn down another aisle and head for a large collection of paperbacks. Unfortunately, they're old Westerns. Why on Earth would a high school have books only a seventy-year-old man would enjoy? It's like they put no thought into what students might like to read for fun. Instead, they raided the bargain bin at the used bookstore just to fill up their shelves.

I turn the corner to try another aisle, but skid to a halt. Paige is there, casually sliding books out and analyzing their covers.

I slowly turn around, afraid any quick motions will draw her attention. I think I'm successful until I hear the annoying voice I've come to loathe from behind me. "Cadet Evans." I close my eyes and groan.

"What do you want?" I ask, not bothering to face her.

"Two laps for not greeting me properly."

*Greeeeat.* I must be up to at least ten now. Tomorrow's athletic time will be a blast. I take a step away from her.

"Are you done with your homework?" she asks.

"Yeah."

I turn the corner to go down a different aisle and breathe a sigh of relief when she doesn't follow. I've landed in the naval book section. The first one I pull out is about knot tying. I flip through the book and find myself strangely fascinated. Who knew there were so many ways to put two pieces of rope together?

"I'd like you to join a couple club activities." I jump at the sound of her voice. I was so enthralled by the bowline knot, I hadn't heard her sneak up.

"Huh?"

"When we're done with the gym, you'll have personal time again. Either I can monitor you or you can join some clubs where you'll be under the supervision of one of our teachers," she says, looking over my shoulder at the book. "There's a knot tying club, if you want to do that."

"Seriously?"

"Uh-huh. Though they only meet once a month."

"Will I ever be allowed to spend personal time by myself again?" I ask, slipping the book back onto the shelf. It's not like there's anything great to do during personal time, but I'd rather stare at a wall than deal with Paige or join a pointless club.

"Once you earn back our trust."

Running my hand over my head, I think about my options. I don't like either, but a club might be the lesser of two evils.

"What other clubs are there?"

"Yearbook, band, debate team, community service, robotics, public speaking—"

"What's the community service club?" It sounds like something Mr. Needleham would want me to do.

"They go into town every Saturday to volunteer someplace."

"Off campus?"

"Yeah."

"Every Saturday?"

"Yeah."

"Sign me up."

"Okay, great."

I turn and step over to the bookshelf on the other side of the aisle. A book with a bright orange spine catches my eye. I pull it out, only to be disappointed: *Weaponry of the Civil War.*

"Would you mind signing up for band, too?" she asks in this weird, kind of shy way that catches me off guard. Well, it's actually a combination of her voice and the mention of band that catches me off guard. I haven't played an instrument in years and have no desire to.

"It's my favorite club," she continues. "The dean offered to make other arrangements for you during our practices, but I told him I'd take care of it."

"Are there other clubs that meet at the same time?"

She shakes her head. "No. It's okay if you're not musically inclined. The band leader will be happy just to have another person."

"I'm not really into band," I say. "But maybe someone else can babysit me during that time?"

"I won't pawn off my responsibility on anyone else," she says, blowing out a breath as her shoulders slump. "I'll let Captain Reynolds know I can't be there for a few weeks. Hopefully it won't mess up our winter concert too much."

And just like that I'm considering band. Why? To make Paige—annoying Paige, who has been driving me crazy—feel better? It hardly seems worth it. Yet, I hate seeing the disappointment in her eyes, especially since I know I'm the sole source of it. What is it with me and girls? I'm such a freaking pushover. I might as well lie down and let them smush me flat with a two-thousand-pound steamroller.

Actually, that might be less painful than band.

"Can I just play the tambourine or something?" I ask with a sigh.

"Um . . . yeah, probably."

"Okay, fine."

"Good," she says with a nod and a small smile. My lips start to curve up, but I quickly stop them. I just agreed to band. To help Paige. There will be no smiling. "We meet on Wednesday nights," she continues. "I think we've made enough progress on the gym so far that we can afford to take an hour off tomorrow night for practice."

"Yeah, sure, whatever," I reply absently as I think about what I agreed to. As long as I'm able to hide in the back it might not be so bad. And if they play decent music, I guess it could be entertaining.

Plus, there's still the community service club. That one has real potential. I'll actually get to escape Wallingford for a few hours. Sure, I'll have to work, but for the first time in my life, the thought of manual labor doesn't seem so bad. In fact, I can't think of a single job I wouldn't jump at the opportunity to do if it meant crossing through those Wallingford gates.

Four more days.

If I can make it four more days, I'll finally get a little freedom.

# CHAPTER 8

# LOGAN

**The next day,** during personal time, I'm hiding in the back of the band room as the other cadets warm up.

Compared to the band at my junior high school, this is lame. There are only like twenty cadets and some instruments aren't even represented while others, such as clarinet, have five people. Paige is first-chair clarinet. Of course she is.

There are two trumpet players next to me. They're both blowing air through their lips, warming up, as I'm reclined in my chair.

Just then, an older instructor-looking woman, who must be the bandleader, walks through the door. We all stand at attention when the cadet closest to the door announces her arrival.

"Good evening, everyone," she says as she strolls to the front of the room, chatting with the cadets she passes. It's a much more casual atmosphere than classes, which is kind of nice.

Paige stands and joins the woman at the front of the room. After a few seconds, the woman looks in my direction and smiles. "Welcome, Mr. Evans. I'm Captain Reynolds. We're glad you're joining us. Keep warming up," she says to the class. "Play your scales for a few more minutes."

While everyone else sits back down and pulls their instruments to their lips, she starts walking my way. "What instrument did you have in mind?" she asks when she's standing right next to me.

"Tambourine."

"Oh . . . interesting choice," she replies, twisting her lips as if deep in thought. "We've never had a tambourine player, and it's not a typical instrument for a jazz band. I could probably make it work for a few of our pieces, but you'd be sitting out on a lot of songs."

"That's okay," I say with shrug. It's actually better than okay. I'd be thrilled to sit out during all the songs.

She shakes her head. "No, no. I want all my students involved in every song. What else can you play?"

"Umm . . ." I look around me and say the first thing I see. "Trumpet." It should be easy enough to fake. I'll just pretend I'm blowing into it as I randomly press the keys.

"Great!" She goes to the rear of the room, grabs a trumpet from the wall, and brings it back. "Let's see what you've got," she says, handing it to me.

"Right now?"

"Yes. Play me something."

So much for pretending. I practically groan as I shoot daggers at Paige, but she's practicing the clarinet and not paying any attention to me.

"I'm actually not very good," I reply.

"That's okay. I'd love to see what we're working with."

"Right," I murmur, and lift the instrument. I tentatively blow, but no sound comes out. I try again a little harder with the same result.

"Slow down and focus," she says. "Your lips aren't positioned correctly."

No kidding. It's because I have no idea what I'm doing.

"Pretend you're saying the letter 'M,' then blow raspberries."

I try again, using her tip and the most horrendous squeak comes out of the trumpet at an earsplitting level. It causes everyone in the room to stop what they're doing and stare at me.

Captain Reynolds is standing with her hand partially covering her lips. The side of her mouth inches up slightly, but I have to give her credit, she doesn't laugh her ass off like she should.

A few of the cadets do chuckle, though.

"That was a good try. We just need to work on your technique. Have you taken classes before?"

I blow out a long breath and shake my head.

"Well, I couldn't tell," she says with a wink. "I'll schedule extra sessions to teach you the basics."

"Extra sessions?"

"Of course. I want all my students to master their instrument."

Shit. "Oh . . . uh . . . I don't really want to master the trumpet. Or the tambourine. Or any instrument, really."

"Why are you here, then?"

"Lieutenant Commander Durant wanted me to come."

"I see," she says, glancing over her shoulder at Paige. "Well, if she wants you to learn an instrument, then you better learn an instrument. I can meet with you Saturday for our first private lesson."

"No," I say a little too quickly. Saturday is my chance to escape campus—I'm not about to miss that. "I mean . . . I've got community service on Saturday . . . Maybe I should play something else."

She raises her right eyebrow. "What'd you have in mind?"

"Guitar," I mutter under my breath. God, I hate this place. I gave up the guitar years ago. It was more of my plan to avoid my dad at all costs. It worked. I had two less dad interactions a week once I quit lessons. And we had one less thing he'd try to do with me when I was forced to stay at his place. Sure, I'd still hear him playing in the living room, but I could easily ignore it if I turned the TV up high enough in my room.

Now, four years later, here I am voluntarily—well, not totally voluntarily—getting ready to strum the freaking strings again. Really? Can life get any more annoying?

She points me toward the back of the room where acoustic and electric guitars hang from hooks. After taking my time selecting an electric one and the amp, I sit in the first empty seat I pass and plug things in.

Captain Reynolds stands next to me once more. "What are you going to play for me?" she asks.

"A riff from my favorite group."

I get my fingers in place and practice moving them over the neck, but they feel stiff. They aren't used to it anymore. I try a couple more times before I feel a little more confident. "Ready?" I ask.

"Whenever you are."

I strum the guitar, but it sounds horrible. "Sorry," I mumble as I tune the strings. I try again and make a few more adjustments before I'm happy.

Then I play the riff I've probably played a thousand times before and listened to at least another thousand times. It feels better than I'd like, which makes me scowl at myself.

Captain Reynolds, however, isn't scowling. She's clapping. And all the cadets are staring at me again, only their mouths are hanging open this time, including Paige's.

This is so not how band practice was supposed to go.


On Saturday morning, I wake up with an unusual feeling. Excitement. I'm finally escaping this hellhole, at least for a few hours.

Surprisingly, the excitement lasts through formation, PT,

breakfast, and study hall. A week and a half ago, that never would've happened.

I try Lora's number as I cross the quad toward the bus because this is the only time we'll have to talk today. Immediately after community service, we'll have lunch, then Paige and I have to start buffing the gym. Apparently buffing is more time-consuming than applying the wax, so we'll be spending the rest of the day there.

"Hey, babe," Lora says when she answers.

"Hey. How's it going?"

"Okay, but I've missed you. You really can't call me during the week?"

"No."

"Text?"

"No."

"Email?"

"No, nothing. I told you, this place is like juvie. It's horrible," I say, kicking a pebble off the path.

"Can you come home for a weekend?"

"Maybe. After I earn off-campus privileges."

"When will that be?"

"At least a month."

She sighs again. "I'm no good at long-distance relationships."

"You could come up here."

She groans. "I asked my mom, but she said no. She—never mind."

"What?"

"She's kind of down on you right now. Because of the hit and run."

My mouth drops. It's her hit and run. I'm just covering for her.

"Yeah, I know," she says in a rush of words. "It's messed up. I tried to explain how it was an accident, but she didn't really want to hear it."

"Loooora," I complain.

"I know! I'm sorry. I'll keep working on her. By the time you come back, I'm sure she'll like you again."

"You have like eight months to convince her."

"Eight months? Is it really that long?"

"Yeah. Graduation is in June."

After a long pause, her voice comes out only slightly above a whisper. "June is a long time from now."

No shit. It sucks. "Well, it's June or years apart with me locked up," I say with annoyance.

"You're mad at me."

I take a deep breath. Yes, I'm mad, though it's not necessarily at her. It's more the situation. And Wallingford. And her mom.

"Do you want to break up?" she continues.

"What?" I ask, stopping in the middle of the path. A guy crashes into my back and apologizes as he goes around. "No. Of course not. Why . . . do you?"

"Nooooo," she says in a drawn-out way that makes the inkling of a suspicion grow into something more serious.

"What the hell, Lora?" I ask, my voice growing louder. "I thought we had something good, and you're going to break up with me the first chance you get?"

"I said no! I just . . . I miss you. I hate being apart. It's really hard."

My eyes grow wide and practically pop out of my head. It's hard for her? She's got to be kidding me. She should try one day here. She'd never make it.

"Logan? You there."

"Yeah, I'm here."

"We're good, right?"

"Yeah, we're good. Look, I've got to go do something. I'll call you tomorrow."

"Okay. Love you."

"Love you, too," I say automatically before ending the call and staring at my phone in disbelief. She's going to break up with me. I honestly didn't see this coming. We've always gotten along well, hardly ever fought, spent a ton of time together. We seemed to be in a good place. At least we were until the accident.

And now I'm going to lose my girlfriend in addition to my freedom.

Can life get any shittier?

I continue obsessing about the impending demise of my relationship the rest of the way to the bus and as I select a seat in front of Noah.

"You're in this club?" I ask, sitting down and leaning against the window.

"Court-mandated. You okay?"

With a sigh, I reply, "I think my girlfriend is going to break up with me."

"Sorry, man. Same thing happened to me."

"Yeah?"

"Yeah. Absence doesn't always make the heart grow fonder. In my case, it made her stab me in the back."

I raise my brows.

"She hooked up with this guy I've . . . had issues with in the past."

"What kind of issues?"

"We had a falling-out over my prescription painkiller acquisition and resale hobby."

It takes a moment for his words to register. When they do, I study him more closely than I ever have before. He still doesn't look the part to me, although the camouflage pants and shirt, cammies as everyone around here calls them, could play a big role in that. "You're really a drug dealer?" I never would've guessed. As much trouble as Gordy gets into a school, it's over stupid stuff like truancy. I've never known anyone involved in truly illegal behavior before, and I'm not exactly sure how I feel about this new piece of information.

"I'm nothing now, but I preferred to call myself an entrepreneur back in the day. Why are you here?"

"Hit and run," I say.

"Bummer. Manslaughter?"

"No! No one died—just some injuries and bad damage to a building. And I didn't do it. My girlfriend did. I let her convince me to cover for her."

"And now she wants to break up with you?"

"I think so."

"Wow. She's even worse than my ex."

A commotion draws our attention to the door. Jernigan is there with Paige and a couple of other students, and they're all laughing at something he said.

My frown deepens when I see her. I didn't realize she was also in this club. I thought I was getting away from Wallingford and *her*.

Jernigan puts his hand at her lower back, and she smiles at him, says something, and then takes a big step, putting space between her and his hand before taking the seat at the front of the bus. He slides in next to her. If I didn't know any better, I'd say he has a thing for her and she . . . well, I can't tell. She's impossible to read. The way she looked at him says yes, but the slick way she evaded his touch says no. Then again, she's acting very relaxed right now, not the Paige I'm used to seeing.

"Are Paige and Jernigan together?" I ask Noah.

"I'm not sure. Hey, Eddie," he whispers to a guy sitting behind him. "Are Alex and Paige together?"

He shakes his head. "No, but he wants to be."

"Sorry," Noah says with a shrug, "but I'd stay far, far away from her if he's interested."

"What? Oh, no, I'm not . . . I was just wondering. I can't really see her dating anyone."

"Dating isn't easy here," Eddie says. "With the whole no-PDA rule on campus, it's not exactly a dating paradise."

I'm sure that's what the administrators were going for. I continue watching them as they talk and laugh. Commander Jernigan sits too close to her, and she scoots back whenever he turns around. It's still not conclusive, but it's looking more like she's not interested. I'm not sure why I would care one way or the other, but the growing smile on my face as I watch her makes me realize I do. Maybe it's because Jernigan is a prick, always finding fault in something I've done. He's even worse than Paige. Where Paige will usually wait to assign my punishment until we're mostly alone, Jernigan will bark it out during formation or in the middle of the hallway between classes. For him, the bigger the audience and embarrassment, the better. The thought of him being shot down by someone may be the highlight of my day. Possibly my week.

Luckily, the two of them ignore me all the way to the animal shelter and they work in a different group than me. While they're carrying hundred-pound bags of dog food from one storage room to another, I help other cadets disassemble tables and desks so they can be moved to the new reception area. It's not exactly fun, but Noah and I talk the whole time, there's no senior officer shouting orders, and there's a TV hanging on the wall playing an old movie. Back home, I'd be thinking about ways to get out of this, but right now I'm trying to figure out a way to do community service every single day. Maybe twice some days.

About an hour and a half later, all the furniture has been moved and reassembled, so we're sent to a fenced-in area outside to play with the dogs. I grab a tennis ball and chuck it for a big black Lab with plenty of drool. She jumps and snags it midair before racing back to me and dropping it at my feet. Our game continues for at least twenty minutes while the rest of the cadets trickle in as they finish their work. Eventually, my new buddy gets tired and lies down next to my feet. Following her lead, I lower myself to the ground and then scratch behind her ears. She must like it because she moves closer and lays her head on my lap.

"You're a good dog," I say, patting her shoulder. She lifts her head and gives me a big, wet, sloppy kiss on the face. I wipe the drool from my cheek with my sleeve. "But not a very good kisser."

With two wags of her tail, she pushes her nose under my arm, encouraging me to pet her head again. When I do, she yawns and appears to settle in for a nap. I wasn't feeling especially tired today, but her yawn must have been infectious because I'm now doing the same. I scoot back about a foot until my back rests against the fence and then close my eyes, too.

Not even two minutes later, before my mind even has the chance to grow groggy with sleep, I feel something tugging on my boots. Then two things. Then three things.

I peel open one eye and can't help but laugh. Down by my feet are three pudgy brown-and-white puppies, attacking my shoelaces like they're prey to be taken down. I yank my boots away, then roll the biggest one over and rub his belly. His brother tries to attack my fingers, so I use my other hand to do the same thing to him. Then the third clambers onto my lap, yipping and pawing at my chest as though he doesn't like being left out. Soon, I'm rolling on the ground, laughing and fighting off the three energetic puppies and the black Lab, who has decided she needs to be part of the action, too.

I haven't had a dog since I was eight and never really missed it since I have my cat, Coconut, but I'm suddenly wishing I could adopt all four of these guys. I'm sure Wallingford has a strict no-pet policy, though.

"If you're still here in June," I say, spinning a puppy around as it tries to attack my shoelace again, "I'm taking all of you home with me. Mom won't be thrilled, but I can probably convince her."

A deep bark across the grassy area draws my eyes away. It's from one of those massive dogs with way too much skin. He's wagging his tail and nudging Paige's hand, which holds a Frisbee, but she's not paying attention to him. She's staring at me with . . . not quite a smile, but not her usual frown, either.

I offer her a small nod but stop when Jernigan steps next to her. He follows her gaze and immediately narrows his eyes when he notices me.

I quickly lower my head and focus on the puppies again.

That doesn't stop him from coming over, though. I feel his presence only a fraction of a second before he says, "Stand up, cadet, so I can inspect your uniform." I inwardly groan. He'll find something wrong.

"Did you just realize your inspection three hours ago was inadequate?" I ask as I stand.

He ignores my comment like he always does as his eyes slowly roam up and down me, looking for anything out of place. He must not be happy with what he sees because he says, "Show me your hands."

I hold them out for him. "Check out my right one. I've got some gnarly new calluses from all the pull-ups."

He clenches his jaw as he inspects every single finger. "You've got dirt under your nails."

"That's impossible," I say, turning my hands around so I can see. I scrubbed my hands for like five minutes after working on the furniture.

Damn. He's right. There's dirt under two of my nails. "It's from playing fetch," I say. "It will be gone as soon as we're done here."

"Yes, it will because you now have dish-washing duty. You'll help our kitchen staff clean the lunch dishes today."

"That's not fair," I say, my shoulders slumping. Paige is going to kill me when I'm late to the gym this afternoon.

I glance over to her, and she's got her hands on her hips and is shooting daggers at one of us. Probably me. I'm sure she's annoyed I screwed up again. But, seriously, did they really expect us all to have spotless hands while playing outside in a field with dogs? It's totally unreasonable.

"Complain and I'll assign you dinner, too," Jernigan says.

I shake my head and bite my tongue so I don't make it worse. I can't believe this new punishment is going to make me late for my previous punishment, which will likely land me another punishment. I can't win. Even off campus.

This place *is* hell.

# CHAPTER 9

## PAIGE

**Evans finished lunch** an hour and a half ago and still hasn't made it to the gym. Weekend dish duty generally takes a little over an hour, so he should be here soon. I couldn't admit it to Alex, but I was annoyed by what he did. He knew Logan and I have to wax the gym floor, and yet he assigned him an excessive punishment for what really shouldn't have amounted to an infraction. He was playing fetch. Of course his hands were going to be dirty.

The door slams open, and Logan, looking frazzled, rushes in, holding a tray. "Sorry I'm late," he says. "Commander Jernigan made me wash dishes, but I finished as quickly as I could. And I brought a peace offering. Please don't assign me anything else for being late. I'm having a hard time keeping up with all the punishments as is."

"We're not allowed to have food in the gym," I say.

"Of course that'd be your first comment," he mutters under his breath as he shakes his head. At least he doesn't roll his eyes. I may have finally been successful in curbing one of his irritating behaviors. "Not 'Thanks, Logan, how thoughtful,'" he continues, "or 'Yes, I love the red velvet cake the cooks keep for special visitors, how'd you know?'" He turns around as he keeps talking to himself. "Just another thing you can—"

"Thank you," I say, interrupting him before he says something that would absolutely require me to take corrective action, which would further delay our work on the floor. Plus, it *is* a nice gesture.

He gives me a half smile. "Was that so hard?"

"How'd you know red velvet cake is my favorite?"

"Al told me."

That makes sense. Al, the main cook, knows all the student officers' favorite recipes so he can make our birthdays a little special. I'm tempted to eat the cake now, but we should wait. There will be time for cake when we're done.

"Let's finish the buffing, then take a break," I say, getting back to work.

He sighs, then nods before lowering the tray to the ground and stepping inside the gym. After grabbing a rag, he starts on the opposite side of the gym. It's our usual routine. We put as much space between us as possible.

I have no doubt he hates me and Wallingford. All DQs do at first. Eventually, he'll come to the realization everything I've done has been for his own good.

Three hours later, after no more words between us, we finish.

I walk into the hall and find the cake, along with a bowl of melted chocolate ice cream with sprinkles and a cherry floating in the liquid.

"Who was the ice cream for?" I ask as he steps through the door.

"Me."

"Sorry." I bite my lip. He should've told me his dessert wouldn't last.

"Whatever," he replies with a shrug. He moves the plate with the cake onto the floor, then picks up the tray and starts walking for the outside door.

"Wait," I say.

He pauses but doesn't turn around.

"We can share the cake," I offer.

"I'm not hungry." He continues to the door but stops after opening it. Turning back around to face me, he says, "Thanks for not punishing me for being late."

I nod. "Thanks for the cake."


The next day, we meet again to start on the second coat of wax. We're halfway done and our time is halfway up, so we're right on schedule.

Evans grabs a five-gallon pail of wax and starts to head for his side of the gym but stops midway there, lowers the container, and pops off the lid. I know the issue before he says anything. It's the pail I was using for the last coat, and it was just about empty. The one he had was brand-new and is still about three-quarters full.

"We can both use this one," I offer, lifting the other pail and walking toward him.

"Okay," he replies, sliding the empty container out of our way. I settle onto the floor next to him, and we silently begin working side by side.

Two hours into our task, we've exceeded my expectations. We're both getting faster, him even more so than me.

He stands and stretches his hands over head before twisting his back to the left and then the right. "May I take a quick bathroom break?" he asks.

"You don't need to ask my permission to use the restroom."

Once he's gone, I stand and stretch as well. This is backbreaking work, crawling around on our hands and knees. Since we're well ahead of where I wanted to be at this time, I also take a break and head to the water fountain in the hallway.

While I'm getting a drink, he exits the bathroom and steps behind me, waiting.

After finishing, I start toward the gym, but stop and watch Evans instead. Something has changed. Over the past week, he hasn't been nearly as disagreeable. He still says rude things occasionally, but it's not as bad as it was.

It almost feels like he's starting to accept Wallingford.

Have I done it? Have I transformed him into a respectable cadet?

He stops drinking and straightens up.

"What?" he asks after wiping his mouth with the back of his hand.

"You're coming around," I say. "I like it."

"You mean you like that I've given up? After days of constantly being ordered around and ridiculed and made to feel like a third-class citizen, it was bound to happen sooner or later."

His words cause my self-congratulatory back patting to stop. Yes, he's supposed to be ordered around, but not be ridiculed. As a mentor, I'm supposed to build up his confidence and show him he can succeed here. If he thinks I'm demeaning, then . . . I'm not doing a good job at all.

"You think I've ridiculed you?"

He shrugs and waves off the comment as he steps back inside the gym. "I know it's your job. Tear me down to build me up, right? You can't fix us until we're at rock bottom. The good news is I'm about there. Any day now I should be a crying mess, lying in the fetal position on the floor of my room."

I give him an intense stare. Is he serious? Or trying to be funny? I wish I could read him better. He certainly doesn't look like he's on the verge of a complete mental breakdown. We had one cadet reach that point, and he was not rocking the guitar at band practice or rolling around on the ground as puppies licked him during our community service. Of course, I still don't know what Evans did to be sent here. It's serious, that much I know, so could the combination of those troubles along with Wallingford be enough to push him over the edge?

"I can't read you," I say bluntly. "Are you serious or joking?"

He cracks a smile and laughs, which makes me lean toward joking.

"That," he says, pointing his finger at me, "may be the only thing we have in common. I can't read you, either."

"I'm confused right now," I say so there will be no ambiguity. "If you're serious about reaching rock bottom, we should go to the nurse. If you're joking . . . well, that's not something to joke about."

"I'm joking," he says before leaning against the wall with his foot propped up on it. "I would never melt down on the floor—it's much too uncomfortable. I'd at least do it in my bed . . . or maybe that big blue mat they use for high jump. That looks nice and comfy."

I continue watching him, feeling unsure of myself. It's an unfamiliar and uncomfortable feeling I don't much care for. "I need you to be absolutely, one hundred percent, serious with me right now."

He laughs again. "I'm good," he says.

"Your problems from home aren't getting you down?"

He shrugs.

"Am I being too tough on you?"

He shrugs again.

"Okay, come on," I say, waving my arm. "We're visiting the nurse."

He smiles and shakes his head. "I was trying to be funny. I'm not going to off myself if that's what you're worried about."

"Mental health is not a joking matter."

His face becomes more serious. "You're right. Sorry."

"There's usually some truth to what people say when they're trying to be funny."

He looks out the doorway, takes a deep breath, and then meets my gaze. "You want the truth? The truth is I'm homesick," he says. "I miss my mom. My cat, Coconut. My girlfriend. My friends. My body is exhausted from our ridiculously long days and all the push-ups and pull-ups and lunges and running and everything else I have to do, when I'm used to being a couch potato. My mind is exhausted from having to learn how to change everything about myself. I'm tired of constantly being on guard whenever Jernigan is within ten feet of me, I'm tired of fighting with you, and I'm tired of wondering when my girlfriend is going to break up with me."

He starts to run his hand through his nonexistent hair but stops when he seems to realize it's been shaved off. "I'd love to have my hair back," he says, confirming my suspicions. "I'd love to escape these prison walls for ten minutes for something other than community service. I'd love to be able to take a shower again without forty other naked guys walking around, and I'd love to be able to sleep in until even eight o'clock at least one day. And would it kill the school to have a vending machine? Do you have any idea what I'd give for a Reese's Peanut Butter Cup right about now?"

I shake my head.

"Like fifty bucks! I'm worn out and angry and frustrated and sad and lonely and have a serious chocolate deficiency." His shoulders slump, and he takes a deep breath. "But I'll make it because I have no other choice. I just need to do my best to keep my head above water as I tread from one day to the next, making as few ripples as possible."

"That I believe," I say quietly.

"Good."

He's been here a week and a half, and this is the first time I feel like I've gotten a glimpse into the real Logan Evans. He's struggling, like all DQs do, and they each handle it differently. He's tried to hide it or maybe cope with it through his dry sense of humor. I suppose there are worse coping mechanisms. And I probably should have realized this earlier and been a better mentor.

"I can't control most of your issues with this place," I say, "but I'll try to stop fighting with you. I don't enjoy it, either. And I'll try to be more lenient with your . . . sarcasm. But please be judicious in its use. I don't want it coming across as being disrespectful to me or others."

An unusual expression flits across his face—maybe surprise or appreciation. It was too quick to know for sure.

Then he gives me his trademark smirk as he says, "Can I roll my eyes again?"

I cringe.

"C'mon," he says, knocking his elbow into me. "It's nonverbal sarcasm."

I rub my temples. This is going to cause me physical pain every time he does it. "Okay, fine. But please keep it to a minimum."

"Did you just give in to something?"

"As hard as it may be for you to believe, I'm not completely unreasonable, especially if I see a DQ trying. I do understand how difficult it is the first few months."

His smirk transforms into a genuine smile. "So I'll work on showing more respect and you'll better appreciate my sense of humor and we'll both stop fighting?"

I nod. "Let's get back to work . . . Logan."

"Hey, Leah, you awake?" I whisper to the blue-and-white-striped mattress above me. Lights-out was twenty-five minutes ago, and we should both be asleep by now.

"Huh," she replies groggily.

"Can I ask you a question? About Logan?"

Rather than answer, she climbs down from her bunk and plops herself in the middle of my bed, seeming much more awake than she was moments ago. I draw my legs to my chest and sit up, resting my chin on my knees. It's dark, but I can just barely make out her face from the orange glow of my alarm clock. She's smiling.

"It's Logan now? Not Evans?" she asks, tilting her head.

"Oh, yeah, we had a . . . breakthrough in the gym tonight."

"What kind of breakthrough?"

I readjust my position so I'm sitting cross-legged. "He let down his guard. Admitted to how hard this has been for him."

"That's good."

"Yeah, but it made me think I haven't been as supportive as I could be," I say with a sigh. Seeing all those emotions from him made me feel bad for him. And disappointed in myself.

"There's a fine line between getting them where they need to be and being supportive," Leah says.

"I don't think I walked the line very well. I was all drill sergeant and no friend."

"I wouldn't be too hard on yourself. The dean put you in a difficult situation. Most DQs have two weeks of boot camp before being partnered with someone. I think all their anger comes out then, so it's easier for us to be a friend afterward. You know, when they've quit fighting."

I nod. "I guess so."

"You got the angry, resistant Logan, the one the drill sergeant usually gets."

I nod again. "Although I don't think he's angry or too resistant anymore. Just sad and lonely."

"Resigned to the way things work around here?"

"Yeah, for the most part. He's accepted it but doesn't like it."

"Then it seems like you gave him an appropriate boot camp under unusual circumstances."

Maybe, though I still feel like I was too rough on him. And it's not like all my other stress helped. Between my dad and the CFA, and Alex now wanting me to help him and some artist design new rank insignias, I'm constantly worried about something. I want to be a perfect mentor, I do, but apparently it's not as easy as it used to be when I had fewer responsibilities. Unfortunately, poor Logan took the brunt of my anxiety.

"Anything else bothering you?" Leah asks.

"Mostly my dad and the CFA."

"You'll easily pass your CFA. And I told you to talk to your dad weeks ago."

"I know," I groan.

"He's going to notice when August rolls around and you head to Colorado instead of Maryland."

"Ugh," I say, flopping back on my pillow and staring at the bottom of her mattress again. "What if he tells me I'm joining the Navy whether I like it or not."

"I don't think he'd do that."

"You realize we're talking about my dad, right?"

She pats my knee. "I know he's kind of controlling, but this is important to you. He loves you and will want you to be happy."

I wish I felt as optimistic as her, but he's not "kind of" controlling—he's thoroughly controlling. My dad was a Navy SEAL. My grandpa was a quartermaster in World War II. My great-grandpa was a gunner's mate in World War I. I'm next. If I'm not marching around reciting "Forged by the Sea" next year, the whole Durant family line may come crashing down. In my dad's eyes, at least.

"Plus, it's not like you're completely avoiding the military—you're just going to a different branch."

I hope she's right, about my CFA and my dad. And Logan—the current reason why I'm not getting any sleep.

Sitting back up, I say, "So you don't think I scarred Logan too much already?"

She laughs and shakes her head. "No, he seems pretty tough, though it sounds like he's ready for a friend."

"A friend," I murmur, wondering about the chances of that happening. "Do you really think he and I can be friends?"

"Yeah, sure."

"You're just being optimistic, Leah, like you always are."

"No," she replies, shaking her head. "I really believe it."

"Why?"

"Because I like both of you. And if I like both of you, then you should like each other. Isn't that the transitive property or something?"

I wrinkle my nose at her. "You don't even know him."

"He's in a couple of my classes. I know him a little. All right, I've got to get some sleep," she says, swinging her legs over the edge of my bed, "but let me know if you're having boy troubles again. Or dad troubles. Or any other troubles."

"Thanks, Leah," I reply with a smile as my mind starts to settle a little. Maybe she's right. Maybe Logan and I can turn this all around and have a more typical mentor-mentee relationship.

We say good night to each other, and Leah climbs back into her bed. I close my eyes and try to forget about Logan for the moment so I can get some rest. Unfortunately, I end up tossing and turning for another hour, which is not like me. I'm usually exhausted from my packed day and immediately fall into a deep sleep. Right now, my body feels exhausted like usual, but my mind refuses to give in, instead replaying my earlier conversation with Logan and trying to figure out a way to make him less miserable while still maintaining appropriate cadet conduct. It's what a friend would do, and I need to take on that role now. I owe it to him.

It's not until I have a couple of ideas that I finally begin to drift off.

# CHAPTER 10
# LOGAN

**It's Friday afternoon,** and I've survived almost another week at Wallingford. I still hate it here, but true to her word, Paige chilled out a little, which helps make it slightly more bearable. Since our talk, I haven't received any push-ups from her and only a couple of laps for "loafing it"—her words—during athletic time. Apparently she's able to count my sit-ups even when she's on the other side of the workout room.

Jernigan is still an ass, but whatever. I've started learning his routine and avoiding him whenever possible. And Noah's been helpful. During hygiene time, he'll warn me if Jernigan is in the head and I'll either delay going in there until the last possible second or even skip a shower until after athletic time. I can't completely avoid him, especially since I'm in his battalion and we share a lot of the same classes, but even one less interaction a day is nice.

I'm currently sitting in my Introduction to Business class and sneaking a peek at my watch every twenty seconds. We still have thirty-five minutes, and I'm sure it will feel double that.

"Here's the case study," the teacher says, holding up a stack of papers. "You'll each work with a partner of your choice and will have the rest of this class period and Monday to finish your analysis. It will likely take longer, so plan accordingly over the weekend. Any questions?"

When no one raises their hand, he begins passing out the papers and then students start pairing up. Unfortunately, Noah's not in this class. Honestly, the only people in this class I really know are Paige and Jernigan. I hang low in my seat, waiting for another straggler with no friends, but Paige heads in my direction.

"Hey," she says when she's standing next to me. "Want to be partners?"

"Seriously?"

"Sure."

"You honestly think we'll be able to complete a class project together without killing each other?"

"We're almost done waxing the gym floor and we're both alive."

"Okay," I say with a shrug. If she's not worried, why should I be? "But you better pull your weight. I don't want you *loafing it* and me having to do all the work."

She purses her lips but keeps her mouth shut.

"You realize I was joking, right?" I ask. "I doubt you've ever loafed it in your life."

"I haven't."

"That's why it's funny."

"Mm-hmm," she replies before turning around. "Let's work in the library," she says over her shoulder.

I start to follow her when Jernigan squeezes past two desks to stand directly in front of her. "We're not working together?" he asks, his eyes darting between her and me.

"Oh, sorry, Alex," she says. "I decided to work with Evans. I figured it made sense with me being his mentor."

"I see." The muscles in his much-too-thick neck flex, and he runs his tongue along his teeth while staring at me.

"Excuse me, Commander Jernigan," I say as I walk past him, giving myself as wide of a berth as possible in between the desks. It's not like I expect him to tackle me, but he looks pissed. Of course he does—I just stole his private time with his wannabe girlfriend. Actually, I didn't steal it; she avoided it, and I had nothing to do with it. "I'll meet you in the library, Lieutenant Commander Durant. I've got to get something out of my locker."

She nods and says something else to Jernigan, but I don't stick around to hear it. A few minutes later, we're both seated at a table in the library with a couple of our classmates working nearby.

I skim through the case study—it's comparing two businesses with different models and we have to predict a number of outcomes for each. Then, on Monday, we get more information about the actual outcomes and have to analyze the situation using what we've learned in class so far. It seems like a huge pain in the ass.

"This seems like fun," Paige says when she sets down the paper.

"That's *exactly* what I was thinking."

"So how do you want to do this? Each take a different question or work together to answer each one?"

I shrug. "Whatever you want."

"Or maybe we should each answer all of them, and compare our answers. Then we'd only have to discuss where we're in disagreement."

"That seems like more work than necessary."

She taps her fingertips on the table. "Maybe we should talk through them first?"

"Okay."

"So this first business—Gadgets R Us—is considering how to decide which products to carry."

"They should carry whatever their customers will buy."

"Exactly. That means they need to know what their customers

are thinking. It doesn't do any good to offer something no one wants."

I smile at her choice of words and, for once, wish Jernigan were here right now. Maybe he could learn a thing or two since he's clearly offering himself and she doesn't seem to want him.

"Why are you smiling?" she asks. "Do you disagree?"

"No, you're absolutely right."

"Good. So what do you think is the best approach for the market research? Online survey? Analysis of sales trends? Hitting the street and talking to potential customers?"

"Just asking them straight up if they're interested?" Yep, Jernigan really needs to be here.

She nods. "Maybe show photos of some of the products with the key features." I have to bite my lip to keep myself from laughing as I imagine Jernigan giving her a photo with all his stats—six foot four, two hundred pounds, brown hair, brown eyes, interests include making cadets miserable and sucking up to everyone else.

"Or even putting the items on display," she says.

My mind automatically pictures Jernigan strutting the catwalk in his cammies.

"Okay, we can go in a different direction. It was just a thought," she says.

"What?"

"You're laughing at me."

"Oh, no, sorry. That's fine. I was picturing something else."

"What?"

"You really want to know?"

She gives me a perplexed look. "I wouldn't have asked if I didn't."

With a half grin, I say, "I was picturing Jernigan in a fashion show, modeling this year's amazing new line of cammies."

Her perplexed look doesn't change. "Huh?" she asks.

"It's all this talk of market research."

"What?"

"He knows what he wants, but obviously has no clue what she . . . you want. He should've done a little market research with you."

Paige leans back in her chair and crosses her arms over her chest. "I'm so confused right now."

"He's clearly in love with you."

She laughs. "No, we're good friends. Have been since freshman year."

"Uh-huh."

"What's that supposed to mean?"

"He wants more. At a minimum, friends with benefits."

"Oh . . . no," she says, shaking her head. "He doesn't want that. He's like a brother to me. That's just . . . gross."

I laugh. I can't help it. It comes out way louder than it should in the library and everyone turns to stare at us.

"Sorry," I mumble to no one in particular. Leaning across the table, I whisper to Paige, "I guarantee he doesn't find you gross."

I can't imagine any guy finding her gross. Her attitude, yes, but not her looks.

She frowns, then studies the papers in front of her. After a minute, she says, "Let's get back to work so we're not stuck doing all this over the weekend."


On Sunday afternoon, after finishing most of our class project, Paige and I meet in the gym yet again. Two more hours and we should finally be done with the floor, easily meeting Paige's deadline.

"Hey," I say to her before collecting my rag and heading over to where we had left off yesterday. Then I yawn. One of those prolonged yawns that keeps going and going.

"Tired?" she asks.

"Yeah. I've never run so much in my life." I was unsuccessful in avoiding Jernigan at dinner last night, and he assigned me ten laps for a snide comment. That was what he said anyway. I'm sure the real reason was because I worked with Paige on the class project.

She looks up at me. "I saw what happened. It was only supposed to be five laps, but you had poor impulse control."

It's true. I might have flipped him off because his punishment was ridiculously harsh for a minor comment.

"Besides, the mileage was good for you," she says. "My dad always told me, 'What doesn't kill you, makes you stronger.'"

"Wallingford may kill me," I reply.

She smiles. "To my knowledge, there have been no deaths in the sixty years it's been open, so you're probably safe." After refolding her rag, she asks, "If you weren't here, what would you be doing right now?"

I glance at her. She's hard at work, not really even paying attention to me. To an outsider, it'd probably seem like a simple question between friends. To me, it's weird. This is the first personal question she's asked me. She's playing it off like it's nothing, but it's not nothing. It makes me feel . . . weird. There's no other way to describe it.

"Something adventurous, no doubt," I reply.

"Really?" she asks, interest lighting up her face. "Like what? Skydiving? Bungee jumping? White-water rafting?"

"Uh, no. I was kidding. My life is the complete opposite of adventurous."

"Oh. How so?"

"You want to know exactly how unadventurous my life is?" Why now, all of a sudden does she have an interest in me? We've spent hours upon hours together over the last few weeks, and the topic of hobbies has never come up. The topic of anything even remotely having to do with my life outside of Wallingford has never come up. Why would it? It's not relevant to her job of turning me into a good cadet.

"Yeah, sure," she says.

"Okaaaay . . . my life back home consisted of school, way too many video games with my friends Gordy and Nate and Lora, a reading addiction that would make any librarian proud, and a shitload of TV, especially when I was forced to spend weekends at my dad's. That's about it."

"Your parents are divorced?" she asks.

"Yeah."

"How was that?"

"Awful."

"That's too bad."

I nod and rub the wax in a little harder than I need to. How did we get talking about my parents? The only people who know about what happened are Gordy, Nate, and Lora. Nobody else needs to know.

"You live with your mom?" she asks, not taking the hint I'm pretty much done with this conversation.

"What about you?" I ask to change the subject. "Are your parents still together or divorced?"

"Neither. My mom died a long time ago."

Aaaaand I'm a complete ass. "Sorry," I mumble.

She shrugs. "Like I said, it was a long time ago."

We continue the monotonous job of buffing the floor, now silently working next to each other. This feels normal. This is the way we work together in the gym. Of course, the silence used to be tainted by mutual hatred. The hatred is gone. I'm not sure when it started to fade or when it disappeared completely. All I know is one day I was cursing her name and now . . . I'm just trying to keep the peace. I feel like we're in some sort of nebulous gray area. Not really friends but no longer enemies, either.

"What's your plan after Wallingford?" she asks from out of the blue.

"I'm still weighing my options," I reply, not wanting to get into the fact it's actually the court weighing my options for me. "You?"

"The Air Force Academy."

Of course. I should've guessed a military academy. She's in for life.

"Why Air Force?" I ask while stifling another yawn.

She slides to a new section of floor. "I want to be a pilot."

"The Navy has pilots, right?"

"Yeah, but I'm not into living on a ship for months at a time."

I tilt my head to the side and raise a brow at her. "You do realize you're at a Navy boarding school, right?"

She grins. "I didn't have much of a choice. My dad went here."

"Yeah? Did he join the Navy afterward?"

"Uh-huh. Then he was a Navy SEAL for a long time."

So it's a family thing for her. That could explain a lot about her personality.

"But, honestly," she continues, "there's only one Air Force high school and it's tiny compared to Wallingford. Even if I had the option, I would've chosen Wallingford."

Sitting back on my heels, I grin and say, "So size matters?"

"Of course," she replies stone-faced, obviously not getting it. Gordy would've appreciated my joke.

"That was supposed to be funny," I point out.

"What?"

"That size matters to you."

Her forehead scrunches up, and a little line appears across the top of her nose. It's funny how nothing around here—not our classes, not the military lingo, not completely disassembling and reassembling a rifle—confuses her, but this one joke does her in.

"I don't get it," she says, shaking her head.

I smile as I work my rag over the wooden floorboards. "You know, I kind of like that about you." She doesn't strike me as a person who will admit she's wrong, or doesn't know something, or doesn't get something very often. The fact that she does makes her seem . . . imperfect. Apparently I like imperfection. Maybe it's because I've got imperfection down to a science.

We continue chatting, which makes the time go by much faster than it has been. In what feels like only minutes, we're finally done with the floor. Three weeks of work done in two, just like Paige promised.

As soon as we put away the supplies, she says, "I've got good news."

"Yeah?"

"My weekly mentor meeting is with the dean tomorrow. Due to your good behavior, I'm going to recommend you no longer need to be monitored during personal time."

"Oh, okay." It is good news, though, honestly, I haven't minded spending time with Paige the past few days.

"Please lay off the video games."

I nod, as I wonder how I'll occupy my time with the floor being done. Maybe I should join more clubs. Or have my mom send some decent books. It will be nice to have some downtime to do something else. Or nothing at all. I could lie in bed and listen to music. Actually, that would be really nice.

"And it gets better—you've got ten minutes to change into civilian clothes and meet me in the parking lot."

"What?" I ask, sure I heard her wrong, as we step into the hallway.

"You can go off campus for a couple of hours."

"Really?"

She nods.

"Seriously?" There's no way. It hasn't been a month yet, and it's not like I've been a perfect cadet since I've been here. In the back of my mind, I was actually worried there was a chance I may never get to leave for anything other than community service. Don't get me wrong—the community service trips are nice and much better than campus, but it's not like I get to do whatever I want during those times.

She nods again and laughs. "Yes. I got permission from the dean as a reward for finishing the gym."

No freaking way.

My arms automatically fly around her, engulfing her in a hug. I feel like I won the lottery. Or was just cured of an incurable disease. Or was granted parole from prison. Okay, that last one is actually kind of accurate.

"All right, that's enough," she says, stepping away from me and smoothing out her hair, though not a single strand is out of place. Her cheeks are tinted a rosy color, and she stares at the ground as she says, "It's not a big deal."

But it is a big deal. She has to know it is.

Going from absolute freedom to absolute captivity has been the hardest thing I've ever done in my life. Even ten minutes outside these gates will be like heaven. I'll get to wear my own clothes. I'll get to walk around without the constant worry of forgetting to salute someone important. I'll get to do whatever I want or absolutely nothing at all. I'll finally be, at least for a little while, back in control of my own life.

I'm tempted to hug her again, but she's already headed for the door.

I sprint to her side, having the most energy I've had in weeks despite all my running this morning. She didn't need to do this for me. I have no idea how much effort it takes to get permission from the dean, but even two minutes of effort is more than she had to do. In fact, it's more than anyone has done for me since I arrived here.

As much of a pain in the ass as she's been, I suddenly have a . . . slightly more than lukewarm feeling when I look at her. It's not a full-on warm fuzzy, but damn if one little thing didn't just make my whole image of her transform in a fraction of a second.

She just might not be the cold, heartless robot I had pegged her for.

# CHAPTER 11
## PAIGE

**"Did you sign** up for the CFA next week?" Leah asks as we walk to my car in the student parking lot.

"Not yet."

"How come? I thought you were going to do it on Thursday?"

I remove my hat and gloves. It was cold this morning during PT, but now, with the sun out, it's turning into a beautiful fall day. Much nicer than we've had lately and a perfect day for a hike in the mountains. "I know," I say to Leah. "I meant to, but I ended up getting cold feet. I want to feel confident before I sign up."

"How can you not feel confident? You're in great shape."

"My shuttle run time is still too slow."

We reach the parking lot, which is almost empty of cars now, since everyone is already enjoying their few hours of freedom.

"Want me to time you?" she asks as she reaches for the front passenger side door. She pauses and then takes a step back and opens the door to the rear seat instead.

"You can sit up front," I say.

She waves me off. "Logan can have it. I don't mind."

After I join her inside, she says, "So, tomorrow? Should I time you?"

"Yeah, that's a good idea. Thanks. I need to see where I stand now. Last time, I was three-tenths of a second above the goal."

I scan the parking lot for Logan but don't see him yet. I still can't believe the dean agreed to let him leave campus. The rule is a month of good behavior before it will be considered. I must have been persuasive.

"Hey," I say, looking at Leah over my shoulder, "what about your application? Have you heard back from your congressman or senator about the nomination?"

"Not yet."

I offer her a reassuring smile. "You still have plenty of time."

"When did you hear last year?"

"September."

She slumps in her seat. "That's why I'm worried. It's the middle of October. What's taking them so long?"

"Maybe they consider Naval Academy nominations later in the year. Remember, Alex didn't hear about his until November."

"Maybe," she says with a sigh.

I glance outside again, and there's Logan at the edge of the parking lot. He's wearing worn jeans, a white shirt, and a denim jacket. On his head is a black beanie. He doesn't look anything like the Logan from ten minutes ago.

My heart does a double beat, and my hand immediately reaches up to cover it.

"Man, he's hot," Leah says from the back seat.

"Huh?" I ask, still preoccupied with the fluttering in my chest.

"Logan."

I take a couple of deep breaths and am pleased when my heart returns to its strong, steady beat. "Sorry, what'd you say?"

"Logan. Hot. I could stare into his eyes all day long. Does he have a girlfriend?"

I twist in my seat to face her. "What about Steve?" Steve is from her hometown. They've been together for two years, despite the hundreds of miles between them for nine months at a time.

"Not for me! For you."

I laugh at her words. Not only because it's Logan—the guy I either bickered with or ignored up until last week—but also because I am not interested in having a boyfriend. School is hard enough without the added nuisance of a guy. And then I'll hopefully be moving all the way to Colorado for the academy. There's absolutely no room in my life for a boyfriend. Not now. And probably not for at least the next five or six years. Once I'm a fighter pilot, I can start thinking about frivolities like a boyfriend.

"You don't think he's hot?" Leah asks.

I glance out the window as he spots me and starts walking our way. I have to admit he looks like someone out of a magazine, not someone from Wallingford. And his pale green eyes are nice. What draws my attention, though, are his lips. The upper one has this prominent dip in it. It makes him seem like he's got a permanent smirk, which initially irked me, but I'm beginning to realize it's just his normal appearance. His normal cute appearance.

My heart does that double beat again. Crap.

"You okay?" Leah asks.

I nod just as Logan opens the door.

"Don't worry," I say, looking at Leah in the rearview mirror, as I try to forget about Logan's lips and eyes. "You'll get it."

"Get what?" he asks as he slips into the front seat.

"A nomination to the Naval Academy," I say. "It's not enough to just apply. You need an influential politician to recommend you."

"Really?" he asks, buckling his seat belt.

"Yeah."

"Sounds like a lot of work."

I ease out of the parking spot and head for the exit. "It is, but completely worth it."

"So you can have four more years of Wallingford?"

"Some of us actually like it here," I say, motioning between myself and Leah behind me.

He sits up straighter, and with a half wave to the back seat, says, "Good afternoon, Lieutenant Commander Culver."

"It's 'Leah' outside of school."

"Right." He turns back around and asks, "So where are we headed?"

"Granary Point," I reply. "There's a nice four-mile hike up to a lookout. We're going to meet some other cadets there."

"More exercise? I thought we were going to hang out in town. Maybe stop at the Piggly Wiggly so I can overdose on chocolate."

"That reminds me. Look in the glove box."

"Why?"

"Just do it."

He pulls down the door, and it becomes clear when he sees what's in there for him. "I take back every mean thing I've ever said or thought about you," he says, drawing the orange package out. "You even got the king size."

"I figured you deserved a little reward for making it through three weeks here."

"Do I owe you fifty bucks for this?"

"No," I reply with a laugh. "My treat."

He tears open the package, takes out one of the peanut butter cups, and stuffs half of it into his mouth. He closes his eyes while he chews, and I get the sense this might be the very best moment he's had since arriving at Wallingford.

"Hmm . . . this is good. Thank you." He eats the rest of that piece and then says, "So, hiking? Not a movie?"

"The nearest theater is over ninety minutes away. We'd never get there and back in time for dinner."

"We could eat out."

"Can't. My dad's coming for dinner tonight."

"We could sit at that burger place and watch Netflix on my computer."

Besides a couple documentaries in the summer, I haven't watched television in three years. It was hard initially, but after a while, I realized I was able to get much more done without TV in my life. Now I don't miss it.

I look at him out of the corner of my eye to see if he's serious. He's watching me with a grin—the one I used to find annoying but for some reason I'm now starting to find appealing. "Can't. I got permission for you to go on a hike. That's all."

Just then, there's a buzzing sound and Logan pulls his phone out of his pocket. He glances at the screen, then turns it over on his lap.

"Reese's?" he asks, holding out the package to Leah in the back. She declines; then he offers me one. I also decline. I'm not having withdrawal from normal life like he is. He needs all the chocolate he can get.

His phone buzzes again. He looks at it, silences it, then turns it over once more.

"You can get that if you need to," I say, tilting my head toward his lap.

"Nah. I'm good. No sense ruining this nice afternoon with my imminent breakup."

"You're breaking up with your girlfriend?"

"No, I think she's breaking up with me. She keeps texting me and asking me to call her because *we need to talk.*' Everyone knows 'we need to talk' is code for 'you're screwed.'"

"That's not true. Maybe she misses you and wants to hear your voice."

"Doubtful."

"Maybe she's planning on visiting you and wants to know the rules."

"Unlikely."

I tap my fingers on the steering wheel as his phone buzzes again.

He ignores it and my tapping increases. "You're not going to text her back?" I ask.

"Nope."

"That's rude."

"You don't even know her. Why do you care if I'm rude?"

"Because it's disrespectful. Plus, you're just delaying the inevitable. Don't you want to know what she has to say? Good or bad, it's better to know so you can move on. Instead, you'll continue to obsess over it and get yourself stressed. She might have a good reason to be texting you."

He rolls his eyes. "Fine, I'll write her back. Just to get you off my back."

He types something into his phone as I focus on the curvy road ahead of us, following it down the mountainside to where I'll join the interstate for a few miles.

We're silent while he finishes and we wait for her response. My tapping fingers continue, and my stomach is a little tighter than normal, which is ridiculous. Why am I nervous about this?

After a few moments, the buzzing returns, and he holds up his phone and reads the screen. "She's sending me a care package and wanted to know what's allowed."

"Oh, that's sweet," Leah says from the back seat. "I wish my boyfriend would send me something."

"So we can get them?" he asks, looking over his shoulder.

"Yeah. The rules for what we can get are on the Wallingford website. Have her look there."

He types into his phone again, then puts it back in his pocket.

"See, you were worried for no reason," I say.

"Yeah, I guess so."

I'd expect him to be beaming right now, but he's biting his lower lip and staring out the window. Obviously something is still on his mind. I gently knock his arm with my elbow. "Anything you want to talk about?"

He shakes his head, then gives me his trademark grin. "I'm outside of Wallingford, and I've got chocolate," he says, holding up the remaining candy. "What could possibly be wrong?" He reaches for the stereo. "Let's see what kind of music Paige likes."

The British band Leah introduced me to comes on full blast. It's one of their heavier songs, so the bass practically shakes the vehicle.

"Sorry," I reply, quickly turning it down. "I was in here by myself last time."

"You listen to hard-core rock at concert-level volume?"

I shrug. "It's a good song."

"It is," he agrees, turning it up a little. "You know, Paige," he says loudly to be heard over the music, "you never cease to surprise me."

# CHAPTER 12

# LOGAN

**Paige pulls off** the side of the road and parks on the gravel shoulder behind a red truck. When Jernigan exits from the driver's side of the truck, I groan.

"Who invited the douchebag?" I mumble.

"What?" Paige says with a frown, removing the key from the ignition.

I tilt my head toward him as he walks in our direction. "What's he doing here?"

"He's a good friend," she says, frowning at me. "We always come here together."

"*Fantastic*," I say, suddenly wondering if I would've been better off staying at Wallingford.

"All right," Leah says, probably trying to break the tension. "Who's ready for some fresh mountain air?"

I nod and reach for the door. Paige continues watching me. "What?" I ask with annoyance.

"He's a good guy."

"No, he's not. He's been harassing me since day one, and it's only gotten worse."

"He's trying to make you into a respectable cadet."

"Yeah, right," I scoff.

Leah silently exits the car, apparently not wanting to get into the middle of this.

"Look, I don't like him, okay? I'm allowed to not like people, right?"

She purses her lips but eventually nods. "You can't be disrespectful, though."

"I'll take the laps," I say. "He's a power-hungry asshole. A dickwad. A brown-nosing overachiever." I meet her eyes, not willing to let her win this one.

Surprising me, she smiles. "You're jealous."

I roll my eyes and let out a good laugh. I would never want to be like Jernigan. He's too much like my dad. "You're delusional."

"Mmm-hmm," she says, putting her keys into her pocket. "Please keep your colorful thoughts about Alex to yourself from now on."

My brows rise. "No laps for today?"

She shakes her head. "But it's still mean and undermines your otherwise charming personality."

"I think what you meant to say is it enhances my sarcastic personality."

She shakes her head and reaches for her backpack on the seat behind her. I only get a glimpse of her face, but I'm pretty sure I saw the slightest hint of a smile. I must be growing on her.

She opens the door and steps out. Right into Jernigan's personal space. He's all smiles. All smiles and muscles. His biceps and pecs stretch the fabric of his green Wallingford sweatshirt, and my annoyance grows.

I quickly exit the car and join some other students by the start of a trail but keep my eyes on the two of them. They say a few words, then join the rest of the group.

He ignores me as he walks past to take the lead. I expect Paige to follow him or join Leah, who is also at the front of the group, but she steps next to me.

"I wish you two could get along," she says with a sigh.

"That's never going to happen. He has it out for me. Has from the very beginning."

"No, he just has high standards for anyone in his battalion."

Uh-huh. Especially any guy who happens to spend a lot of time with his precious Paige, even if it's totally innocent and not the guy's idea or necessarily his preference.

"So has he professed his love for you yet?" I ask.

She smacks my arm and gives me a pointed look. "Shhh! Someone might hear you and start spreading rumors."

"I think most people here already know." How could they not? He's obvious. Then again, how could she not know? Of course, she's not denying it now like she did in the library. Maybe she's finally seen the light after my prodding.

"Come on," she says, leading me up the path toward the others, who have already started along the trail.

The "easy" four-mile hike turns out to be excruciating. For me, at least. The others don't seem to have a problem chatting nonstop while speed-walking up the steep switchbacks for two hours with no break. I guess that's what years of Wallingford PT will get you.

About halfway up, when I'm huffing and puffing and Jernigan is swinging from branches like some freaking Tarzan, I make a resolution to double my cardio workouts. It may kill me, but I'd rather die out on the track by myself than on a hike with Jernigan watching me. And Paige. I don't know why I care what she thinks, but I don't want to seem like a total wuss next to her and her friends.

"You okay?" she asks when we finally reach the summit.

I nod and lower myself to a large boulder, where I fall back and close my eyes. My legs hurt. My lungs hurt. My back hurts. My feet hurt. I honestly can't think of a part of me that doesn't hurt right now.

"Here, drink some water," she says. "It'll help."

I hold out my hand to accept the bottle but can't quite muster the energy to sit up so I can drink it.

"You're missing a fantastic view," she says, plopping herself next to me.

I open one eye. All I can see is her face in profile, her neck, and her chest. She's taken off her sweatshirt and is wearing a tight athletic shirt. I suddenly realize just how unflattering her polyester uniform is. It hides every single curve that is now evident. Her body is . . .

Shit. I've got a girlfriend. Lora would be furious with me if she knew what I was thinking and rightfully so.

"Here, eat a protein bar," Paige says. "You'll need the energy for the trip down."

"We have to go down?" I ask, easing myself onto my elbows so I can look at something other than her. All the cadets are scattered around eating, talking, or just enjoying the view. "Can't we stay up here all night? Camp under the stars?"

She smiles at me. "That would be nice, but, ya know, the whole lights-out thing."

I roll onto my side and then into a sitting position before accepting the bar. After tearing it open and eating half of it, I start to feel a little better and can appreciate other aspects of the view besides Paige's body.

We're on top of the tallest peak for miles. Around us are rolling hills, separated by streams and green valleys filled with farmland. The sky is a brilliant blue. It's very peaceful. It's not the beach—my happy place—but I have to admit this is almost as calming as waves lapping at the shore.

"There's Wallingford," Paige says, pointing to the left. "Those teeny-tiny buildings down there."

I have to squint to see what she sees. On the top of one of the smaller hills is a collection of brick buildings. The track and football field are actually the easiest things to make out. From up here, you can truly appreciate how isolated we are from the rest of the world. There's not a single decently sized town anywhere in sight.

"Sorry about the hike," Paige says, rocking her shoulder into me. "We've done this so often, I forgot it can be a little difficult the first time."

"It's all good," I reply. I'm not about to admit the agony of the climb to her.

I take another bite of my protein bar and then chug half of the water.

"You know, hiking is not only great exercise but also a great way to clear your mind," she says once I set the bottle down. "Maybe you should take it up when you go back home. It might help with whatever you've got going on there."

"Hiking's not going to make the felony charges disappear."

Her head snaps to me. "What?" Her expression goes through what appears to be a series of emotions—shock, confusion, sympathy. Finally, she says, "It's none of my business, but if you want to talk, I'm all ears."

"There's nothing to talk about. Just some stupid charges that will hopefully be reduced."

She gulps, and I can only imagine what she's thinking. Actually, she could be thinking much worse. I don't know why it matters to me, but I don't want her to think I'm a murderer or something. "Do you want to know the charges?"

"Only if you want to tell me."

"Hit and run," I say, happy to set the record straight.

"You killed someone with your car?" she asks, her eyes wide.

"No, I didn't do it. And no one died. Just some injuries, but he's fine now."

"You . . . wait . . . how . . . what?" she asks.

"Long story," I say with a shrug. Why am I getting into this with her? I should've kept my mouth shut.

"What do you mean you didn't do it? If you're innocent, you can't be held responsible."

"It's nothing."

"Either you did it or you didn't. If you didn't, then there should be no trouble for you."

"I confessed, okay?"

"You confessed to a crime you didn't commit?" she says with a frown.

I nod.

"That's just . . . moronic. Why would you do something so stupid?"

I give her a dirty look, although it's the same question that's been running through my mind lately. "My girlfriend asked me to," I say quietly. In my head it doesn't sound nearly as bad as it does out loud.

"So you were doing something else, minding your own business, when she crashed your car?"

"Yeah. I was playing video games with my friend Gordy all night. He's got this dream of making it big as a live streamer, but most of his followers are in Asia. That means we play in the middle of the night a lot."

"How did you find out what happened?"

"When Gordy dropped me off at home, the cops were waiting. I was arrested and spent the rest of the night at the police station."

"She needs to come clean and get you off the hook."

I ignore her. I really don't want to be having this conversation.

"Or you need to take back your confession."

When I still don't say anything, she pulls her phone out of her pocket. "Should I call the police for you?"

"Look," I say, holding up my hands. "She's got some outstanding charges against her for weed. It'd be worse for her. If I graduate from Wallingford, it shouldn't be too bad." That's how she convinced me to take the heat. In addition to smashing into a building, she had left her stash in my car. She swore I'd get off with a slap on the wrist, but she'd end up in jail for another drug issue along with the accident. Had I known a "slap on the wrist" would require me to move all the way across the state and subject myself to cruel and unusual punishment on a daily basis, I might have used better judgment the night of the accident.

"It's admirable you're covering for her—very sweet—but she doesn't deserve it. No one would deserve this," she says, shaking her head. "Plus, it's totally inappropriate for her to have asked this of you in the first place. She's the one who messed up that night, and she'll face no consequences while you'll be punished? In what universe is that even remotely acceptable?" She stares at me, waiting for a response, but I have nothing to say. She's right. I know it, but there's nothing I can do about it now. After a long moment, she adds, "You need to rethink your plan. She doesn't deserve it."

"Hey," I reply, ready to defend Lora's honor, but, honestly, I don't have the fight left in me. I'm exhausted and sore, this conversation is making me grumpy, and I'm still pissed Lora might be thinking of breaking up with me. I don't really buy her care package story. She's not the kind of girl who randomly gives sweet gifts, so there has to be more. Like she feels guilty about something that's coming.

"Yes?" Paige asks, eyebrows raised, inviting me to disagree.

"I screwed up, okay?" I say quietly.

"You can still make it right."

That'd be nice. For me, at least. It'd suck for Lora. Could I really do that to her? No, of course not. It's easier for me to deal with this hellhole than get her into trouble. That's just the way it is. Even if she breaks up with me.

I tear off another piece of the protein bar and chew it with more force than necessary. Isn't talking things through supposed to make you feel better? What a load of shit that is. I feel more frustrated by my situation now. I'd like to blame it on Paige, but it's not her fault. She didn't say anything I haven't already thought myself.

Then, to really brighten my mood, Jernigan lowers his ass to the rock on the other side of Paige. There's not nearly enough space for his big frame, though. If I weren't still pissed about the Lora discussion, I'd probably laugh as she scoots closer to me, rather than letting him lean into her. "Easy hike today, huh? We sure took it slow," he says, smirking at me.

What a prick. Always looking to rub my nose in something, like how out of shape I am compared to Mr. American Ninja Warrior himself.

"I guess," Paige says with a shrug.

"Maybe we should jog down," he says, grinning.

There's no way I could convince my legs to run all the way down. He knows it, too.

"You're in a big hurry to get back," I say. "Afraid of running into a bear? Or getting stuck up here in the dark?"

He scoffs at me. "Hardly."

"Hey," Paige says, giving me a warning glare before focusing on Jernigan. "We don't have to all go down together. Let's split into a couple of groups."

Why would I get the warning glare? He's the one trying to start something. Like he always does.

"Yeah, sure. Whatever," Jernigan says. He stares over the edge of the cliff for a moment before looking back at Paige. "You ready for our meeting with the dean tomorrow?"

"Uh-huh," she says, nodding. "Of course."

He's still frowning in my general direction, which makes my stomach drop. Is this the meeting Paige was talking about earlier? The one she needs to have with the dean about me? If so, why is Jernigan going? Because he's my commander? So much for unmonitored personal time. I'm sure he'll make sure that never happens for me.

"Don't forget to highlight all the issues we've been dealing with," he says, still frowning.

"I won't."

"The dean needs to understand how difficult it's been."

"I know," she replies shortly, as if she's either lost her patience with him or is trying to end the conversation. Maybe she's trying to end it so I won't realize her words from earlier were a complete lie. She told me I was getting a good report, but clearly she and Alex have other plans.

"And how unhappy we've been with the progress," he says.

"I know, Alex. We've already been through this ten times. I've got it, okay?"

He nods. "You're right. Sorry. I trust you."

I shake my head as my jaw clenches. I can't believe she throws the damn Honor Code in my face all the time but then lies to me about my report. Why pretend you're going to do something nice when you're not? Did she not think I'd eventually find out?

Jernigan stands and gives me one last nasty glare before saying, "We should probably start heading back."

If I weren't a hundred pounds lighter than him and about a million times weaker, I'd be really, really tempted to tackle him right now. Yes, I get it—he's in love with Paige—but he can't blame me if she doesn't feel the same. It has nothing to do with me. Up until about a week ago, I couldn't even stand to be around her.

If he keeps convincing her to give me bad reports, I'll be screwed. There's no way my lawyer will be able to get the plea bargain. The real kicker is I'm actually following the damn rules. I'm being good, but they're still going to say I'm not.

I don't even know how to fix it at this point. Is there anything more I can do?

I continue to mull over my life the entire way down the mountain. Luckily, it's much easier than up, and we do it in half the time. Despite my foul mood, I keep up with the others better and Jernigan maintains his distance—not really jogging but staying well ahead of me the whole time. All in all, it should have been a more pleasant experience, but I kept thinking about how Paige lied to me about my report.

We're now in her car, heading back to Wallingford. It's been quiet because Leah caught a ride with someone else so she could stop at the Piggly Wiggly, I'm still irritated, and Paige apparently has nothing to say.

*Thwap. Thwap. Thwap. Thwap.*

"Do you hear that?" she asks, slowing down.

"Yeah," I reply, looking in the side mirror. "You've got a flat."

"Crap," she murmurs before putting on her turn signal and easing onto the shoulder of the mountain road leading to Wallingford.

We both exit the car and then stare at the right rear tire for longer than necessary.

"It's flat," she finally says, stating the obvious.

"Yep. You got a spare in there?"

With a nod, she says, "I think so."

She opens up the tailgate and then glances around. After a moment, she grabs what looks like the floor and pulls up, revealing a donut and the jack.

"Okay," she says, clapping her hands in front of her. "I can do this. It can't be that hard."

She grabs the donut and lowers it to the ground.

I reach in for the jack and then take it back to the tire before assembling it and setting it in place. She follows behind me. "Do you know what you're doing?" she asks.

"Does it look like I know what I'm doing?" With a few turns of the crank, the car starts to rise. When it's high enough, I remove the hubcap and start on the lug nuts. She squats down next to me.

"Do you want me to do that?"

"Do you want to do it?"

"No, but it is my car. There's no reason for you get dirty when I can do it."

"And be out here all night while you figure it out?" I hand her the first nut. "No, thank you." I guess I should be appreciative my dick of a dad made me prove I could do this before he'd take me to get my license, but I refuse to give him credit for anything.

I expect her to have a holier-than-thou response to my not-exactly-nice comment, but she keeps her mouth shut and continues to accept the nuts. When I'm done, she hands me the donut, which I put in place. As she begins passing lug nuts back to me, she says, "Are you mad?"

I shake my head.

"Why have you been so quiet, then?"

"Tired."

"Does that also explain why you're about to snap the wrench in half?"

I pause. My knuckles are white. And I do have a layer of sweat despite the cool temperature.

"I'm fine," I reply, getting back to work.

"A cadet will not lie. It's in our Honor Code."

I pause again and shake my head. "Unbelievable," I mutter.

"What?"

I lower the wrench and turn to face her. "You may be the biggest hypocrite I've ever met."

. "Excuse me?"

"You constantly tell me not to lie, but you have no problem doing it to me."

"I've never lied to you."

"Ah, your report to the dean about me? My good behavior? Ring a bell?"

"Yeah, why?"

"You and Jernigan have been plotting how you can ruin my life with that report!"

Her eyes grow wide and her arms drop to her sides, causing the remaining lug nuts to spill to the ground. "Wh-what? We . . . no," she says, shaking her head. "We're not doing that."

"Right," I say with a roll of my eyes. "He made it very clear up on the mountain."

Her mouth drops open, and she stares at me.

"Whatever," I say, shrugging my shoulders. "I don't care. I should probably thank him for being honest with me, you know? Since you obviously aren't."

She takes a deep breath and rubs her temples. "You're a jerk, you know that? And after all the nice things I did for you today. Ten laps tomorrow." She turns on her heel and walks behind the car.

Shit. Now I'm only making things worse. I don't need her adding this to the already bad report.

"Look, Paige," I say, following her as I run my hand over my head and clench my teeth. "I'm sorry. You're right. I'm being an ass."

"You are," she says. Despite the calm way she walked away, there's still anger brewing in her eyes. She jabs her finger into my chest. "How dare you accuse me of breaking our Honor Code.

I have never in the almost three and a half years I've been here broken that code, and I never would. Ever. It's in my core. It's who I am."

"I said I was sorry, okay?" I try to push her finger away, but she leans in closer and grabs my hand.

"Do you have any idea how insulting your accusation was?"

Her nose is only inches from my face, and I realize it has a small dent in it midway, like maybe she broke it at some point. A far as I can tell, that may be her only flaw. Her clear skin is smooth and nicely tan, despite it being October. Maybe it's not a tan. Maybe she's just got a better complexion than my ghostly one. And her bright green eyes are striking at this distance, especially since we stand eye to eye.

"Alex and I weren't even talking about your report," she continues. "It's a totally different meeting."

"Really?" I ask, my brows furrowing.

She nods. Then her unblinking eyes lower to my mouth, before shifting back up.

"So I got it all wrong?"

"Yes."

"And you're not plotting with Jernigan to ruin my life?"

"No."

I gulp, my mouth suddenly dry. "I probably should've asked for clarification earlier," I mumble.

She nods before biting her lip and continuing to stare at me. Shit.

Her lips are totally kissable. How have I not noticed this before?

I gulp again. "Um . . . so . . . uh . . . this other meeting is about something else?"

"New rank insignias." Our bodies are practically touching, and her breath tickles my cheek. "We're working with an artist. She's not doing a good job," she whispers.

When her gaze drifts down to my lips again, I realize she must be thinking the same thing I am.

"That's . . ." I swallow. ". . . too bad."

"Yeah, it's been a pain."

Our conversation is over. She should let go of my hand and I should step away from her, but neither of us moves. We continue staring into each other's eyes. One week ago, we were tearing each other's throats out—hell, one minute ago we were tossing insults back and forth—and now we're . . . We're what?

She licks her lips as a car passes by.

She wants me to kiss her.

And I . . . don't find it nearly as repulsive as I would've thought. In fact, I'm not finding it repulsive at all right now.

Slowly, I close my eyes and tilt my head before aiming for her mouth, giving her at least a few seconds to push me away if I'm reading her completely wrong.

She doesn't push me away, but a long, loud honk followed by whistles causes my eyelids to fly open. A car with cadets hanging out the window, looking back at us, speeds up the road. At least it wasn't Jernigan's truck.

"Sorry," I mumble, taking a step back as I realize what a stupid idea this was. I hope she was right about cadets not spreading rumors. I really don't need Jernigan hearing about this. With how he feels about her, I'm sure his barely concealed hatred for me would quickly become unconcealed.

"Me too," she replies, smoothing back her hair. "Let's finish the tire. Dinner's soon."

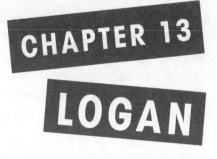

# CHAPTER 13
# LOGAN

**Back on campus,** we each went our own way with no more talk about the almost kiss. Hopefully we'll never mention it again. What was I thinking? Clearly I wasn't thinking at all. I've got a girlfriend. Plus, she's . . . well, she's Paige. Definitely not someone I should be kissing.

After changing back into my cammies, I head to the mess hall for dinner. As I'm spooning chili into a bowl, I feel a large presence behind me. Rather than turn around, I slide down the buffet line, adding cheese and sour cream to my bowl.

"Evans," a deep voice says. "In the hallway. Now."

I gulp.

Jernigan is always an ass, but he sounds like a royally pissed-off ass right now. Not a good combination.

"I just got my food. Can't it wait until after dinner?"

"No."

I take a deep breath and slide my tray to the end of the line before turning around and following him out. Paige was wrong about the rumor mill. It's been less than fifteen minutes since our almost kiss and Jernigan already knows.

And now he will proceed to kill me.

I take slow, short steps, trying to delay the inevitable, but it's only like ten feet to the doorway, and before I know it, I'm in the hallway staring at a pacing, knuckle-cracking Jernigan.

It really would've been nice to spend my last few days alive back home, not at Wallingford.

When he spots me, he marches over, flames practically coming out of his nostrils and steam out of his ears.

"What in the hell did you do to her?" he says, barely above a whisper. I'd expect him to be yelling, but somehow, this is worse.

I gulp again and shake my head. "N-nothing. I swear."

"Danny saw you. Said you had your hands all over her."

I shake my head again, more forcefully this time. "No, we were arguing about something stupid. That's all."

"I trust Danny a hell of a lot more than I trust you," he says in that eerily calm voice as he comes even closer.

I back up but hit the wall. He takes another step toward me. Then another. His face is so close to mine I can make out each individual pore on his nose as his nostrils flare.

"Whoa, whoa, whoa, what's going on?" a male voice asks. I take the opportunity to move three steps to the side.

Rushing toward us is an older man who looks vaguely familiar.

"Alex, what's the problem?" the man asks.

"Evans was caught . . . being inappropriate with Paige."

"What?!" the man says, stepping beside Alex, now glaring at me, too.

"No!" I say, holding up my hands. "We . . . nothing happened. I swear!"

"Daddy! Alex! What are you doing?" a welcome voice says. And suddenly I realize why the man looks familiar. He often sits next to Paige for dinner on the weekends.

"Putting Evans in his place," Alex says, the veins in his neck big and blue.

"For what?"

"For whatever he did to you."

"He didn't do anything to me. And even if he did, I don't need you two to put him in his place. I'm more than capable of taking care of myself." She steps between Jernigan and her dad, then uses her arms to push both of them away from me. "Stop it—you're scaring him."

"Danny said he had his hands all over you."

A slight blush appears on the top of her cheeks. "Um, no. That's not exactly what happened."

"What exactly happened?" her dad asks, hands on his hips as he stares down his daughter now.

"Nothing. We were arguing and then we almost . . . kissed."

"Kissed?!" Jernigan and Paige's dad say together, staring at her.

"Yeah," she says with a shrug, like it's no big deal.

"He tried to kiss you?" Jernigan says, cracking his knuckles again.

"No. Yes. I mean . . . we . . . it was mutual."

"Mutual?" her dad asks. "Can I have a word with you?" He grabs her shoulder and steers her down the hallway and around a corner.

While Jernigan's distracted by their departure, I sneak back into the mess hall. Things have gone from bad to worse. It's not enough to have Jernigan on the warpath. I now have a Navy SEAL out to get me, too. At this point, prison might be the better option.

I grab my forgotten tray from earlier and head to my typical spot next to Noah.

"Oh man, you look like you're about to piss your pants," he says as soon as I sit down. "What happened?"

"My life may be over."

"Why?"

"Paige and I almost kissed. And Jernigan found out. Then her dad."

Noah face lights up like he was just granted off-campus privi-leges. "Hold on. You kissed the Ice Queen? She kissed you?"

I shake my head. "No, we almost did."

"And Jernigan knows?"

I nod as I stare at the chipped tabletop.

He lets out a huge laugh while a couple of other guys at the table chuckle a little less enthusiastically; then they all stop at once.

"Evans," a soft voice calls from over my left shoulder.

I sit at attention. "Yes, ma'am," I say to Paige.

She makes a face I can't quite read before saying, "Please come join me at my table. I'd like you to meet my dad."

"Actually, I feel we're pretty well acquainted. Thanks, though."

I start to push a crumb around the table, when she gently touches my elbow. "Please?"

I glance to the table, where I expect to see Mr. Durant shoot-ing daggers at me, but he's deep in conversation with Jernigan. "I really don't think it's a good idea."

"I talked to him. He wants to apologize."

"Really?"

She nods. I want to believe her, but if he really wanted to apol-ogize, wouldn't he come over here? It seems weird the apologizee has to go to the apologizer.

"Please?" she asks again with a hard stare, and I realize I have no choice. It was never a question; it was an order.

I stand, grab my tray, and follow her to the round table in the corner.

There's only one empty chair; it's next to Jernigan and directly across from Mr. Durant.

Jernigan stiffens when I sit down but doesn't say anything.

"Mr. Evans," Paige's dad says, drawing my attention to him. "My daughter would like me to apologize. Sorry I scared you."

I almost laugh at his "apology." I have never heard a less sincere one.

Jernigan angles himself toward me and leans over so his lips are practically touching my ear. "I'm not sorry," he whispers. "Keep your hands off her from now on."

I ignore him and take a bite of chili. He doesn't need to tell me twice. I will never make the same mistake again.

"Dad," Paige says, "Mr. Evans is my new DQ. He came here from . . . actually, where are you from? I can't believe I don't know."

"Chesapeake," I mumble.

"I heard," Mr. Durant says, his jaw tight.

"From who?" Paige asks, facing her dad.

"Commander Anderson. He told me all about Mr. Evans before assigning him to you."

"Oh, I didn't realize." Her voice is quiet, and her jaw tenses, just like her dad's. It seems they're both pissed now. Everyone at the table focuses on their meal, shoveling bite after bite into their mouths to prevent them from having to speak.

All of them except for Jernigan, that is. "Mr. Durant," he says, like he doesn't notice the uncomfortable silence, "I've submitted my application to the Naval Academy, but I'm wondering if there's anything else I can do now to start preparing myself for BUD/S?"

"You'll be on the swim team again this winter, right?"

He nods.

"Keep up with that, your running, and your upper and lower body calisthenics. Physical fitness is going to be most important for making it through the SEAL training."

"What about the selection process to get into the training? It's tough competition, right?"

"It is. Usually by senior year at the academy, interest has

dwindled to around sixty, but there are only thirty spots. You need to make a name for yourself at the academy . . . like you've been doing here at Wallingford. I'm sure you won't have a problem becoming a SEAL," he says with such goddamned pride for Jernigan, I want to puke.

"Excuse me," I say, standing. "I just remembered I have another commitment. It was a pleasure meeting you, Mr. Durant," I add without a trace of truth. I'm sure the look on my face makes it clear, but at least I'm saying the words required of me.

I throw my mostly uneaten dinner in the trash, place my tray and dishes on the conveyer belt, then head for my room, ready to forget about the last thirty minutes. I guess I'm lucky Paige found us when she did. Otherwise, I might be a nothing more than a white outline on the hallway floor.

I flop myself on the bed and pull out my phone to catch up on email and texts. There are two texts from my mom, wanting to know how I'm doing. Rather than write her back, I dial her number since I haven't talked to her once since coming here.

"Hey, Mom," I say when she picks up.

"Oh, Logan, honey! I've been waiting to hear from you. How are you? Are you getting enough to eat? They're not pushing you too hard, are they?"

"I'm fine," I say. "It's exhausting and demanding, but I've met a couple nice people. And classes aren't too bad."

"Good. So you're making friends?"

"Yeah, this guy Noah lives across the hall from me and he's cool. And this girl Paige and I are starting to get along."

"A girl?"

"Yeah."

"Are you . . . Did you and Lora break up?"

"No. Paige and I are just . . . friends." Really? Are we friends now? We're not more, and I guess we're not less. She has been acting mostly friendish lately. But what about the almost kiss? You don't kiss a friend. Especially not when you have a girlfriend. I knock my head into the wall behind me. I can't believe I was so stupid earlier.

My mom's quiet on the other end of the line. She's never said anything, but I get the impression she's not a huge Lora fan.

"What's Paige like?" she finally asks, trying to sound interested but not too interested.

"She's a play-strictly-by-the-rules kind of person."

"Oh."

"Very no-nonsense. Kind of cold . . . actually, I take that back. She seemed cold at first, but she's been pretty nice lately, especially today. She got me permission to leave campus."

"That was nice of her."

"Yeah."

"Well, hopefully I'll get to meet her sometime. I was thinking about coming up to visit in a few weeks. Would that be okay?"

"Sure."

"It won't be embarrassing for you if your mom shows up, will it? I don't want to make things harder on you."

"No. Paige's dad comes up a lot. And I've seen other parents here. It'd be . . . nice to see you," I say, feeling heat creep up my neck. We don't really have heart-to-heart discussions.

"Okay, good. I've got a big project at work right now, but once that's over, I'll plan the trip."

I nod, though she can't see it. She's always got big projects. As soon as one ends, the next one begins, which means it's unlikely she'll ever make it up here. I'm used to it, and at home, it never bothered me because the more she worked, the more freedom I had. For some reason, the thought of her not keeping her word now stings. I'll never tell her, though. She already feels guilty enough for being a single parent.

"Your dad asked me if he could visit, too."

"No."

She's quiet for a moment before saying, "I'll let him know. Oh, I talked to Mr. Needleham yesterday. He wants you to give him a call."

"Okay."

"I love you, honey."

"Love you, too."

As soon as I hang up, I press the contact info for my lawyer with shaky fingers. We haven't spoken since the video game incident. I haven't gotten into any more trouble with the dean, so hopefully this is just a standard catch-up call. I really can't handle any more issues today.

"Hello?" he answers after two rings.

"Hi, Mr. Needleham. It's Logan. Logan Evans," I say in a nervous voice. "My mom told me you wanted me to call."

"Yes, I did. How are things going at Wallingford?"

"Fine."

"Have you gotten into any more trouble?"

"Um . . ." I pause. How should I answer his question? If Paige were here, she'd tell me honestly. "I haven't gotten into trouble with the dean again," I finally say. I don't think trouble with Paige and Jernigan counts.

"Good, good. That's what I want to hear. I talked to Commander Anderson yesterday, and he said he's pleased with how you're doing. Said you've acclimated nicely since the rocky start. Great job."

"Thank you," I say, feeling a small pang of pride, despite my horrible afternoon.

He's quiet for a moment, and I imagine him writing something on his notepad with a bunch of arrows pointing at it. He's a big doodler. Every time we meet, he fills three pages of paper with notes, except those notes contain only about ten words total. The rest is squiggles and triple underlines and exclamation points.

I hear people taking in the background, like he just walked from his office into the waiting room. Or maybe from his car into a Starbucks since it's Sunday. He always had one of their mega cups sitting on his desk when I met with him.

"I've talked with the commonwealth's attorney's office, and they're willing to consider a plea bargain at your pretrial hearing in mid-November."

"That's good, right?"

"Yes." I hear a beep, then a whistling sound and someone yelling a name. Definitely Starbucks. "I'm trying for a reduction in your felony charge to a Class 1 misdemeanor. I'd like them to agree to a suspended license for a few months, a small fine, and some community service," he says. "In addition to you graduating from Wallingford, of course."

"Okay." This is what we talked about before I came here. I can handle no license for a while and community service. Actually, the community service requirement might be fulfilled through my club. "So no jail?" I ask, hoping to have him put my mind at ease.

"We'll have to see. There will be significant negotiations, but I will try everything I can to keep you out of prison."

"Thank you." His words aren't exactly reassuring, but at least we're on the same page.

"I'm coming up to Wallingford this week to meet with some of your teachers. I want to get as many good reports as I can for the prosecutor."

"Okay," I reply. I've never caused a problem in class, so hopefully this will help.

"I'll see you then. Keep up the good work, Logan."

"I will."

"Oh, one more thing."

"Yes?"

"Are you getting involved in extracurricular activities?"

"Yeah, a few."

"Good. The more the better. We want to show you're giving it your all at Wallingford."

"Okay."

We say goodbye, and when I hang up, there's an unwelcome feeling in my chest. You'd think I'd be thrilled hearing my lawyer's happy with how I'm doing, but there's a tightness inside me. Like my heart is heavier than usual and hanging lower than usual. I stare out the window at the mostly bare trees and the quad with only a few students returning to their dorms. The sun is setting, but it's not one of those pretty sunsets with oranges and purples. It's just a gray sky, getting darker and darker. That's kind of how I feel. Today started out okay and was really promising with being able to leave campus, but it's just been getting darker and darker as the hours wear on.

I miss home. My mom. My friends. My car. My freedom.

And, strangely, I miss that brief moment Paige and I shared before the car of cadets distracted us. It was wrong, I know, but I can't stop thinking about what almost happened.

And the fact that she seemed totally on board with it.

# CHAPTER 14

## PAIGE

**I can't believe them**. How could they? Poor Logan was scared out of his mind. Of course he was, he had Alex and my dad ganging up on him like sharks circling a capsized boat.

And for no reason. Logan didn't have his hands "all over me," like Danny said. He almost kissed me. That's it. And even if he had done something worse, why would my dad and Alex assume I couldn't handle things myself? I'm stronger and faster than Evans—than a lot of the guys here—and I would have no problem knocking some sense into any of them if I had to.

Equally bad, though, is I was practically begging Logan to kiss me, which adds embarrassment to my anger. I shake my head, trying to erase the memory of me drooling over his cute lips. Lieutenant commanders do not drool.

"Did you sign up for the CFA Captain Baldwin is offering this week?" my dad asks, interrupting my thoughts. We're in the rec hall with a few other cadets who are playing air hockey. My dad lines up his pool cue. I wait for him to take his shot before answering.

"No. I'll do it next week."

"Paige Rachel Durant." He lowers his cue to the floor and purses his lips. "You can't keep pushing it off. The sooner you get it done, the sooner you'll get your acceptance letter." To the Navy. That's what he's thinking, and I know I should bring up the Air Force, but I don't have the energy after everything else this evening.

"I know. I just want one more week of practice. Leah's offered to help me."

He nods. "Fine. One week. That's it. No more excuses."

"Yes, sir," I say, then approach the table. It probably makes more sense to tell him about the Air Force after my CFA anyway. There's more than enough stress with the CFA. I don't need to add more on myself until the test is over and I know whether it's good enough to even be considered for admission.

I take my shot. The four ball drops into the side pocket, and the three ball rolls close to the corner pocket. I tap that one in and then bank the eight ball into the opposite corner.

My dad whistles. "You've been practicing," he says before starting to rack the balls.

I haven't played in a few weeks. The real reason for my skills tonight is that I always perform better when angry, whether it's cross-country or pool.

He holds out his hand, inviting me to break, but it's getting late and I'd rather be alone. "Actually, Dad, I should get going. I have some homework I need to finish."

"Of course."

We step outside into the dark evening and head toward the parking lot.

"So I assume you've gotten Evans's behavior under control?" he says as we cross the quad.

"Yes, sir."

"You two aren't . . . don't . . . have anything else going on, do you?"

"What do you mean?"

"You're not . . . dating or anything are you?" Earlier today, when we talked right after the incident in the hallway, I had explained to him Logan and I almost made a mistake, but quickly came to our senses. He seemed satisfied with my answer at the time and hasn't said anything else about it until now, two hours later.

"No, of course not," I say, feeling my cheeks heat up. At around age ten, my dad and I developed an unspoken agreement we would not discuss uncomfortable topics like anything related to puberty or boys. He dutifully signed me up for classes and gave me a credit card to purchase whatever I needed. It's worked well for the past seven years, and I have no desire to change our agreement now.

"Okay, good. You're too young for a boyfriend."

"I know," I reply to get him to drop the subject.

When we reach his SUV, I wrap my arms around his shoulders and give him a kiss on the cheek. I always enjoy seeing him, but, tonight, it will be nice to get away from his stifling dad routine. It's bothering me much more than usual. "Thanks for coming today."

He nods. "Love you, pumpkin."

"Love you, too."

I wait until he disappears into the dark before heading back to my dorm. It only takes me half an hour to finish my homework; then I contemplate what to do until my yearbook meeting. I've got an hour and should probably read ahead for one my classes, but I can't stop thinking about Logan and what almost happened earlier today. I could ignore it, but I know that's not the right thing to do. We need to talk about it.

I head back to the rec hall, but he's not there. I ask a freshman to see if he's in his room, but he can't find him anywhere in the boys' dorm. After checking the library, the mess hall, and the track, I'm at a loss. It's like he disappeared. The longer and longer

I look, the more concerned I become he just got up and left. If he went AWOL, he's in serious trouble. Leaving campus without permission is even worse than an Honor Code violation.

The last place I check is the band room. I don't have much hope since, every Wednesday night, he acts like band practice is a fate worse than death, but it's the only place I haven't looked.

I hear the music before I open the door. It's loud and hard and immediately recognizable. It's the song we listened to on repeat in my car only a few hours ago.

After slipping through the door, I stand in the corner as Logan quickly slides his hands up and down the guitar, playing along to the music coming out of his phone. He hits a wrong note and shakes his head before stopping the song and letting the guitar hang from his neck as he runs his hand over his head.

I remain silent. Despite acting like he hates band, he obviously loves playing the guitar. And he's amazing. I've been first chair clarinet for nine months now. It's an accomplishment I'm proud of, but seeing and hearing Logan play makes me realize I'm an amateur, surrounded by even more amateur musicians.

He plays a few notes, furrows his brow, then checks a sheet of paper lying on the chair next to him. His foot taps rhythmically as his eyes wander the page, left to right, top to bottom. Then he starts the music and plays along again. This time, it's perfect.

He grins, turns off the music, then plays the entire song by himself. After the elaborate ending, I can't help but clap.

He jumps in his seat and spins to face me. "Jesus, Paige," he says, shaking his head. "How long have you been there?"

"Long enough to see how talented you are."

He frowns and shakes his head. "Not really."

"You taught yourself a new song in a matter of what? An hour?"

"No," he says, "I used to play this. I . . . refamiliarized myself with it."

I cross the room, turn a chair in front of him around to face him, then sit down. "Play something else?" I couldn't stare into his eyes all day like Leah, but if he were playing the guitar non-stop, I could watch him all day. It's mesmerizing, probably partly because of him and partly because I love his choice of songs.

He lifts the guitar and starts something much slower, this time singing along quietly. There's no crazy riff or complicated chords, but his performance is equally impressive. And his voice is nice. It's not the same as the lead singer of the band, but it's far better than I could do.

"I've never heard that one before," I say when he's finished.

"It's from their first album. I prefer their older stuff."

"I like it."

"I can put it on your phone, the real version, if you want."

I nod. "Thanks. I take it you like rock better than jazz?" We only play jazz during band. He's just as good but not nearly as enjoyable to watch then.

He nods but says nothing. After unplugging the guitar, he asks, "Were you coming here to practice? I'm done, you can have the room."

"No," I say, shaking my head. "I was looking for you."

He stills. "Why?"

"So, this afternoon," I say, keeping my eyes on the amp near his foot. "I'm . . . sorry about what happened."

"It's not your fault. Jernigan and your dad were worried. I can't blame them."

"No, not about that." I meet his eyes. "I mean, yes, I'm sorry about that, but . . . I was more thinking about what happened before."

"The almost kiss?"

I nod. "I'm sorry I put us in an uncomfortable situation. It was wrong. I'm an officer and I know better, but I had a momentarily lapse in judgment. I blame . . . never mind," I say, shaking my head.

"You blame what?"

"I should get going. I have yearbook."

"You blame what?" he says, his body stiffening. "Me? You had plenty of time to shove me away."

"No, not you in general, more . . ."

When I don't finish my thought, he says, "Do I need to remind you a cadet will never lie?"

I shake my head. In certain situations, withholding information would be considered lying, though not here. Still, I have to give him credit for trying. "Our argument, okay? And standing too close to each other. And holding your hand. And your eyes and smile. It all clouded my judgment, and I'm sorry."

"My eyes and smile?" he asks as a grin gradually builds on his face. I'm sure this wasn't the answer he expected, but he seems to like it.

"Yes. I apologize for my inappropriate behavior, and I promise I won't let it happen again. I have already assigned myself head duty to make up for the indiscretion."

The grin vanishes. He stares at me with a blank face for much too long.

"What?" I finally ask.

"You're making yourself clean a nasty bathroom because you like my eyes and smile?"

"Yeah."

With a shake of his head, he says, "You are such an odd person."

"What's that supposed to mean?"

"Well, a normal person, would say, 'Gee, you're cute. Want to go out sometime?' An odd person would say, 'Gee, you're cute. I better clean a toilet so I don't think about you again.'"

"We're at Wallingford. The normal response isn't realistic."

"Sure it is."

"Ah, no, it's not. Who has time for dating here?"

"You're telling me no one has ever dated at Wallingford?"

"A few have tried, but it never ends well."

"You don't strike me as someone who shies away from a challenge."

"I don't," I say, straightening my shoulders. I meet every challenge head-on and always rise above, whether it was memorizing all the US presidents the summer after third grade because my dad told me I couldn't or meeting the guys' PT requirements freshman year because, as a girl, I didn't want to be treated any differently. Failure is never an option for me.

But this is different. This isn't a challenge. And why does he care anyway? Unless . . . "Wait, are you saying *you* want to date *me*?"

"No!" His answer comes out quick and loud. "I mean, I've got a girlfriend. I'm just saying if you did find someone you liked, you could probably make it work."

"I don't want to make it work."

"Why not?"

"I need to focus on school and getting into the academy."

His brow furrows as he watches me. "That doesn't seem like a twenty-four/seven job."

"It is."

"Then you shouldn't leave campus for your personal time."

"Why?"

He picks up the amp and returns it and the guitar to the back of the room. When he rejoins me, he says, "Your personal time should be spent focusing on school and getting into the academy, not hiking with friends or eating ice cream."

I shake my head. "That's downtime to help me relax after a hard week."

"You don't think dating would be relaxing?"

"No. Because inevitably I'd let my boyfriend borrow my car and he'd crash into something and then the police would get involved and all my dreams would be turned upside down."

"Touché," he says with a chuckle. "You do have a point; however, things were good with my girlfriend before the accident."

"I'll have plenty of time to date after I finish the academy. And become a pilot."

"When will that be?"

"Six years or so," I reply with a shrug. It's really not *that* long.

"You're not going to date at all until you're like twenty-four?"

I nod.

"Some people are married and have a kid by then."

I shrug again. "Not me."

"Wow."

Again he stares at me with that blank face that says nothing and a million things all at once. "What?" I ask.

"Have you ever even kissed a guy?"

I shake my head.

"Never?"

"No. Why?"

"You almost kissed me today."

"I already told you it was a momentary lapse in judgment."

"You don't think you'll have any more of those in the next six years?"

I start to shake my head, then stop. How can I guarantee such a thing? I never thought I'd be tempted to kiss Logan, but it happened when I least expected it.

"You're totally out of touch with reality," he says. "And your hormones. At some point, you're gonna find a guy so hot all your ridiculous rationalizing will fly out the window."

"I don't think so."

"Okay." He has a straight face, but his pale green eyes twinkle under the fluorescent lights like he's laughing.

"You don't believe me," I say.

"Nope."

"I would never risk my career for a guy."

"And . . . there's the ridiculous rationalizing. Why does it have to be one or the other? I bet you're a great multitasker."

"I am, but that's beside the point."

"*That* is the point, right? You're afraid if you spend time with a guy then you won't study as hard or work out as much, right?"

Yes. But if I agree, he'll tell me my plan is flawed, which I don't need to hear. Even if there were only a small chance of dating interfering with my future, I wouldn't risk it. "Why do you even care about this?" I ask.

He opens his mouth, then closes it. After a moment, he says, "You're right. It's none of my business, and last time I stuck my nose where it didn't belong, you almost kissed me. I'd hate for you to have another momentarily lapse in judgment so soon after your last one. I'd never forgive myself if I ruined your chances at the Air Force Academy."

"Don't worry," I say with a grin. "It's not going to happen again." Yes, his lips are still nice and I'm finding his musical ability quite attractive, but admiring from afar will be the extent of it from now on.

My dad and the CFA are big enough obstacles; I can't let anything else interfere with my dreams.

# CHAPTER 15

# PAIGE

**"Nine point six seconds,"** Leah says with a sigh.

I pound my fist into a stack of football pads laying on the side of the track while my labored breaths come out as white mist in the cold afternoon air. Two-tenths of a second too slow. The CFA has clearly defined goals. If I don't reach nine point four seconds, I don't reach the goal, which would likely mean no academy—Navy or Air Force. I've been practicing every day this week and still can't get to where I need to be.

"Let's try again," Leah suggests. "You're not turning your hips all the way on the pivot. Get them facing back the way you came."

I nod and catch my breath. "Okay, one more time." I take my place behind the start line and wait for Leah's command.

"On your mark . . . get set . . . go."

I take off as fast as I can, my legs pushing off the ground and propelling me forward. When I reach the other line, I remember Leah's words and concentrate on bringing my hips all the way around as my fingertips on the ground steady me. Then I push off again and repeat two more times.

"Nine point five!" she says, giving me a high five when I finish. "You looked much better that time."

"I'm still too slow."

"Maybe try alternating your pivot leg? I read that can help."

"I'll try anything at this point." I wipe my forehead with my sweatshirt and take a couple deep breaths. While I'm doing that, I see Logan enter the track on the far side. He does a few stretches and then starts a slow jog.

"Ready?" Leah asks.

"Yeah," I reply, focusing back on my task with a newfound sense of confidence. Perhaps alternating my pivot leg is all it will take. Unfortunately, it turns out to be harder than I expect, and my time shows it. Nine point nine seconds. The worst time I've gotten in weeks.

I shove my hands through my hair, messing up my braid, and groan in frustration. I'm successful in everything I do. Sometimes it might take weeks of practice, but I'm always successful. Until this. I don't know what it is about this exercise, but I seem incapable of conquering it no matter how much time and effort I put in. I've never given up on anything, but I'm beginning to wonder if this might be a first. Of course, then I could kiss the Air Force goodbye. I have no choice. I have to do this. I have to pass no matter what.

"Everything okay?" Logan asks when he approaches us on the track.

"No," I say with a groan.

He slows to a stop and comes closer. "What's wrong?"

"The shuttle run is kicking my butt. The best I've done is still one-tenth of a second too slow."

"That's really close," he says. "You'll get it."

He doesn't understand. "Close only counts in horseshoes and hand grenades, not the shuttle run," I say, grinding my teeth together.

"Okaaay, Lieutenant Commander Grumpy-Ass."

My eyes grow wide and my jaw tenses. He hasn't been so

overtly disrespectful in a while, and I really don't want to hear it right now. Pointing to the track, I say, "Add on five laps to your daily run."

He turns around and starts jogging away but flips me off over his shoulder.

"Make it ten!" I yell to him. This is just what I need. Annoyance at Logan on top of frustration at myself for my ineptitude. I face Leah and say, "One more time?"

She gives me the command, and I pump my arms and legs harder, taking out some of my anger. Just when I was beginning to think he had turned the corner, he goes and does something to show me he still doesn't respect the chain of command here.

"Nine point four," Leah says, jumping up and down when I finish. "You did it! You did it!"

"Really?" I grab the stopwatch to see for myself. She's right. I finally got the goal.

"What did you do differently?" she asks.

"Nothing . . . I . . . I was thinking about Logan and how annoyed I was at him."

"Then you two need to get into a massive fight the day of the test."

I scoff at her, but she may be right. Just like with pool and cross-country, I also seem to do best at the shuttle run when I'm upset.

"Want to try it again?" she asks.

I shake my head. "No, I want to end on a positive note today. Can you help me again tomorrow?" It's a relief I finally reached the goal time, but I'm not naive enough to assume I'll be able to easily reproduce this on test day. I won't feel confident until I consistently reach my goal in four out of five attempts. The problem is I only have a week, which means there's a good chance I won't be going into the test confident.

"Sure," Leah says. "I'm gonna run a couple miles now. Want to join me?"

I nod, and we take off at a leisurely pace around the track. Despite our slow speed, we still catch up to Logan after two laps. I plan on ignoring him, but Leah says, "She did it! She got the time!" as we pass by him.

"Nice!" he replies holding out his hand for a fist bump, obviously not harboring any resentment toward me. I tap my knuckles against his as he says, "I told you you could do it."

"You told me a lot of other things, too," I say as Leah speeds up and away from us. It's almost like she planned on getting us to run together. Normally, I wouldn't mind the time with him, but I'm still irritated by his earlier behavior. Of course, his behavior led me to finally getting the time I needed, so I shouldn't be too annoyed. "Enjoying your extra laps?" I ask.

He shrugs. "I was planning on a longer run today, anyway. In fact, I can still earn another five laps before it's longer than what I had planned. What should I do?" He taps his finger against his chin as if he's deep in thought.

"That's not a good idea."

"I'm only kidding," he says, knocking me with his elbow as we round the corner of the track.

"Cadet Evans," a loud voice calls from the fence. We both look in that direction and see the dean with an older man carrying a briefcase and wearing wire-frame glasses, a scarf, and an unbuttoned trench coat revealing an expensive-looking suit. "Please come here," the dean says.

"This ought to be good," Logan mutters under his breath.

"Who's that?"

"My lawyer."

"Oh."

Without another word, he jogs overs to the fence as the dean walks away. I continue around the track, speeding up on the parts where I'm facing away from them and slowing down on the parts where I'm facing them. It doesn't help, though. My view is of Logan's back and the lawyer's front, but the lawyer's face doesn't give anything away.

After three laps, Logan motions for me to join them.

"This is Lieutenant Commander Durant," Logan says when I reach the fence. "She's my peer mentor and can attest to how well I'm doing here." He briefly meets my eyes, and I get the sense he's pleading with me to say the right words.

"Good afternoon, Ms. Durant," the lawyer says. "I'm Arthur Needleham, Mr. Evans's attorney."

"It's a pleasure to meet you," I say, holding out my hand. He shakes it and then asks to speak to me privately, so Logan goes back to the track and slowly starts another lap.

"How is Mr. Evans doing here at Wallingford?" the lawyer asks in a cheerful tone as he takes a notepad and pen out of his briefcase.

"Good," I reply. "From what I've seen academically, I'd say he's in the top ten percent, maybe five."

"Yes, yes, he's always excelled in the classroom. Is he getting into trouble here?" He still sounds cheerful, but his stiff posture and intense gaze make me realize the importance of this question.

"What kind of trouble?" I ask cautiously.

"Disobeying rules? Breaking the law?"

"To my knowledge, he's not breaking the law."

"What about Wallingford's rules?"

"Um . . . what rules?"

"Any of them."

I gulp and look over my shoulder, but Logan is on the far side of the track. I know he wants me to say the right words, but I also have to adhere to the Honor Code. I must always be honest, no exceptions.

"He's not gone AWOL, which would be the worst offense," I say, shifting my weight from one foot to the other.

He writes something on his notepad, and I bite my lip. I'm being honest but not entirely forthcoming. Still, Logan doesn't even belong here if he's being truthful about the accident, which I believe he is. I can't make things worse for him.

"He hasn't hidden any contraband in his room," I continue, happy to list all the positive things he does on a daily basis, "and he's never late for classes or formation. Compared to other DQs . . ."

"DQs?"

"Delinquents. It's the nickname we give those who are sent here against their will. He's clearly not a delinquent, though."

He looks up from his notepad. "Why do you say that?"

"He told me what—" I catch myself before I divulge his secret. I don't agree with him confessing to a crime he didn't commit, but I also don't want to be the one to set the record straight. He needs to do it. Or his girlfriend. "Um . . . it's a feeling I've got."

"Okay," he says, looking much less interested now, "so getting back to his behavior here . . ."

"He's joined the community service club. He's great at the guitar. He's becoming more and more physically fit. He's easily running five miles now, and he could barely do a half mile when he started."

"This is good information," he says underlining something on his pad three times. "Anything else?

"He shows appropriate respect for—" I'm about to say superiors, but he still has his moments with me, like fifteen minutes ago. "Our instructors," I finish. That's true.

"Okay, great. I'll continue to check in to see how he's doing. Do you mind if I reach out to you again?"

"No, not at all."

We shake hands again, and then he leaves. I lean against the fence and watch Logan on the track. At least he's doing better now, so I had some good things to share. Part of me feels a little guilty about leaving out the video game incident and his bouts of disrespect, but honestly, how relevant are those now? His disrespect is only directed at me and Alex. It doesn't seem fair to potentially hurt his future over a few eye rolls and middle fingers when he never committed the original crime in the first place. If he had, I'm sure I'd be more inclined to be completely open with the lawyer.

Of course I would.

# CHAPTER 16

# LOGAN

**It's study hall,** and I just finished tutoring a sophomore in algebra, which leaves me about an hour to finish my own homework. Luckily, there's not much tonight—just some physics problems and a few chapters for my literature class.

As I'm finishing the problems, Paige comes strolling in to the library. She often studies here and will usually sit near me. I'm still shocked by how nothing changed after our almost kiss. It's like it never even happened, which is good.

Even more surprising is how Paige admitted she thinks I'm good-looking. Okay, she said she likes my smile and eyes, but I'm assuming that can be extrapolated to my looks as a whole. Maybe not. Maybe it really is just my smile and eyes. Even so, those aren't bad parts of you to be attractive. It's certainly better than your feet or ears.

Luckily, I didn't have to admit to anything. Saying I'm beginning to find her hotter and hotter the more time we spend together would feel like I'm cheating on Lora. Instead, I try to ignore it. Some days it's easier than others. Civilian clothes days are rough.

"Hey," she whispers as she pulls out a chair across from me and lowers herself into it.

"You're later than usual."

"My dad sent me this great book. I started reading it earlier today and couldn't put it down."

"Yeah? What kind of book?"

"Nonfiction."

"Shhh!" says the one other guy sitting at our table as he sends a nasty glare our way.

"Sorry," Paige mouths to the guy. To me, she whispers, "I read mostly history, but I like memoirs, too."

Of course she reads boring shit, not best sellers. "So what was this riveting book about?" I whisper.

"A woman who held the record for the fastest known time on the Appalachian Trail. She did it in forty-six days—Maine to Georgia. Can you even imagine?"

"No."

The guy from earlier slams his book shut and sends another glare in our direction before moving to a desk at the back of the room.

Paige leans across the table and says more quietly, "She averaged forty-seven miles a day. That's almost two marathons each day."

"I'd die on day one."

She laughs and drags her backpack onto the table. "Not if you trained beforehand. I think I'd like to try it sometime. Can you imagine how awesome it'd feel to accomplish something like this?"

"Nope. I can't even imagine thinking about doing something so crazy."

She smiles as she pulls a textbook out of her bag. "You need more ambition."

"If I can get a job that puts food in my stomach, clothes on my back, and gas in the car, I'm good."

"There's got to be some big goal you have in life?"

"Nope."

"Nothing?"

"Nope."

"Become fluent in a foreign language?"

I shake my head.

"Travel to every continent?"

"No."

"Get a black belt in karate?"

I give her a sideways glance. That sounds more like a goal *she'd* have.

"Nothing? Absolutely nothing?"

"I mean . . . I guess a goal is graduating from Wallingford and staying out of jail."

"Well, at least that's something, but goals should be about setting a high bar for yourself, not a bare-minimum bar."

I shrug. "There are two kinds of people in life—the Paiges and the Logans. I'm totally comfortable with who I am and see no reason to improve upon what is already perfection," I say, waving my hands down my body like a game-show model. "You, on the other hand, seem to have serious self-esteem issues with your need for constant self-improvement."

She rolls her eyes.

She freaking rolls her eyes.

My mouth drops open and I point my finger at her.

"What?" she whispers.

"You rolled your eyes."

"No, I didn't. I would never do that."

"You did! I swear." I *am* rubbing off on her. Miss Proper is starting to crack and turn into a normal teen right before my very eyes.

With a shake of her head, she says, "You're delusional, too, in addition to being *'perfect.'*"

"At least we're in agreement on my perfection." I give her a wink as I open my book. She has to know I didn't mean anything I said. I'm about as far from perfection as one can be, and I've never met someone with more self-esteem than her.

She meets my eyes and offers me a small smile before starting on her own physics problems. I try to focus on my book—*1984*—but I've already read it twice. Instead, my eyes are repeatedly drawn up to watch Paige. She taps her pencil on the table as she reads the problem, and I immediately recognize the rhythm. Her lips silently move to the lyrics of the song, and I wonder if she has a good singing voice.

I'd love to see her at a school dance, letting loose. Back when we first met, I'd have sworn she would never let loose, but I'm beginning to think there's a wilder Paige under the regimented facade that has been perfected over the years. It's been suppressed and pushed deeper and deeper, but it's not totally gone yet.

Maybe, if I'm lucky, I'll get to see it someday.

I erase my answer and start over. This is an easy problem, so I don't know why I'm having difficulty. Scratch that—my lack of sleep last night is why. Paige convinced me to read that damn memoir, and I was up until one in the morning finishing it. She was right—it was riveting. I still have no desire to speed walk the Appalachian Trail, but it did make me feel a little lazy. Okay, a lot lazy. I could probably run a little farther during athletic time or do a few more reps in the weight room.

I roll my neck and take a deep breath. On top of being tired, I have a kink in my neck from trying to hold the book and a flashlight under my covers after lights-out. I really need to invest in one of those clip-on book lights if I plan on continuing to be rebellious. Of course, it'd probably be confiscated during our room inspection since I'm sure Jernigan would figure out its purpose.

Someone knocks on the door and then enters the classroom. All of our heads snap up to see the visitor so we can determine if we need to stand at attention or not. We don't. It's a freshman who's about as low as me on the totem pole of cadet ranks. While he talks to the teacher, I focus back on the problem in front of me.

"Mr. Evans," the teacher says.

"Yes, sir?" I reply, standing.

"You're wanted in the main office."

"Yes, sir." And just like that, my palms grow sweaty. What have I done now? I glance at Paige on my way out, hoping she might be able to shed some light on what's going on, but she shrugs her shoulders and looks as confused as me. I then pass by Jernigan, who's watching me with narrowed eyes.

Great. Just great. Apparently I've angered him yet again. Did he report me to the dean for something? God, I hope not. As much of a dick as he's been, he's at least kept it between us. I do not want the dean involved. I can't have Jernigan ruin everything for me.

When I get to the office, only the secretary is there, which makes me hopeful. If it were something really bad, I'm sure the dean or the headmaster would be waiting for me.

"Oh, Logan," she says, looking up from her computer. "Your lawyer is on the phone. He said it's very important." She passes me the handset.

"Hello," I say, trying to hide my nerves. What does he want? What if the plea bargain is off? What if he tells me it's time for an orange jumpsuit?

"You need to dump her ass, Lo!"

It's Gordy, not my lawyer. I take a deep, relieved breath.

"Um, Mr. Needleham, thanks for calling." I angle myself away from the secretary, but the cord is only so long. I can't get totally out of earshot. Hopefully she can't hear Gordy's end of the conversation.

"Nate and I went to the movies last night and Lora was there, hanging all over some guy!"

"I am disappointed to hear that," I say.

More like pissed.

Did the past year not mean anything to her? I go away for like a month, and she moves on? Already? I should've known something was up the moment I received the care package. She included one of my old sweatshirts I had given her, saying she was worried I might need it up in the mountains. I thought it was unusually sweet. She wasn't being sweet; she was clearing me out of her life.

"We confronted her, and she begged us not to tell you. Said it would be too hard on you with everything else going on."

"That's very considerate of her to look out for my best interests," I say, grinding my teeth together. And here I was feeling guilty for almost kissing Paige and thinking about how hot she is. It sounds like Lora's been doing at least that, if not more.

"Right? She doesn't deserve what you're doing. Break up with her, come clean. Then you can come home and be done with all this military school shit."

"That does sound appealing."

"So do it," he says, calmer now.

Can I do it? Two weeks ago, the thought of breaking up with her was really depressing, but now . . . not quite as much, especially if she's fooling around with another guy. It was nice thinking she was at home, waiting for me, and come June we could fall back into our easy routine, but was that ever a possibility? Could we ever really get back to what we had before the accident?

Which brings me to the bigger question. Can I turn her in? Even though I'm not a huge fan of her right now, I don't want her to go to prison. I still like her. Maybe not necessarily as girlfriend material, but what we had still means something to *me*, even if it doesn't mean anything to her.

No, I can't ruin her life. It sucks, but, like Mr. Needleham said, in the grand scheme of things it's only eight months of my life. A prison sentence would affect her for the rest of her life.

"I see your point," I say.

"Good."

"I'll take care of as much of it as I can this weekend. Thanks for calling, Mr. Needleham."

"Later, Lo."

"I look forward to speaking with you again soon."

I hand the phone back to the secretary.

"Everything, okay?" she asks, the wrinkles around her eyes turned down in what seems to be genuine concern.

"Yeah, thanks."

As I walk back to class, I think about it some more. Maybe this is a good thing in disguise. The whole one door closes so another one opens, right?

Maybe this is a little good cosmic karma finally raining down on me. A sign I can find a better girlfriend. One who wouldn't make me take the heat for her mistakes. One who wouldn't forget about me the minute I leave town.

One who may have a stick up her ass but would have my back. Shit.

What am I thinking? Paige is absolutely not girlfriend material. And I don't need to jump from one girl to another. I could use a little break. I need to focus on school and staying out of prison anyway. That's what's most important at this moment.

*And now I even sound like her*, I think, rolling my eyes.

It's Saturday, and I just finished morning study hall. I'm starving and want to head to lunch, but I need to get this phone call out of the way first.

With a sigh, I pull my phone out of my pocket and lower myself to the floor outside the mess hall. I never thought I'd be the one calling it off, but here I am.

I tap my fingers on my knee while I wait for Lora to pick up. As soon as I hear her voice, my whole body tenses. "Hey. It's me," I say.

"How's it going?"

"Okay. How are you?"

"Fine."

Then it's silent, which is another sign we're over. We never used to have silence between us.

"So, uh," I say, tracing a dark brown spot on my cammies, "this long-distance thing isn't really working for me."

"What? Why?" she asks. I can't tell for sure, but it seems like there's some relief in her voice, mixed in with the surprise.

"I think a relationship requires being able to see each other, or at least talk to each other, more than two days a week. Don't you?"

"Oh, well, I guess so. I mean, it's not what I want, but if you think it's best, then okay."

I probably should call her out on the other guy, but it's not like I'm totally innocent myself.

She continues. "We'll still be friends, right?"

"Yeah, sure."

"I . . . I know I owe you big for what you're doing. Maybe when you come home for Christmas, I can take you out to dinner or something. As friends."

Yeah, that ought to cover my time at Wallingford. "Sure."

"Okay."

"Okay."

"Let's keep in touch," she says quietly.

"Sure."

"You're a good guy, Logan. I miss you and wish things could've turned out differently for us."

"Yeah, me too." It would be great if I were at home right now. And she hadn't crashed my car. And we were snuggled up on the couch watching something on TV, but that's never going to happen again. The night of the accident changed everything, and there's no going back.

We say goodbye, and then I end the call. Despite thinking I would be okay with this, there's a small empty feeling in my chest. Not big enough I regret what I did, but also not small enough it's easily ignored. I'm going to miss her.

I quickly type out a text to Gordy and Nate: *It's done. Lora and I are through. Thanks for the heads-up.*

Nate replies first. *Sorry, man.*

Then a message comes in from Gordy: *Is she going to admit to the accident?*

*No. I didn't ask her to do that.*

*Why not?!* Nate's reply is first, but Gordy sends a similar one only seconds later.

*I'm not going to ruin her life*, I type. *I can't do that to her.*

Gordy writes: *I can't believe you're staying there for her*, while Nate writes: *You're too nice. I've always said that.*

I pocket my phone without texting them back and take a deep breath. No more Lora. One less tie to home. Slowly but surely, Wallingford may remove all outside influences on me. I'm sure that's more of their plan.

"Good afternoon," a familiar voice says.

I look up to see Paige walking down the empty hall toward me. I quickly stand at attention and reply, "Good afternoon, Lieutenant Commander."

"What are you doing?" she asks as she approaches me.

"Breaking up with Lora."

"Oh." Her smile fades, and that cute line appears at the top of her nose. "Sorry. Want to talk about it?"

"Not really. Why are you late to lunch?" I ask as we walk into the mess hall together.

"I was talking to my dad."

"How is the Navy SEAL?"

"Fine," she says with a chuckle. "He's coming earlier than usual tomorrow. Wants to go to the shooting range. Do you want to join us?"

I shake my head. I have successfully avoided it so far and hope to do the same for the rest of my time here.

As we step up to the buffet line, she asks, "Have you ever been to a range?"

"Nope," I say as I grab a tray and then hand one to her. I'm not into killing animals and have no plans of going to war, so why would I need to shoot a gun?

"It's only open a few times each semester. You should come and watch. It's fun."

"I'll think about it," I say to be nice as I spoon green beans onto my plate. "Oh, hey, that book you lent me?"

"Yeah."

"You were right. It was good."

"See? Made you feel like you could climb Mount Everest, right?"

"Uh, no. But maybe run a 5K race or something."

She knocks her elbow into me. "I hate to break it to you, but you've already run more than a 5K. Aim higher, buddy."

"By now you should realize I don't aim high. I aim completely horizontally. Smack-dab at average. Maybe a little lower."

"We need to change your mediocre tendencies. You have too much potential to be average."

I pause in line and turn to face her. She can't be serious. I expect her to be smirking, but she meets my gaze with hard eyes and her soldier expression. "You're mistaken," I say before turning around.

"No, you are."

It's only three little words and they aren't exactly nice words, but they cause my lips to curl upward just a bit. I don't know why. It's not like I want to do anything great with my life, but it's kind of nice to have someone think you can. It's like she can look past the lazy person I am to see something that maybe once was there.

My parents don't anymore. My dad's been too busy trying to buy my happiness after he cheated on my mom, and my mom thinks I still need space to mope around and be pissed at the world.

And it's not like Gordy and Nate are exactly go-getters. They're my best friends, and I can't imagine not having them around the past five years, but to them "making something out of your life" would be reaching a *Fortnite* global leaderboard. Granted, I'd be pretty psyched if I did that, too.

I'm sure that's not what Paige had in mind when she said I have potential, though. I'm sure she was thinking some ridiculous athletic feat or moving up the ranks at Wallingford or breaking some archery record.

I suppose any of those *would* be nice.

And it's not like I have anything better to do with my personal time. Plus, dedication to something might help convince the prosecutor the plea bargain is a good idea. The whole Wallingford-transformed-me-from-a-lazy-troublemaker-to-an-eager-over-achiever idea.

God, I'm going to end up just like Jernigan.

And my dad.

How in the hell did this happen? I groan and shake my head. Wallingford has a way of sneaking its way into your life whether you like it or not.

## CHAPTER 17

## LOGAN

**That night,** after study hall, I change into my stylish Wallingford sweats, put in my earbuds, and head toward the overhead lights of the football field glowing in the dark. It's a balmy forty degrees. *Perfect* running weather.

Apparently I'm not the only one who thinks so. There are three other cadets out on the track. Two are jogging next to each other while the third is doing sprints along a straightaway.

I touch my toes a couple of times and then start off at a slow jog.

This is a first for me: voluntarily running during personal time for no reason. Usually during this time, I'll either practice the guitar or lie in bed and listen to music. Every now and again Noah and I will hang out, but he usually still needs to finish homework.

I don't really have a plan or a goal for this, other than to run until I'm too tired to continue. I have no idea if that will be ten laps or fifty laps.

A faster song starts, and I turn it up. It's got a strong beat, and before long, my legs are pounding the track in time with the music. It's nice to have music. It's not allowed during athletic time, which leaves my mind to obsess over how many laps I have left. Now I focus on the songs instead.

After I complete five laps, the sprinting cadet leaves and the other two move from the track to run up and down the stairs of the bleachers. At some point, they also leave, though I don't notice when. The cool air, which initially burned my lungs and stung my face, now feels refreshing against my flushed skin. I take in long, deep breaths as I switch to a new album, and then eventually another.

When two of the four overhead lights blink off, I know it's time to head back to my room so I don't miss lights-out.

As I'm jogging along the empty path, almost to my dorm, two girls suddenly emerge from around a corner, and I nearly trample them.

"Sorry," I say, grabbing an arm of each of them to keep them steady. "Oh, good evening. Lieutenant Commander Durant, Culver," I say as soon as I recognize Paige and Leah. I stand at attention, and they return my greeting.

Paige looks me up and down, then asks, "Were you running?"

"Yeah," I reply with a shrug, like it's no big deal.

"Voluntarily?"

I nod.

She grins and asks, "How far?"

"I don't know. I didn't keep track."

"How long were you out there?"

"Um . . . maybe a little over an hour."

Her jaw drops, and she just stares at me.

I shrug again. "I had good music. Running doesn't seem nearly as bad with music."

"That's true. You probably ran at least seven miles."

"Huh." It didn't seem nearly that far.

"How'd it feel?"

"Okay." I never once got out of breath, probably because I wasn't really pushing myself too hard. My legs did start to get sore toward the end, and I'm sure I'll pay for that tomorrow.

"You should register for a half marathon."

"Maybe." There's still a big different between seven miles and thirteen miles.

"We could do it together."

"You want to run a half marathon with me?"

"Sure. I've never done one—it'd be a nice thing to accomplish. Leah, you in?"

Her friend shakes her head. "I max out at ten."

"So?" Paige says, looking back at me.

"Maybe," I reply with a shrug. "I'd need to find one and sign up and figure out how to get there . . . There could be some logistical challenges." Like my complete inability to drive with a suspended license.

"There's one in my hometown every April. The dean will give you permission, and I'll drive you there," she says as if reading my mind. "My dad would probably do it with us. He loves running with me."

"Slow down there, eager beaver," I reply, holding my hands up in front of my chest. "I haven't agreed yet." And the addition of her dad isn't exactly a selling point. I'd be happy to let my one and only interaction with him be my last.

"Sorry," she says, smoothing her hair back though I can't find a single strand out of place. "I'm just happy to see . . . you . . . this . . ." She waves her hand in front of me.

"What?"

"You're acting like a real cadet."

It takes all my self-control not to roll my eyes. She's right, though. I am acting like a real cadet. That right there should be enough for me to throw out the idea forever, but Mr. Needleham wanted me to sign up for more activities. He'd love to know I'm training for a half marathon. And if it'll help me get the plea bargain, it's probably a no-brainer. I should do it. Still, it's thirteen miles. Thirteen miles in a car can take a while. Can I seriously go from couch potato to serious runner? "Let me sleep on it," I finally say.

"Of course."

"Five minutes till lights-out," Leah says, tugging on Paige's arm. "C'mon."

While still watching me, Paige takes a couple of steps in the direction of their dorm. "I'm proud of you, Logan."

She waves goodbye and then takes off at a sprint with Leah by her side.

I stare after them for a couple seconds and then realize I need to do the same or face the wrath of Jernigan. I bolt to my dorm and up to my room in record time.

Peering out the window, I see the two of them as they slip through the door. The windows in the stairwell allow me to watch them run up two flights before disappearing through another door. I continue staring as lights start to dim in each of the rooms. In one room, however, the lights go on and someone peeks through the blinds. I'm too far away to see the person's eyes, but if I had to guess, I'd say they're a bright green.

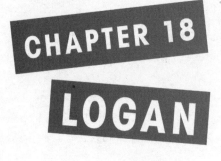

# CHAPTER 18

# LOGAN

**The next day** is Sunday, and just as I suspected, my legs are killing me. It takes every ounce of energy to haul myself out of bed for formation. Then PT is excruciating. At least study hall should bring some relief.

I plan to go to the library like usual, but the thought of sitting in a hard wooden chair is too much. Instead, I spread out on my bed with my books scattered around me and start with the three chapters for my literature reading.

Just as Winston and Julia are apprehended by the Thought Police, there's a knock on my open door and Noah walks in. "Hey, man."

"Hey," I say, sitting up and lowering the paperback.

"You helping out with the haunted house tonight?" he asks.

I nod. It's Halloween, and apparently Wallingford has a tradition of turning itself into a haunted house for local kids. Each classroom is transformed into a different scene and cadets dress up and act out short skits in each as the children walk by.

"Want to help me? We finished decorating our room last night. It's for the teenagers, so lots of gore."

"What's the theme?" I ask.

"Mad scientists experimenting on human subjects."

"Sounds like fun."

"Yeah, should be. We need one more person. Do you think Paige would do it?"

I shrug. "I don't know. I can ask her."

"Thanks," he says. He starts to turn around, then stops himself. "You don't have to answer this if you don't want to, but are you two . . . like a thing now?"

I laugh at his seriousness. "Uh, no. I don't think Paige will be a *thing* with anyone for a long time. Maybe ever."

"Really? She's been acting so differently the last couple of weeks. I just assumed . . ." His voice trails off, and he looks out the window.

"Assumed what?" I ask.

"I don't know," he says, focusing back on me. "I guess I thought maybe she's chilled out because she was finally getting some." He smirks, and I throw a pillow at him, which he easily catches before it hits his face. "I take it that's a no?"

"Yeah, she's not getting any. At least not from me . . . and I doubt from anyone else."

He takes a step back into the hallway, looks both ways, then sticks his head inside again. "We'd all know about it if Jernigan finally got lucky," he whispers.

He's trying to be funny and it *is* funny, but the thought of Jernigan and Paige together makes my stomach churn.

"Well, my money is still on you," Noah says. "No one else has been able to melt the Ice Queen like you. Just give it more time."

My brows raise as he turns around. "Wait," I say.

He looks over his shoulder.

"Never mind." I shake my head. I don't want to get into a discussion of me and Paige. Yes, I find her hot. Yes, I'm starting to really enjoy spending time with her. Yes, she likes my smile and eyes. But there are about a million reasons to leave it right there. Which is what I need to do.

We say bye, and then he crosses the hall to his own room.

I try to focus back on my book, but he got me thinking of Paige, which reminds me I need to make a decision about the half marathon. Last night, before bed, I was leaning toward doing it, but now that my body is dealing with the aftermath of seven miles, I'm not so sure anymore.

Although if it helps with the plea bargain, it'd be worth it.

I could sit here all day going back and forth or I could get an answer immediately. I grab my phone from my desk and dial my lawyer's direct number.

"Hello?" he answers.

"Hi, Mr. Needleham. It's Logan Evans."

"Oh, hi, Logan. How are things?"

"Fine."

"Are you in trouble?" he asks.

"No. I just wanted to get your opinion on something."

"Sure."

"I'm kind of thinking about maybe training for a half marathon, but it's a lot of work. I'm not sure it'd be worth it. Do you think it'd help with the plea bargain?"

"Absolutely. Anything you do to show you have positive interests and hobbies will help prove to the court you're on the right path now."

"Okay," I reply with a sigh. I guess part of me was hoping he'd say it wouldn't make a difference. "So you think I should do it?"

"I do. I'm glad you called because the date for your pretrial hearing was changed. Give me a second," he says, and I hear shuffling of papers. "Let's see . . . it was moved back to November twenty-ninth."

"What happens there again?"

"That's when I'll present the plea bargain to the prosecutor. Hopefully she'll agree to the terms we've discussed and then you'll just have to finish up at Wallingford. Continue to stay out of trouble between now and then, okay? We want the strongest case possible."

"Yes, sir."

He chuckles. "I see Wallingford is having a positive effect, in multiple ways."

"I'm sorry?"

"This is the first time you've called me 'sir.'"

"Oh, yeah," I reply with a small laugh of my own. "I guess it's second nature now."

"That's not a bad thing."

"No, I suppose not."

"Keep up the good work, Logan."

We say goodbye and then realization sinks in. I'm running a half marathon. A freaking thirteen-mile half marathon.

A couple hours later, Noah and I and a few other DQs are at our normal table in the mess hall for lunch. I haven't had a chance to tell Paige about my plans, so I scan the room for her. She's going through the buffet line with her dad right behind her.

I expect her to take her dad to the table in the corner where she eats dinner with Jernigan and Leah and other officers, but she heads our way.

As soon as she and her dad pull out chairs, Jernigan appears like an excited little puppy. He's never sat at our table before.

All the cadets mumble their greetings to the two officers, then shoot me an annoyed glare. I shrug my shoulders to no one in particular. It's not like I invited Mr. Durant and Jernigan over. I'd be just as happy if they were across the room.

"Are you staying for the haunted house, Mr. Durant?" Jernigan asks, acting like it's perfectly normal for him to be at our table.

"No, I can't make it this year."

"That's too bad. Paige, you're joining my room, right?"

"Ye—"

"I thought you were helping us," Noah says.

Paige's brows furrow in confusion.

"Sorry, I was supposed to ask you," I say, giving Paige and then Noah an apologetic look. Though it's not like I had any opportunity to talk to her before now. "It's mad scientists. Lots of gore."

"Oh, that sounds like fun," she says.

"C'mon, you can't mess with tradition," Jernigan says. "We've been doing this together since freshman year."

"That's true, but . . ." She looks at me. "But I think I'd like to try something new this year. I perfected the headless horseman two years ago; it's time for something different."

Yes. *In your face, Jernigan.*

No.

Shit.

As awesome as it is to see her reject him, this will only make things worse. He'll up the torture.

I sneak a look across the table, and sure enough he's sending a death glare my way. I know I should ignore him and focus on my food, but my lips have a mind of their own and damn if they don't rise into a patronizing smirk he's deserved for a very long time.

"Plus," Paige continues after swallowing a French fry, "it's time for an underclassman to step up and take on that role. I think Catherine would be great. I'll talk to her." She continues on as though nothing monumental just happened. Maybe in her mind it didn't, but to everyone else around the table, she just snubbed Jernigan for me. Her lowly DQ.

Why would she do this? Is it as simple as she's more interested in Noah's room? Doubtful.

I'm not going to lie, her dig on Jernigan feels about as good as a day of sleeping in would feel, but there's more to it. I get she's my mentor and is required to spend time with me, which I'm sure is why she continues to eat meals with me and sit with me at study hall, but this is totally different. It feels much more . . . personal. Kind of like her offer to run a half marathon with me.

"Sure, that'd be great," Jernigan grumbles, still frowning.

"Did you sign up for your CFA?" Mr. Durant asks Paige.

"Yes, sir. It's on Thursday." Her smile is betrayed by her cracking her knuckles. Either she's pissed or nervous. I still can't read her very well.

"Good. Is anyone else taking it?" He glances around the table, then must realize it's filled with DQs, none of whom have military aspirations, because he says, "This chicken's delicious. Al really outdid himself."

All the cadets murmur their agreement.

Mr. Durant takes another bite, then looks at me. "Evans, my daughter said you're thinking about running the Blue Ridge Half?"

"Yes, sir," I reply with a nod and a gulp. This is the first he's talked to me since his "apology."

"It's a gorgeous course. Right on the Parkway. If you're only going to do one, that'd be my pick."

Jernigan's head snaps up. "Even over the Marine Corps?"

"Well, they're both nice, but yes, I'm a nature guy. I'd rather run through the mountains."

"So did you decide?" Paige asks, facing me.

I nod. "Yeah, I'll do it."

"Nice!" she says, holding up her fist. I bump it and then focus back on my food, though I can feel Jernigan's eyes on me. Between the haunted house and this race, I'm doomed. I'll need to avoid him even more from now on. It may require no more showering, but really, cleanliness is a small price to pay to avoid cruel and unusual punishment, Jernigan-style.

I remain quiet the rest of the meal while the other cadets relive stories of past Halloweens. I wasn't expecting much out of this because, let's face it, it's Wallingford, but the more I hear, the more excited I start to become. It seems as though everyone chills out a little and has fun with it. I could definitely use a little fun around here.

A few minutes later, lunch is over, Jernigan has thankfully left, and Paige and I are about to head over to the classroom building for the haunted house.

"Bye, Dad. I'll see you next weekend," she says, and gives her dad a hug.

"Bye, pumpkin. Have fun tonight."

After he leaves, I knock her arm with my elbow. "Can I call you Lieutenant Commander Pumpkin from now on?"

"Only if you like scrubbing toilets," she replies with a grin.

"What makes you decide between toilets and laps?" It's a legitimate question. She's only given me laps or push-ups, which I appreciate. If I were forced to scrub toilets early on, I probably would've stopped with the attitude much sooner.

"It depends on the offense and what I think will better curb the undesired behavior. 'Pumpkin' isn't nearly as disrespectful as other things that have come out of your mouth."

"So you think laps work better for me with bad offenses?"

"Yeah."

"Interesting." I guess it makes some sense, especially early on. I did come here about as lazy as a person could be.

"Am I wrong?" she asks.

"Nope," I say, popping the "p." Even with my sore legs, I'd run all day long over cleaning nasty toilets, but I'll keep my aversion to human excrement to myself.

We reach the classroom building, and I hold the door open for her. She stops in her tracks and stares at me with a wrinkled nose and brows, almost like she's been hit by a horrible smell.

"What?" I ask, sniffing the air. It seems fine to me.

"Don't do that," she says.

"Do what?"

"Hold the door for me."

I laugh and roll my eyes. Only she would fault me for doing something nice. "Why?"

"It's demeaning."

"No, it's not. It's nice."

"Would you do it for a guy?"

"Well . . . no."

"Exactly." She steps behind me and grabs the handle, then motions with her hand that I should go first.

"I also wouldn't kiss a guy, but you didn't seem totally opposed to the idea a few weeks ago."

This is the first we've mentioned the almost kiss since agreeing it was momentary lapse of judgment. I expect her to blush, but she seems totally unfazed. "Those are two entirely different scenarios. One infers I'm unable to open the door myself; the other . . ."

I put my hands on my hips and tilt my head. She trailed off, but it'd be nice to her what she was thinking. I'm sure it's surprising and possibly a little cringeworthy. "What exactly does the other mean to you?"

"A kiss?"

"Yeah."

"It's . . ."

I raise my brows, waiting for her answer.

She takes a moment, then says, "It's a sign of mutual interest. A test of physical compatibility. An expression of intimacy between two people who care for each other."

I grin.

"What?"

"You have a warm, mushy heart in there after all, don't you?"

"What'd you expect?"

"Nothing," I say, shaking my head. She doesn't need to know about my Tin Man thoughts from weeks ago. "So just to be clear," I say as I enter the building, "is opening the door for you only demeaning on campus or always?"

"Always."

"Then you can feel free to open it for me. One of us should be nice, and since you won't let me do it . . ."

She enters behind me. "You're hilarious, you know that?"

I smile at what may be her first use of sarcasm ever. Score another point for Logan. "I like to think so."

She shakes her head, but I catch the half grin before she turns away. She thinks I'm hilarious, even if she won't admit it.


"Is this real?" I ask, shaking a jar with a brain. Noah and Eddie, his roommate, have transformed the classroom into a creepy lab with numerous vats of bubbling liquid, blinking lights atop what look like torture devices, and a variety of skeletons from the animal to the human kind. There's also smoke seeping out of the red strobe-lit closet. The whole thing is actually a little freaky, and it's hard to imagine I sit in here every fourth period for physics.

"Yep," Noah says proudly. "Got it from the butcher. It's a goat brain. He said we could eat it after we're done."

"You're joking, right?"

He shakes his head. "I'll give you twenty bucks if you do."

"In your dreams."

He laughs and then claps his hands once. "Okay," he says. "Logan and Lieutenant Commander Durant will take the far table, and me and Eddie will take this one. We've only got twenty-five minutes before go time. Let's get costumed up."

The sun is setting, which means the younger kids will be leaving and the older ones will be arriving soon. Paige and I walked through the tame halls, enjoying the cute Charlie Brown, Casper, Garfield, and other cartoon scenes. I was surprised by what an awesome job the cadets did, although I shouldn't have been. They put 110 percent into everything, so why would this be any different?

"Here's your blood," Paige says, handing me a tube.

"And a tattered shirt for you," Noah says, tossing me what looks like scraps of white fabric.

I exchange my cammies top for the shirt from Noah, then climb onto the table. After opening the tube of blood, I start squirting it on my chest. It dribbles down, looking eerily realistic. We decided Paige would be implanting computer chips inside me, so I need to make what looks like a nice long incision.

"Hey, did you want to implant my chest or my belly?" I ask, glancing in her direction. She's got her white lab coat and fake glasses on. It's nerdy but cute. A huge change from soldier Paige, yet equally . . . nope. Not gonna go there. Student officer. Mentor. Navy SEAL dad. Pain-in-the-ass guy friend. Way too many reasons for me to not think about how adorable her eyes are in the black frames. Or how the lab coat is hanging open to reveal a white T-shirt that's tight across her chest and cinches in at her waist, giving me a taste of those nice curves that are usually hidden.

She walks to my side and inspects my body, her eyes roaming from head to toe. She's watching me keenly.

Very keenly.

Too keenly.

I gulp.

This is worse than the almost kiss. That was in the middle of the afternoon and we were alongside the road. Now we're in a dark room and I'm lying on a freaking table. It's too easy to imagine . . .

Nope. I shake my head.

"How about chest?" I say.

She nods. "Sure."

"Great," I reply, completely ignoring the elephant in the room. I maneuver around the fabric scraps as I squirt a line from my throat to below my ribs. It all runs downhill and doesn't look anything like an incision. I glance over to Eddie. He's lying on his back as Noah uses his fingers to paint with various colors of costume makeup in between the shards of his shirt.

"Hey," I yell to them. "Can we have some of that?"

Noah chucks a few tubes at us. I open them and start working on a line with the red and black, trying to make it look three-dimensional like Noah's doing, but I failed art class in seventh grade.

"You're making a mess," Paige finally says, grabbing a tube from my hand. "Lie down."

I do, and she spreads the tatters of the shirt and tries to fix the damage I've already caused.

"Hey, we're all set," Noah says from across the room, "so we're going to check out a few other scenes. We'll be back in ten." The soft thud of the door closing would be impossible to miss.

Dimly lit room? Check. Lying down? Check. Hot girl touching me? Check. Completely alone? Check.

Paige's fingers lightly trace a line down my sternum. My mouth goes dry. My heart starts to speed up. This is so not good.

"You know how a cadet won't lie?" I say, watching her.

"Yeah."

"Well, I'm finding you especially hot right now." If I lay it out there, she'll surely say something to knock my hormones back down to where they belong.

"What?" she asks, her eyes going wide.

"This nerdy thing you've got going on," I say, waving my hand in front of her, "is a good look. But I get it. There's Jernigan. Your dad. Your carefully crafted twenty-year plan or whatever it is. So no kissing tonight. No matter how badly you want it," I whisper.

"You think I want to kiss you?"

"I was trying to be funny."

"Oh."

"Do you want to kiss me?" I ask, goading her into the mood-ending comment I know she has in her.

She bites her lip and stares at the makeup on my chest for a few moments. Then, slowly, her eyes rise to meet mine and she nods. One small, barely perceptible nod.

"Seriously?"

Another minuscule nod.

Un-freaking-believable. She was supposed to bring me back to reality, not hike up the hormones even higher.

"My eyes?" I ask, my heart now racing like I'm on my fourth lap around the track.

She smiles, and some of the tension seems to leave her shoulders. "Yeah. Your lips are nice, too. And now that you're not nearly as disrespectful, I'm rather fond of your personality. Oh, and your musical talent."

I close my eyes and take a deep breath. Are we seriously admitting we like each other right now? In the middle of our physics classroom while in full costume?

"Did you choose me over Jernigan or mad scientist over headless horseman?" I ask.

"What do you think?"

"Me."

She nods again, this one normal-sized. "I like spending time with you," she says with a shrug, seemingly becoming more and more comfortable with this topic. It's like we're talking about our favorite colors, not our budding romantic interest in each other, despite way too many obstacles. "You're different than others here."

"I like spending time with you, too," I admit. She's standing next to the table and those kissable lips of hers are only a few feet away. If I push myself up they'll be reachable.

"So," I say, leaning to my left as I ease myself into a sitting position. "Jernigan's not going to find out if I kiss you tonight, is he?"

Her face goes slack. Apparently talking about liking each other was okay, but actually doing something two people who like each other would do is not? Or she's thinking of one of the other many, many obstacles I'd be okay with ignoring for the next few minutes.

Reaching for her face, I run my thumb down her jaw. Her skin is soft and smooth and only makes me want to kiss her even more.

She swallows and gently takes my hand in hers. With a squeeze, she says, "No, we can't."

I mean to take a breath, but it comes out like a sigh. "Right. Your future. Jernigan. Your dad. The whole balance of the universe."

"No. I mean, yes with my future. But also it's against the rules. No PDA on campus."

Oh yeah. I did hear about that. It seemed like a moot point back then because I had a girlfriend and, really, who would I want to kiss at Wallingford? Certainly not my pain-in-the-ass mentor.

"So no kiss tonight?" I say.

"No."

"What if I get off-campus privileges?"

She shakes her head. "I'm sorry. I was serious. I have too much else to focus on right now. I mean, my CFA is in four days. If I don't do well, and there's a good chance I might not, I can say goodbye to all my dreams. I'm not risking it for a guy. I'm sorry."

"Then why did you even tell me you liked me?" I groan. She should've shot me down at the start of this conversation like I thought she would. Instead, she got my hopes up only to shoot me down for a stupid reason, not because she isn't interested.

"A cadet doesn't lie," she deadpans.

"I could seriously use this to my advantage," I mutter. I wonder what kind of embarrassing things I could get her to admit to?

Before I can ask a question, there's a quiet knock on the door and then Noah and Eddie enter the room, laughing about something. By the wink Noah gives me, I'm sure he assumes Paige and I made more of our ten minutes than we did. Still, it was a nice thing for him to do. And I gotta say, he is quickly rivaling Gordy in friendship status after only five weeks. Although, when you live with someone practically 24/7, things seem to move faster than out in the real world.

"Our room is by far the best," Eddie proclaims. He passes by my table and adds, "Except for your makeup, dude. It's like only halfway done. Noah, he needs help stat."

Noah gets me fixed up and then brings out old-fashioned sausage chains he got from the butcher. We arrange them around my belly and Eddie's like guts. Then it's showtime.

It takes us a few groups to finally get into a routine of Paige pretending to tear into me with a giant machete and then me springing up at the end with a scream that sends the viewers jumping back and rushing away from the doorway. The more times we do it, the more liberties I take. By the end, my springing up also involves grabbing Paige's hand and hauling her toward the door with me to really scare the onlookers.

It probably violates Wallingford's PDA rule, but hey, it's Halloween. Isn't that what Halloween is about? Wear and do inappropriate things under the guise of the holiday?

Tomorrow we can get back to the tedious cadet routine and pretend we never admitted we like each other.

# CHAPTER 19
# PAIGE

**The bugle sounds,** and I finally hop out of bed. I've been awake for three hours, too nervous to sleep. It's Thursday morning, and after reveille, classes, and PT, it will be time for my CFA. I've only gotten under the goal for the shuttle run twice: once when I was angry at Logan and once again yesterday. I hate going into something without 100 percent confidence, but I have no choice. My dad won't let me put this off any longer.

While I'm grabbing my bathroom caddy from the closet, Leah says, "Hey, you got a note."

"What?" I ask, sticking my head back out.

"This was on the floor near the door." She's holding a folded piece of white paper with my name scrawled on it in blue ink.

I take it from her and unfold it.

> *Paige,*
> *Good luck today. I know you'll do great. And, if not, there's always community college. Or I'm sure you'd make a great flight attendant. It's a little more work than piloting a plane, but at least you'd have more space to move around. Plus, you'd get to wear those short skirts. See, lots of benefits, so don't*

*stress about it too much. I'll be cheering you on from*
*the stands. Blow me a kiss or something.*

*Lo*

I smile as I refold the note and then stuff it in the top drawer of my dresser, under my workout clothes. Despite nothing physical happening at the haunted house, something has shifted in our relationship. He's more flirty. I'm more . . . receptive to his flirting. It makes sense. How could everything be exactly the same after we both admitted we like each other? The problem is we're not going to act on the mutual attraction, so we're left in this unusual situation of indefinite flirting.

"From Logan?" Leah asks.

I nod.

"I could tell by the way your face lit up. You've got it bad." Before I can say anything, she shoots out the door.

I do have it bad. Ever since we almost kissed, I spend too much time thinking about him and looking for excuses to hang out with him whenever possible.

Right now, though, I can't think about Logan. I've got to focus on me and the potentially life-changing event coming up in exactly eight hours and twelve minutes.

The morning and early afternoon go by much too quickly, and before I know it, I'm in the newly waxed gym, waiting for my CFA. I'm next in line, and my nerves are starting to ramp up. So much is riding on this one test.

I take a deep breath and pace along the green line of the basketball court, visualizing each of the events. I'm as strong as I've ever been, so all the strength events will be a breeze. I'm positive I'll score the maximum for those. And the mile will be easy. I won't get the maximum, but I will easily surpass the goal. It really comes down to the shuttle run.

I close my eyes and imagine myself sprinting back and forth, fully turning my hips on the pivot like Leah suggested.

"Hey there."

Speak of the devil. "Hey, Leah. What's up?"

"Have you gone yet?"

I shake my head.

"Good. I was worried I missed it. How are you feeling?"

"Nervous."

"You'll do fine."

I nod again, then shake and roll my hands, trying to loosen up my wrists. Then I jump up and down a couple times. The girl in front of me just headed outside for her mile, which means I have about seven minutes until my turn.

"Anything I can do to help?" she asks.

"Make me angry?" I joke. I've never been angry with Leah and doubt it could ever happen.

"Hmm . . ." She crosses her arms over her chest and twists her mouth like she's deep in thought. Finally, she says, "I was so annoyed by your snoring last night, I scrubbed the bottom of my boots with your toothbrush."

No, she didn't. "You're terrible at this."

"Sorry! I'm more about positive motivation. You'll do great! You've totally got this." She gives me a fist bump and then walks over to the bleachers.

I watch her climb up the steps and head to the middle. About midway there, she appears to change her mind and crawls over the benches all the way to the top, where she sits down. Right next to Logan. I've been so focused I hadn't even realized he was here.

I remember his note from this morning and smile. He'd probably love if I really did blow him a kiss, but that will never happen. Student officers do not blow kisses.

He sees me watching him and waves. I return the greeting, then go back to my pacing and visualization exercises as the knot in my stomach grows.

"Durant, you're up!" Captain Baldwin yells a few minutes later.

I jog over to her, my heart suddenly beating a mile a minute. My entire future rests on the next forty minutes. I take one last glance at Leah and Logan for moral support, only Logan's missing. I scan the mostly empty rows and find him at the bottom, sitting next to Kristin, the girl who just finished her CFA. She's sweaty and her face is still red from exertion. He's smiling and says something that makes her laugh.

"Okay, basketball throw," Captain Baldwin says, drawing my attention back to what's important. "On your knees at the line, and then I'll start the timer."

After walking over to the mat, I lower myself and pick up a ball. I take a deep breath and heave it as far as I can. It's a good distance.

Captain Baldwin marks the landing spot; then I repeat it two more times with similar results.

"Take your break," she says, while writing on the form.

I stand and stretch my arms overhead, then do forward and backward arm circles. While I do, my eyes wander back to the bleachers. Logan's still sitting next to Kristin, and they're still talking. How does he know her? We're not a huge school, so you eventually get to know everyone, but I've never seen them talk before.

"Okay, pull-ups. Your time starts now."

I grab on to the bar and easily do seven pull-ups in perfect form with time to spare. That gives me the max score, so I don't waste any energy doing more.

While I'm waiting for the next event, I can't help but glance over at Logan again. My jaw immediately drops. I don't get the reassuring smile I was expecting or a wave or anything. He's not even paying attention to me. Instead, he's reaching up and brushing Kristin's sweaty hair off her forehead. She frowns and scoots a couple inches away from him on the bench.

"One more minute until the shuttle run," Captain Baldwin says, checking her stopwatch.

I nod. And try to place the feeling inside of me. Four days ago, Logan told me he liked me and now he's trying to cuddle up to someone else? I know I said nothing could happen, but he could have at least told me he was interested in someone else. And what about the note this morning? Why do something sweet for one girl when you're obviously thinking about another?

I almost laugh when Kristin stands and climbs over two of the benches before sitting by herself again. Logan's left alone, shaking his head. Looks like he struck out.

"Take your place," Captain Baldwin says.

I line up behind the line and take two deep breaths. I need to forget about Logan for the rest of my CFA. He's not worth it. Like I told him, I'm not ruining my future because of a guy.

"On your mark."

I move my right leg behind my left.

"Get set."

I bend my legs and focus on the line thirty feet in front of me.

"Go!"

I take off at lightning speed, my feet pounding on the wooden planks like well-oiled pistons. My pivot is smoother than it's ever been as my hips twist and I launch myself in the opposite direction. My mind is clear and focused. Getting into the Air Force Academy is dependent on the next few seconds. If I fail, my dream is over.

Those words are the kick in the butt I need to push myself even harder than I thought possible. My lungs sting and my legs burn, but I don't slow down. Not for even a fraction of a second. I need to cut out every minuscule moment that has the potential of putting me over the target time.

When I cross the finish line, I bend over, my hands on my knees as I suck in haggard breaths.

"Nine point two seconds," Captain Baldwin says.

My head snaps up. It's the best I've ever done. By two-hundredths of a second, which is huge in the shuttle run.

All my work paid off. I won't automatically be disqualified from the academy. I'll have a really, really good shot at getting in. I let out a relieved sigh, much of the stress I've put on myself the last few weeks escaping with it.

"Nice work," she adds with a nod. She knows how hard I've been practicing.

The sit-ups, push-ups, and mile run go even better than expected. The whole time, my mind and body relax with relief over the shuttle run.

"Great job, Durant," Captain Baldwin says as I cross the finish line for the mile. "This is a very strong CFA."

"Thank you, ma'am," I pant, then move over to the side of the gym so the next cadet can start.

Leah rushes down to meet me, while Logan saunters over with his trademark smirk. That's when I remember seeing him and Kristin earlier.

"Well?" Leah asks, biting her lower lip and holding her hands clasped together.

"I did great."

"Shuttle run?"

"Nine point two."

"Yes!" She grabs my hands and jumps up and down. "I knew you could do it!"

While we're celebrating, Logan approaches us. "You passed?"

I nod. "I got a good score."

"That's great. I'm happy for you."

I grind my teeth and force a smile. Apparently I'm still annoyed by his behavior, even if I forgot about it for a bit.

"You look awfully pissed for someone who just passed her CFA," he says, raising his brows.

"I'm fine," I reply, turning away from him to grab my parka lying in the corner.

"I'm going to head out," Leah says, sneaking away from our brewing argument.

After picking up my jacket, I put it on and start to walk toward the door, ignoring the silent Logan watching me.

"Come on," he finally whines as I reach for the handle.

I pause and take a deep breath. Can I really be angry with him over this? I know I shouldn't be. I told him nothing could happen. He took that to heart. He should have. It's not like I can tell him I won't date him, but he's not allowed to date anyone else, either. That's not fair.

This is my issue, not his.

I take another deep breath and stand up straight. "I'm sorry," I say, turning around to face him. "I'm just having a hard time . . . you know . . . you and Kristin. But she's great. You two would be good together."

He laughs.

"What's so funny?" I ask with a frown.

"I'm not interested in Kristin."

"You looked like you were."

"Only to make you angry. Leah told me you'd run faster if I made you angry. Did it work?"

Seriously? The two of them were plotting to make me angry through jealousy? It's not Leah's style, which makes me think the bulk of the plan was Logan's. And it's not like it even worked. Once I started my shuttle run, I didn't think about him once.

"No," I reply, crossing my arms over my chest. "I did, however, find it humorous when she walked away from you."

He rolls his eyes. "She wouldn't even hold my hand for fifty bucks! Wallingford has you all so brainwashed. I asked her to break one little PDA rule, and you'd think I asked her to commit a felony." He shakes his head. "You guys need to learn breaking rules isn't always such a bad idea."

"Yes, it is."

"Not always."

"Yes, always."

"Not if you're doing it to help someone with something more important. Don't be pissed, okay? I was trying to help."

"I didn't need your help."

"Good. I'm glad you didn't. And I'm glad you passed. Can we just forget about my embarrassing display from earlier?"

He *was* trying to help, though his method was less than ideal. Still, his heart was in the right place. And it *is* nice to know he's not interested in Kristin. I bite my lip, then nod.

"Good." Now grinning, he asks, "Were you even a little jealous when you saw me talking to her?"

More than I ever thought possible. How can I go from someone who has never been jealous to this? "I didn't like when you touched her hair," I reply, zipping up my jacket.

"I didn't like it, either," he says, his eyes drifting up to my hair. I reflexively smooth it back, but every strand is still tight in my braid.

"You were toying with my emotions on purpose. That's not nice."

"I'm happy to hear you have emotions," he says, putting on gloves. "Sometimes I wonder."

My emotions around him are becoming too strong. They have the potential to cloud my judgment, which is not good. This is why I've never dated or had a boyfriend.

He reaches into his pocket, draws out a folded piece of paper, and hands it to me.

I take it from him and unfold it. There's a bright red heart in the middle of the note with the words "virtual hug" underneath.

"Don't get all stressed out. I know we're just friends, but in a normal, sane environment, I'd hug my friend if she just kicked ass on something so important, so I thought you should know."

A warm wave floods through my chest. The funny thing is, he said it's just friendly behavior but I know it's not. If Alex did something like this, I'd be irritated. With Logan, I'm swooning like a tween at a boy band concert. "You're very romantic, aren't you?"

"I try."

I open the door and step out onto the quad, pulling up my hood in the process. "Thanks," I say. "This note is really sweet. And the one from this morning."

"Better than opening doors for you?"

"Yes."

He removes his beanie from his pocket and puts it on his head before zipping up his parka. "So I have good news."

"Yeah?"

"The dean gave me permission to go off campus one day a week starting next weekend. He said if I don't mess up, he'll increase it to two days in January."

"That's great. Did you make plans yet?"

He shakes his head. "No, I wanted to talk to you. What are the must-dos in this Podunk town?"

"Most cadets eat at the Burger Barn or Dairy Shack, pick up supplies from the Piggly Wiggly, hike, or go home if they live close."

"Can I interest you in a hike and ice cream a week from Saturday?"

"Like a date?"

"No, of course not. I know your aversion to dating. Just two friends hanging out together. We could even have Leah and Noah come along."

"A week from Saturday?"

"Yeah."

I do a quick mental calculation before answering. "Sorry, I can't."

"Oh, okay. Yeah, sure. I get it. It's—"

"It's my dad. He's coming then and wanted to go hiking with me. What about a week from Sunday instead?"

He taps his cheek with his finger. "I'll have to check my schedule . . ."

I jab him in the ribs with my elbow, and he laughs.

"Sure, Sunday. It's a . . . not a date."

# CHAPTER 20

# PAIGE

**"Nice job,"** I say to Logan as we begin our slowdown. It's Sunday afternoon and most cadets have already left campus, but Logan is taking his race training seriously. We just finished six miles and now have to get ready for our "non-date."

"You still want to do a hike?" he asks, favoring his right side a bit as we walk toward the dorms.

"Sure. Unless . . . are you okay?" I ask as he rubs his thigh. "What's wrong?"

"I feel like a crash test dummy with all this running."

"Take some Tylenol. And drink lots of water. We can just go to the Dairy Barn, if you want."

"Nope," he says, dropping his hand. "We agreed to a hike, and I will give you a hike. But can we make it a fairly flat one?"

"Sure. I know the perfect place." There's a short three-mile trail around a lake. It's peaceful and absolutely flat. It's been a while since I've gone there since it is such an easy hike. Most of the cadets find it boring, though I've always loved it.

I turn right toward the dorms with Logan, then remember I need to stop by the rec hall. "You go ahead," I say. "I forgot to check my mail yesterday."

"I'll come with you. Who knows, maybe it will be my lucky day and I'll actually get something."

A freshman approaches us. She salutes and says, "Good afternoon, Lieutenant Commander."

"Good afternoon, cadet," I respond, returning the salute. Once she passes by, I say to Logan, "You don't get much mail?"

"I've gotten the care package from Lora and two letters from my mom."

"You need to sign up for catalogs. Those at least make you feel better when you open up your box."

We chat the rest of the way to the mailboxes, and then I put in my key and turn the lock, not expecting much. I get postcards from my grandparents whenever they head out on a cross-country trip in their RV and newspaper clippings from one of my aunts who's a political columnist. She'll send me her articles or others she thinks I might like, but I just got an envelope from her last week. The most I'll have today is a post card from the Grand Canyon or Joshua Tree.

When I open the door, there's just one thing inside. It's not a postcard but an envelope—a white business envelope, not the big manila ones my aunt uses.

"Empty as always," Logan says, closing his door. "You?"

"One letter." I pull it out and flip it over to see who it's from.

I only read the first word of the return address before my palms grow sweaty and my stomach ties itself into the biggest knot I've ever had.

"What is it?" Logan asks.

I can't speak. I just turn it around for him to see.

"Oh my God! Open it! Open it!" he yells. "What are you waiting for?"

I nod, lick my lips, then tentatively start peeling the flap up.

It's sealed tight and sticks in the middle. My trembling fingers don't help.

"Hurry up," Logan whispers.

I finally get the flap free and pull out the folded piece of paper. I want to open it, but I can't. This little piece of paper puts me one step closer to my dream. When I woke up this morning, I never realized my fate could be sealed before the day is over. If it's a yes, I need to have the dreaded talk with my dad and it's possible, if luck is on my side, I could be on my way to the Air Force Academy and soon be a fighter pilot. If it says no, I'm not sure what I'll do. I guess there's still the possibility of the Navy. I haven't heard anything from them yet, so it's still in contention.

"You're killing me, Paige. Open it," he says.

With a deep breath, I unfold the two sides and then twist the paper vertically. My eyes skim the first few lines, looking for the word I need to read.

There it is.

Third line.

*Congratulations!*

My hands fall to my sides and I lean my back against the wall, then close my eyes.

All my hard work paid off. I did it. I actually did it.

Now I just need to tell my dad.

I feel Logan grab the paper from my hands, and a moment later, he slips something into my palm. When I don't move, he says, "Screw it," and wraps his arm around my shoulders, drawing me off the wall. "Congrats!" he says, squeezing me tight. "You're going to be the most badass pilot there's ever been," he whispers in my ear.

I smile and meet his eyes as he lets go of me.

"Right now, you're the most subdued ecstatic person I've ever met," he says with a frown.

"I think I'm in shock."

"You weren't expecting it?"

I shake my head. "No, not today." I just submitted my CFA a little over a week ago. I figured I wouldn't hear for at least another month, though they did have everything else since September. Maybe they had made a tentative decision and just needed to make sure the CFA didn't change their mind.

"We should celebrate. Ice cream's on me today."

With a smile and a nod, I say, "Thank you. We should get going. I need to call my dad before our hike."

Once we start walking, I finally open my palm to find the note he placed there. It's another virtual hug, and my smile grows. I should punish him for the real hug, but I don't have it in me right now.

My shock dissipates as we pass through the quad and Logan announces my big news to everyone we pass. There are a lot of congratulations and fist bumps. An excited energy builds in my chest and begins to spread through my body, despite the looming phone call.

Back in my dorm, I throw open the door and find Leah in the middle of the room, brushing her hair.

Waving the letter overhead, I say, "I'm in. I did it!"

Her eyes grow wide, and then she runs over to me, grabs my hands, and jumps up and down. "Yay! Yay! Yay! I'm so happy for you!" she yells. "Let me see it!" She rips the letter from my hands and reads the entire thing. "This is so awesome! I can't wait to visit you at the Air Force Academy!"

A couple of our neighbors come over to see what all the commotion is about. "She's moving to Colorado next year!" They immediately know what she means and start squealing along with Leah. It's the most excitement our room has ever seen, and before long, I'm bouncing up and down with them.

"Does your dad know?" Leah asks.

"No." Her words are all it takes to draw the remaining enthusiasm out of me. "I need to call him." Our neighbors head back into the hallway; then I dial his number and take a deep breath.

"Hey, pumpkin," he says when he answers.

"Hey, Daddy. I—I have some good news."

He's silent, which doesn't help my nerves. What if all my hard work didn't pay off? What if he tells me I can't go to the Air Force Academy?

"Do you want to hear it?" I ask, then bite my lip.

"Of course."

"I got an acceptance letter today. To the—"

There's a loud whoop on the other end of the line. "You're one step closer to being a Navy pilot! I knew you could do it!"

"I . . . oh, um. Yeah, about that—"

"Your grandfather is going to be so proud. Should I call him, or do you want to?"

"Um . . . I'll call him."

"I'm really proud of you. Your mom would be, too."

"Thank you," I reply with a gulp. My mom would not be proud of me. She'd be disappointed I'm unable to tell him the truth. Despite my dad being the way he is, she was always in charge and had the final say. She'd want me to stand my ground and tell him I'm joining the Air Force whether he likes it or not.

"I'll let you go so you can celebrate," he says. "Get an extra-large sundae from the Dairy Barn on me, okay?"

"Yes, sir."

"Love you, pumpkin."

"Love you, too."

After hanging up, I take a deep breath. That was not how the call was supposed to go.

"You didn't tell him," Leah says, staring at me with her hands on her hips.

"He didn't give me a chance."

"You need to do it."

"I know," I mumble. Although, at this point, maybe I should wait to hear from the Naval Academy. If I don't get in there, then my dad would have to agree to the Air Force because that would be better than nothing.

Leah wraps her arm around my shoulder and pulls me in for a hug. "Let's forget about him and enjoy today. You got in, which is the hardest part. Everything else will fall into place."

I nod and offer her a small smile. She's probably right.

She has to be right.

An hour later, we're halfway around the trail. Logan and Noah went near the water's edge, but Leah and I found a large boulder close to the creek, which empties into the lake. There's not much water flowing today, so there's only a faint trickling sound and I remember why I like it here so much. It's always been peaceful like this—quiet, beautiful, and free of people.

"You've got a big smile on your face," Leah says with a grin.

I draw my knees to my chest and rest my chin on top of them. "Yeah. I'm happy."

"Is it just your acceptance letter?"

My smile must double in size. *My* acceptance letter. I can't imagine three better words. "Yes. Well, the letter and this place."

She pulls a water bottle from her backpack and takes a drink. "It has nothing to do with your hiking buddies?"

Lifting my head, I give her an apologetic look. "Yes, of course it does. I love hanging out with you. You know that. I'll miss you next year." As much as I'm looking forward to the Air Force, it will be difficult to leave Wallingford—my home for years—and my friends, especially Leah. I'll be starting over. I'll have to make new friends. And make a new name for myself. And move up rank again. It will be hard, but worth it.

Of course, if I went Navy, I'd be with a lot of my classmates, including Alex and Leah. Keeping my dad happy and my same friends are two good reasons to at least consider the Naval Academy.

But then I'd be giving up on my dream.

I can't do that. I won't. It's Air Force for me. It's always been Air Force. I just need to get my dad on board.

"I wasn't talking about me, doofus. Your newest hiking buddy." Leah points toward the lake, but the ferns and shrubs are so overgrown, we can't actually see the guys down there. Still, I know who she means—the cadet who occupies too many of my thoughts.

I rotate to face her, crossing my legs in the process, while she continues staring straight ahead.

"I like him," I admit. It happened on Halloween. In a split second, he went from friend to . . . I want to say "more" but that's not true. We're still only friends, though it's not like with my other guy friends. I don't shy away from his hugs. I don't flinch if he happens to touch my shoulder. And I actually enjoyed all the times he grabbed my hand during the haunted house.

Turning her head to me, she says, "No kidding. And he likes you. So what are you two going to do about it?"

"Nothing."

"Why not?"

"I don't have time for a boyfriend. With school and sports and all my clubs and my focus on the academy."

"Well, you're in at the academy, so you don't need to worry about that anymore."

I shrug. She has point, but I'm not totally in yet. I still need to convince my dad it's a good idea.

"And it seems to me," she continues, "like you've been successful in carving away little bits of time for him already without affecting anything else. You're practically dating as it is. You do realize you're on a date right now, right?"

"He specifically said this isn't a date. That's why you and Noah are here."

She rotates her whole body to face me and crosses her legs like I'm doing. "But it easily could be. That's what I'm saying—nothing will change during the week because, well, it's Wallingford. But on the weekends, you're going to leave campus anyway, it might as well be with him."

"I don't know . . ."

"Why?"

I don't answer her right away. Leah's boyfriend is hundreds of miles away, so there's no way he could derail her future. The only time they're together is during the summer when her biggest responsibility is stocking the shelves of a grocery store. It'd be different, having a boyfriend here all the time.

A bird chirps, then another immediately responds with a longer song. I glance up, trying to find them, but they're elusive. Once it's quiet again, I say, "I didn't plan on dealing with the hassle of a guy until my life was in order."

"Your life is in pretty good order."

"No"—I shake my head—"I wanted to be set in my career first."

"Paaaaaige," Leah says, slapping her hands on her thighs. "That's ridiculous! You're talking years from now."

"I know."

"Logan will be long gone by then."

I shrug. "I'm sure there will be someone else I find good-looking and funny and sweet and too kind for his own good."

"Maybe. Maybe not." She stands and sighs. "Are you sure you want to pass up this opportunity?"

Without another word, she starts working her way back to the water on the overgrown path, trampling the green-and-brown plants in the process. I stand on top of the boulder to watch the guys, who are skipping rocks in the lake. They're both terrible and only get one skip each. Leah joins them, picks up a small pebble, angles her body, and sends it thirty feet away with at least four jumps. That's what growing up on a lake in Minnesota will get you. The guys cheer for her and then try to one-up her but fail time after time.

Sitting back down, I lean on my elbows and allow my eyes to wander up to the sky. It's a beautiful vivid blue with only a few wispy clouds. Although the sun is angled low in the sky, it still provides a little added warmth. I close my eyes to enjoy it.

Is Leah right? Twenty years from now, will I regret having not given Logan a chance? I'm a decisive person—always have been—so this indecision is disconcerting. And part of me feels like if I'm not 100 percent positive about this, then it's not a good idea.

"You look deep in thought," a voice I've come to appreciate says, just as the warmth on my face fades.

I open my eyes and find Logan standing in front of me, blocking the sun.

"Yeah, I am."

"Can I join you or do you want to be alone?"

"You can join me."

He sits down in the spot Leah occupied only a few minutes ago, wincing a little in the process. "Are you still sore?"

"I'm good," he says, rolling his neck. "The Tylenol's helped. And what doesn't kill you makes you stronger, right?"

"Yeah," I reply with a grin.

He looks around us, watching the creek for a few moments before focusing back on me. "So what's bothering you?"

"It's just something Leah brought up."

"That's pretty shitty of her to bring up bad news while you should be celebrating."

"It's not bad news," I say, shaking my head. "And it's not like it's something I haven't been thinking about myself."

"What is it?"

I give him another grin. "You."

"Me?"

"Leah thinks we should date."

"I've always said Leah is one smart cookie." He extends his legs and crosses his ankles.

"You have?"

"No, but she obviously is."

"You want to date me?"

He's silent for a moment, probably letting reality sink in.

"Maybe," he finally says, "but there are a number of . . . obstacles."

"I agree." I hold out my hand and count each one with my fingers. "One, I can't lose focus on my future. Two, I can't loaf it in any of my classes or clubs or teams. Three, I can't give you special treatment. Four, I can't—"

He holds up his hands. "I was thinking more along the lines of keeping me alive. Obstacle number one is Jernigan and Obstacle number two is your dad."

"Alex can't hurt you."

"No, but he can make my life even more miserable."

He's right. Alex hasn't been exactly fair to Logan. "I should have a talk with him. He has gone a little over the top with you."

"What about your dad?"

I take a deep breath. He raises a great question. Logan's a DQ. There's no way my dad would approve of him. Still, I like Logan. Logan likes me. It shouldn't matter what opinion my dad has. "It's really none of his business."

Logan nods his head in an exaggerated way. "Okaaaay, then. I have a feeling he might disagree, though."

"I should be in control of my life."

"Hey," he says, raising his hands in front of himself. "I'm all for you taking control. I just don't want to wind up in the morgue in the process."

"Don't worry," I say, rocking my shoulder into him. "I'm going to face the bulk of his wrath, nobody else."

"I doubt that."

"You'd be a minor issue after I tell him I'm going to the Air Force Academy, not the Naval Academy."

"Wait. What?" he asks, twisting around to face me. "He's not aware of your plan?"

I shake my head. "You know him—it's Navy this and Navy that. He assumed I'd go there. I just need to . . ."

"Grow some balls and tell him?"

"Yeah," I reply with a grin. "But it's easier said than done."

"Remember what you told me about Lora—isn't it better to just do it and know the answer so you can stop obsessing over what might or might not happen?"

He's right, of course. The problem is it's much easier to dole out advice than take it. When I don't answer, he smirks at me and says, "It's kind of like us constantly obsessing over how amazing our first kiss will be. At some point, we're going to realize we should just do it already."

I laugh at his subtle way of bringing us back to the topic of dating. But he does have a point. I spend more time than I'd like thinking about kissing him. For someone who has never once had a fleeting thought about kissing until the last few weeks, this is troubling. Maybe actually doing it would stop my daydreaming.

He's still smirking at me.

Without warning, I lean down and lightly and quickly brush my lips against his. Then I pull back and watch him. His expression changes from surprise to delight.

"You just kissed me," he says, his eyes lit up with amusement.

"Yeah. I realized we should just do it already."

I expect him to have some sarcastic comment, but instead, he grasps the back of my head and pulls me closer. His mouth finds mine, and he makes much more significant contact than I had, with his lips pressing firmly against mine. They're soft and smooth and taste like ChapStick—not a flavor, just plain ChapStick.

As his lips move against mine, it dawns on me I don't know what I'm doing. Had I planned ahead, I could have researched this online first. Or with a magazine. Every time I go to Piggly Wiggly, I see cover after cover in the checkout line advertising "What Your Man Wants" or "Kissing 101." That would have been four dollars well spent.

Logan, on the other hand, seems to know exactly what he's doing and has no reservations.

Rather than obsess over my lack of preparation, I follow his lead. When his hand kneads the back of my neck, I allow my fingers to trail lightly against his lower back. I feel him smiling against my lips, which makes me think I must be doing something right.

"This is nice," he whispers.

"I agree." It *is* nice. But it's a different type of nice than I'm used to. It's not the satisfying thrill that comes with acing a test. It's more of a tingling excitement working its way through my body. It feels like part nervous anticipation and part . . . something I'm not familiar with.

He tugs gently on my lower lip, and my hands begin to wander up his back.

"Hey, Paige, did you—"

Leah's voice causes me to spring away from Logan like a kid who got caught with her hand in the cookie jar.

"Sorry," she says, already turning around and waving her arm overhead. "It's not important."

Logan chuckles next to me. "Are we going to become Wallingford gossip now?"

"No, Leah would never spread rumors."

He takes my hand in his, weaving our fingers together. "Does this mean we're giving the whole dating thing a chance?"

I stare at our hands. Doing this with a fellow cadet, especially one who's my mentee, should make me feel like a horrible officer and at least a little uncomfortable, but those emotions don't make the top ten feelings running through me. "I'm not sure," I finally say. "Maybe we should think about it for a couple more days before we make a decision?"

"Okay," he says, giving my hand two quick squeezes before letting go.

If my disappointment by the loss of contact is any indication, the decision has already been made.

# CHAPTER 21

# LOGAN

**Exactly six days** after our first kiss, Paige and I climb into her CR-V. She removes her coat and throws it in the back, revealing her navy leggings; a thin, silky-looking shirt; a patterned sweater that's open in the front; and brown calf-high boots. My eyes keep alternating between the leggings, which are effectively advertising her sexy legs, and her long black hair, which is hanging to the middle of her back. I've never seen it down before, and I like it. A lot.

"You look great," I say when we're both settled in our seats.

She smiles while putting the key in the ignition. "Thanks."

"And equally important, you were fast, which will help maximize our off-campus time." I've got to say, there are a lot of things I despise about Wallingford, but it is nice how the school has trained girls to shower, do their hair, and put on makeup all in fifteen minutes. Lora used to take over an hour, and it drove me crazy. I can't think of a single movie we made it to on time. There's no way Paige would be late to anything.

"Anyone else coming?" I ask once I'm buckled up. During study hall on Wednesday, she asked me out, though she didn't stipulate whether it was a date or not. I didn't prod her, figuring she'd let me know one way or the other when she was ready.

"Nope. Just us."

Okaaaay.

"Where are we going?" I ask.

"It's a surprise."

"If it's another hike from hell, I should change my shoes." The gray Chucks I'm wearing wouldn't be my first choice for climbing up a mountain.

"No wardrobe change necessary. You'll fit right in where we're going."

Now I'm intrigued. The only places to hang out in town are the Dairy Barn and the burger joint, but they're filled with cadets, so I'd fit in even if I were wearing my uniform. My black jeans and flannel shirt are much more reminiscent of Logan from public school, which makes me wonder if we're leaving this tiny town.

My phone vibrates, indicating I have a message, but I stop it without looking at it. Whatever it is can't be more important than my date. Or non-date. Whatever this is.

"Do you need to get that?" she asks.

"Nope."

"It's fine if you do. I want to call my grandparents anyway."

"Okay. Five minutes and then we're out of here. I need some quality non-Wallingford time."

She nods and grabs her phone out of her bag. I wait until she's talking to her grandparents before I look at my messages.

*Call me ASAP.*

*Where are you? We NEED to talk.*

I dial Gordy's number. It doesn't even ring one full time before he answers. "The new Marvel movie is lit! You gotta see it." Only in Gordy's world would a movie be worthy of an urgent text.

"I doubt it will happen until I come home for Christmas."

"I thought you got partial parole on weekends."

"I do, but I live in the boondocks. No theater within like fifty miles or something."

"What do you do when you leave campus?"

"Mostly hike."

"Hike?" he asks, like it's a foreign word. And, I guess to him, it is. It was to me up until recently.

"Yeah."

"Are you hiking right now?"

"No, I'm on a . . ." I don't want to say "date" with Paige sitting right next to me. Even though she seems like she's concentrating on her call, she might hear me. "Hanging out with a friend. I'm not sure where she's taking me."

"She?"

"Yeah."

"What's her name?" he asks.

"Paige."

"Is she hot?"

"Uh . . . yeah." I know there's no way her grandparents could hear this conversation, but I move the phone to my right ear, just to be sure.

"What's she look like?"

"My height, athletic, long black hair, pretty green eyes."

"What about her ass?"

"None of your business."

He laughs. "Send a picture."

"Okay, hold on." I switch my phone to camera mode and tap her shoulder. She looks at me, then smiles when she sees what I'm doing.

"You should get it in a sec," I say after sending it to him.

He's silent, probably checking his texts.

"Daaaaamn," he says. "She is hot."

"Yep."

"And looks like she could kick my ass."

"Yep."

"What is it with you? You can't go for the sweet and innocent girls anymore?"

"She's sweet and innocent."

"Other than being lethal."

I can't dispute him. Noah told me her aim with a rifle is deadly.

Paige is no longer talking; instead, she's scrolling around on her phone, which is my cue to end this conversation.

"I gotta go."

"I'll expect details tomorrow!" Gordy says.

"Not gonna happen. Later."

"Later, Lo."

I tuck my phone back into my pocket as Paige stuff hers into her bag. "How are your grandparents?" I ask.

"Fine. I told them about the Air Force Academy."

I raise my brows. I can't even believe she went behind her dad's back and applied there. I never would've imagined she'd have it in her.

"They respect my decision," she says.

"Are they going to say anything to your dad?"

She shakes her head. "No. I told them I'd talk to him soon."

"Are you going to?"

"Yeah." After a sigh, she adds, "Over Thanksgiving break. It's time. I need to do it, but I want to wait until we have a few days together." She turns the key in the ignition and pulls out of the parking spot.

"So," she continues, glancing over at me.

"So," I reply, wondering what in the hell we're doing.

She waits until she pulls through the gates before continuing. "After serious consideration, I would like to, assuming you're agreeable, try dating you. On weekends only. We can continue to spend time together during breakfast, lunch, study hall, and our club activities during the week, but that will be the extent of it."

So this *is* a date. She finally caved. After our kiss, I thought this might happen, but then again, Paige is an enigma so I figured there was an equally good chance she'd tell me to get lost.

"Of course," she continues, "there will be no PDA on campus. And I will not give you preferential treatment on campus, so you should continue to respect me as you would all officers. Leah is watching over my shoulder to make sure I don't lose perspective."

She takes a breath, but I remain silent, assuming there's still more.

"And, finally, should either of our grades drop, we will terminate this arrangement."

"Arrangement?"

She nods.

"Did you write up a contract for me to sign?"

"No, but I can. I'll do it tonight, if you'd like."

"I'm joking, Paige."

"Oh, right."

I reach for her hand resting on the console and wind my fingers through hers. She jumps in her seat at the contact. "What are you doing?" she asks, looking down at our hands.

"Starting our date."

"Oh, okay. So you're agreeable?"

Of course I'm agreeable. I still fear for my life a little, but I'm all about living on the edge. Okay, not really, but she made it seem like my safety should be the least of our worries. That's probably true with her dad since he's only here occasionally and it's always on campus where it's not like we can even hold hands. Jernigan is the bigger problem, but hey, if she's got my back, then I should be good. I have a feeling she could easily take him down if necessary.

"Yeah," I say. "Let's give it a shot."

For the next thirty minutes, conversation flows easily as we drive on country roads. Other than holding hands, it's like usual and doesn't even seem like we just agreed to be more than friends. I guess that's the best type of relationship, though—one that so effortlessly morphs from friends to more you don't even notice it happening.

Finally, we catch a small glimpse of life again. She merges onto the highway, and we continue driving for miles. After twenty minutes, I ask, "Are you kidnapping me?"

Smiling, she replies, "No. We're going to Roanoke. It's the closest big city to school. We're almost there, only another ten minutes or so."

It's already 3:30 and dinner is at 5:00, which means we'll only have, at most, thirty minutes there. Hardly seems worth it.

"What are we doing for half an hour in Roanoke?"

She looks confused. "What do you mean half an hour?"

"We've got to get back by five. For dinner with your dad, right?"

She shakes her head. "Nope. I asked him to come tomorrow instead. We've got until eight, when all cadets must report back on campus."

Well, that certainly changes things. An entire three hours in a normal city with normal things to do. I might have died and gone to Heaven.

She's quiet for a moment as she exits the highway and stops at a light. After a couple more turns, she pulls into a parking lot for a mall. By conventional standards, it's not a huge mall, but compared to where I'm living now, this entire town looks like we're in New York City. The bright lights. The people. The traffic.

It's freaking awesome.

"Want to hang out at the mall before dinner?" she asks. "That's a normal thing to do, right?"

I grin and squeeze her hand. "Totally normal. And exactly what I need."

We exit the car and walk through the entrance hand in hand with throngs of other teenagers and some families. "You looking for anything in particular?" I ask.

"Not really. You?"

"I could use some new reading material." We find the map and then search for a bookstore. It's at the opposite end, so we start that way.

"When's the last time you were in a mall?" I ask her.

"Um . . . three summers ago, I think. It was the one week I didn't have a camp to attend, so I decided to hang out with some girls I used to be friends with in middle school. Turns out we didn't have much in common anymore."

"Not a good time?"

"It was fine. I just felt older than them after a year at Wallingford. Their conversations seemed juvenile. Maybe I was being a snob," she says with a shrug. "Regardless, I made sure to have camps scheduled for the entire summer after that. It was too weird going home."

"You don't talk to them anymore?"

"No. My friends are at Wallingford. I don't know . . . There's something about Wallingford that makes friendships seem more . . . profound. Living with someone and going through what we go through makes you know someone much better than seeing them for a few hours at school every day. We see the good, the bad, and the ugly in everyone."

"That's true. I never thought I'd have as good of a friend as Gordy, but Noah's coming close. Wallingford speeds up the friendship process."

She nods. "It speeds up lots of things."

For the next hour, we walk by clothing stores, gadget stores, and smelly soap and lotion stores. I soak in the noise, the chaos, and the freedom to do whatever I want, like slouching as I try out a new video game or kissing Paige's forehead while waiting in line to pay for my books. Who knows when I'll be back so this needs to tide me over for a while.

After the mall, we go across the street to a nicer chain Italian restaurant for dinner. It's delicious but quicker than I thought, and we still have an hour to kill before we have to head back.

"Thanks for dinner. What now?" I ask after she gets her credit card back from the waiter. I tried to pay, but surprise, surprise, she wouldn't let me.

"I have one more thing planned," she says, standing, as we both put on our jackets. "I think you'll like it." There's a twinkle in her eye, which piques my interest.

"Can I get a hint?"

"Hmm . . ." She tilts her head and purses her lips as if thinking. "Just one." She steps closer to me and barely brushes her lips against mine. It's very fast but effective in morphing my interest into anticipation.

"What are we waiting for?" I ask, placing my hand on her lower back and ushering her forward.

This awesome date is about to get a million times better.

# CHAPTER 22

# LOGAN

**We get back** in the car, drive through the small downtown into a residential neighborhood and then up a twisting road that ends at the very top of a large hill or maybe a small mountain. There are signs directing us toward a zoo, but Paige turns the other way, taking us to a park with a gigantic neon star lit up like the sun and a sweet view of the city below. She finds a remote area, backs up her car to a fence, then cuts the engine.

"Uh, Paige, you're facing the wrong way," I point out, craning my neck to see the lights of the city.

"C'mon, this will be better. After exiting, she walks around to the back where she lifts the tailgate and lowers the back seat to make a flat cargo area. She climbs inside and looks at me still in the front. "You coming?"

I don't know exactly what she has in mind, but the bed-like nature of the back gets my feet moving. I spring out of my seat, climb over the console, and settle in next to her, eyeing the blanket she's holding in her hand.

This definitely has the potential to be a very good end to a very good first date.

She hands me the blanket, then scoots to the edge and dangles her feet over the back bumper. I join her and spread the blanket on our legs.

It's cool outside but not as cold as it is back in Wallingford, probably because we're not on nearly as tall of a mountain here. Still, the blanket was a good thought. I tuck it under my leg to prevent it from falling.

"So how do you like the view?" she asks while staring into the night.

"I love it."

We're silent for a few moments before she turns toward me and says, "I had fun with you today."

"Me too. We should do it again sometime."

"I'd like that. Although we might need to tell my dad. He'd be upset if we came here regularly and didn't hang out with him."

"You're from Roanoke?"

She nods.

"Your dad lives around here?"

She points to the left. "About four miles that way."

Huh. Somehow our hundreds of hours of conversation never got around to where she's from. It would explain how she knew her way around so well.

"Is he in the same house you grew up in?"

"Yeah. And my room hasn't changed a bit since the day I left for Wallingford. It will give you a good sense of who I was at thirteen if you ever happen to see it."

"That could be fun." I wonder if she was a mini version of current-day Paige or a more typical girl back then. Are there posters of movie stars on the walls or guns? She did have a mom at some point, so it's not like she never had any girly influence. Granted, she might have died early on. "Did your mom die before or after you came to Wallingford?" I ask.

She faces forward again, and I feel her body tense just a little. "Before. It was the summer between third and fourth grade."

"What happened?"

"Cancer. Lymphoma."

Shit. I can't even imagine.

I've been lucky. I'm eighteen and have never had anyone close to me die. Three of my grandparents are still alive and the other one died before I was born. I can't fathom losing my mom. It's not like we're crazy close, but she's still my mom. "Was it bad?" I ask. "I mean . . . of course her dying was bad, but did she suffer a lot?"

"She said she was never in pain, but she looked awful. For the last month, she was in a hospital bed in our living room. My dad even quit his job to spend every last moment with her. I think he suffered more than her, especially the closer it got to the end. She just slept a lot."

"That had to suck for everyone."

She nods, still staring at the lights below.

I scoot closer and put my arm around her. Smiling, she rests her head on my shoulder and takes a deep breath. "So you hate your dad, right?" she asks.

"Yeah."

"Why?"

"He's a dick."

"How so?"

"He cheated on my mom."

"Oh . . . when?"

"Five years ago. Luckily, I'm eighteen now and no one can force me to see him again."

"You're cutting him out of your life?" she asks, sitting up and looking at me.

"Yep."

"Forever?"

"Yep."

"Hmm," she murmurs, but doesn't say anything else.

"What?"

"Nothing."

"A cadet will not lie," I point out.

She crosses her legs, then says, "It seems like you're not just hurting him. You're hurting yourself, too. Dads are important. I wouldn't be able to survive without mine."

"Your dad never would have cheated on your mom."

"True. But he's made other mistakes and I've forgiven him."

"Like what?"

"Um, hello?" she says, pointing to herself with an index finger. "Controlling my life?"

I chuckle. She's got a point. Still, it's not the same.

"What are you afraid of with your dad?" she asks.

"Afraid? I'm not afraid of anything."

"Then why not forgive him?"

"It would justify what he did."

"No, it wouldn't. You could tell him you disagree with his behavior, but don't want to lose him as a father."

She clearly doesn't get it. "Look, I hate him, okay? I hate everything about him. I've been distancing myself for years and doing everything possible to be the exact opposite of him. I gave up baseball. I gave up basketball. I gave up guitar lessons. I gave up my friends. I gave up everything he wanted or expected of me." I pause and take a deep breath before continuing. "I endured the court-mandated weekends, knowing when I turned eighteen, it'd all be over. Never having to see him again is what I've been trying to achieve for years, and it finally happened in September. I'm free of him. I never have to see him again."

"You're eighteen?"

I nod.

She's silent for a moment, and I watch her chest rise and fall as she takes slow, even breaths. Finally, she says, "Well, you've clearly given this lots of thought."

"I have."

"And were willing to sacrifice your own happiness to prove a point. Your dedication to a senseless cause is to be commended."

"What? No." I scowl. "I didn't sacrifice anything, and it wasn't senseless."

"You love the guitar, are amazing on it, and hadn't played in years until you had no other choice."

I ignore her comment as I lean back on my elbows. It wasn't all bad. I gained Gordy and Nate as friends once I became an outcast as school. And now Paige. That probably never would've happened if my life hadn't done a complete 180 after eighth grade.

"What's your mom like?" she asks.

I take a deep breath and forget about my dad. "She's great. Overworked and stressed all the time, but great. She gives me my space, yet I know I can count on her if I really need to."

"What's she do?"

"Works for a PR firm."

"That sounds . . . really dull."

I laugh. "Right? Sometimes, she'll tell me about her projects, and that's always my thought. What about your dad? What's he do?"

"Works for a private security company."

That makes sense and probably would've been on my list of possibilities if she had asked me to guess. It'd be right under firearm distributor and right above MMA trainer.

A light breeze whips past us, causing Paige to shiver. I fold the blanket from my legs back onto her to provide a little more warmth and then scoot closer until our bodies are touching.

"Thanks," she says. "What do you want to do when you grow up?"

"I don't know. Gordy mentioned something about developing video games. That could be fun. It'll probably end up being something related to computer programming." I check my watch. We only have about thirty minutes until we need to leave. "Come here," I say, reaching for her legs. I pull them on my lap. "Thanks again for the fun date," I whisper in her ear as I lay light kisses along her jaw.

"Anytime," she whispers back before her mouth finds mine. This time, there's not even a moment of hesitation on her part, and I find myself getting pulled in deeper and deeper by that sexy confidence she radiates after only one kiss. One kiss and she's already a pro. It's hot.

I part my lips, hoping she'll accept the invitation. She pauses and pulls away, so I crack open an eye. She's watching me with a look that says she's considering more than a kiss.

"I'm totally willing to go whatever speed you want," I whisper. "You're in the driver's seat."

She swallows and licks her lips. "Can I ask you a question?"

"Sure."

"Have you been with a lot of girls?"

My heart momentarily stills. Why? Why do girls want to know this kind of shit? They always do. I've never given a second thought to my girlfriends' past, but they always want to know mine. I blow out a long sigh before asking, "What do you mean by 'been with'?"

"Sex."

Greeeeat. Just great.

"What would you consider a lot?"

"I don't know . . . maybe with more than one girl or five times total?"

Shit. "Yes."

"To which one?"

"Both."

"Oh."

And now she thinks I'm a man-whore, which is not even remotely true. I've had two girlfriends. That's all. Yes, I had sex with them, but it's not like I was sleeping around. "Is this a problem?"

"No, not a problem. I was just curious."

With any other girl, I'd call bullshit, but with Paige, I believe her. Her devotion to the Honor Code rivals that of a cult follower gulping a gallon of Kool-Aid.

"Why?" I ask, starting to feel better about the situation but now wondering what her point was with this entire conversation.

"Because I'm not going to have sex with you."

I smile as the heavy ball of dread that was sitting in my chest disappears. She just wants to make sure we're on the same page. It's very responsible, and very Paige-esque, of her to set the rules up front. I should've known this was her angle. "I figured it was off the table."

"You're okay with that?"

"Yeah, sure." Honestly, I wasn't even considering going there with her. If her dad or Jernigan ever found out, I'm sure they'd kill me. Like literally kill me.

"Okay, good."

"We'll still kiss, right?" I ask.

"Yes."

"And, maybe, eventually a little more?" She has to realize there's a lot of room for fun between kissing and sex. Or maybe not. Maybe I can be the one to show her.

"Like what?" she asks.

"Second base?"

"Which is?"

I give her a grin. "I get to touch your boobs."

She cracks a smile in return, her white teeth sparkling beneath the neon star. "You want to touch my boobs?"

"Kind of."

She peeks outside her car, twisting her head both ways, and then climbs off my lap and kneels on the floor. "Scoot back," she says.

When I do, she closes the tailgate, giving us even more privacy. Not that we need it; no one else is anywhere near us.

It's much darker in the car now, with the six thousand watts from the star being blocked by the door. I squint to try and read her face, but it's impossible. Did she just give me permission to touch her boobs? My heart starts to beat a little faster at the idea.

"I didn't necessarily mean right now," I say. "Unless you're feeling it."

"You're not feeling it?"

"I'm a guy. I'm always feeling it."

Her hand lands on my shoulder, and then her lips catch the side of my mouth before sliding to the middle. She's wearing peppermint lip balm again. I hate candy canes, but somehow it tastes different on her lips. I may actually start craving the candy if we keep making out. Good thing Christmas is right around the corner.

In a matter of minutes, the kissing turns serious and starts generating some intense body heat in the enclosed space. I peel off my jacket and flannel, leaving me in my white undershirt. Her lips pause, and her eyes roam down my body.

"What are you thinking?" I ask, loving the feeling of her checking me out. Compared to most guys at Wallingford, my body is nothing special, yet it seems like maybe she thinks it is. I don't know why, but I'll take it.

"I like how you make me feel," she says.

I smile. "And how is that exactly?"

"I . . . I feel like I'm standing at the starting line of a cross-country race. There's a tight, jumbly feeling in my stomach."

"I give you a jumbly feeling?"

"Yeah."

Most people would call it horniness, but I'll take her lingo. It's cute. With a chuckle, I say, "You give me the jumblies, too."

She laughs and sits back on her heels, then removes her jacket and sweater, better revealing the silky shirt underneath with only tiny straps holding it up. It's tight across her chest, and I feel second base summoning me.

With a gulp, I say, "For the record, I've got a bad case of the jumblies right now."

"Duly noted. My one condition is our shirts stay on tonight."

Aaaaand I just got tagged out, before I even attempted to steal second.

"Yes, ma'am," I say, giving her a perfect salute.

My eyes have adjusted to the dimness, and I catch her wrinkle her nose. "That's creepy . . . and unnecessary since we're off campus," she says, moving the pile of clothes between us out of the way. "No saluting on dates."

"You're right." It is creepy.

"Is it normal to talk this much while making out?"

"Not with my other girlfriends, but I'm enjoying it with you."

She grins at me. "Did you just call me your girlfriend?"

Is it too soon to be thinking titles? Yes, definitely. But if I didn't want that, I wouldn't be here with her right now. She must realize it and feel the same. "Yeah, you know, a friend who is a girl who I happen to kiss, hopefully a lot. Not like an official title or anything," I say, to downplay what we both must want.

"Got it. So you're my first boyfriend—a friend who is a boy who I hope to kiss a lot."

She totally wants the titles. "That seems about right."

She takes my right hand and lays it on her chest over her silky shirt.

And I'm back in the game.

Using my other hand, I help her lie down while I hover over her, careful to not let my lower body touch hers. I'm fairly confident she's not ready to think about certain parts of my anatomy, one of which is slightly more noticeable now than usual.

Our hands and mouths do their thing, and I'm impressed by her lack of shyness. She's set the boundary but is more than willing to fully explore up to that boundary. Of course, I'm happy to oblige.

With the back seat down, there's more than enough room for us to fully spread out. I've done some things in cars before, but it's usually cramped and uncomfortable and cumbersome. Not my idea of a good time. This is luxurious.

"I'm becoming a big fan of your vehicle," I say between kisses along her collarbone, easing her thin shirt down as far as I can with my chin.

"Archie is practical for a number of reasons."

I tilt to the side and lean on one elbow. "You named your car Archie?" I ask as I sweep a strand of hair off her forehead.

"Yeah."

"After the comic?" That doesn't seem like her at all.

"No, after Alexander Vandegrift."

"Who?"

"My favorite World War II general."

The laugh escapes me without warning. What teenage girl has a favorite general? I probably couldn't even name ten generals. "Who's your favorite World War I general?"

"MacArthur, of course," she answers seriously, obviously missing my sarcasm.

"Of course." I make a face as though any other answer would be pure idiocy.

"We have about two minutes left," she says. "Do you want to talk wars or kiss?"

I have a feeling she can do either equally well, but we have an hour-long drive back to campus during which we can talk. This will be our last chance to kiss for a while. "Kiss. Definitely kiss."

I lower my mouth back to hers. Her lips part, but I can't tell if she's taking a breath or testing the waters. I barely dip my tongue in and wait to see her reaction. When she mimics me, I go a little farther.

She takes my hand in hers again and guides it under her shirt.

"Really?" I ask, surprised but thrilled with the development.

"Yeah. Strictly northern hemisphere, though."

"There are some great geographical features in your northern hemisphere," I whisper as I slide my fingers up her flat stomach until they reach the bottom edge of her bra. I follow it around to the back, searching for a hook, but it's smooth, soft cotton.

"Does your one condition include your bra?" I ask between kisses, my hands returning to the front, still feeling for a clasp, but it's one continuous piece of fabric all the way up to her cleavage.

"Um . . . I'm not sure."

I pause and then lean on my elbow, watching her. "If you're not sure, it's probably a yes."

She nods. "Probably."

We smile at each other, and I settle for some over-the-bra second-base action. While I'm focused on that, she's easily earning her stripes in French kissing.

All in all, I can't imagine having a better day at Wallingford: I had no run-ins with Jernigan; Paige and I basically agreed to a relationship, titles and all; and she's developing an appreciation for some serious private displays of affection.

If this keeps up, I might actually start to like Wallingford.

# CHAPTER 23
# LOGAN

**I'm sitting at** my desk, staring out the window and drumming my fingers on my closed calculus book. Paige and I had our second date yesterday, which was great, but since I can only leave campus one day a week, I'm stuck here while she's out with Leah and her other friends, including Jernigan.

She offered to say here with me, but like a dumbass I told her to go, not realizing she'd be hopping in Jernigan's truck. "I'll be fine," I said. "I've got a million things to do," I said. "You shouldn't miss out on fun because of me," I said.

I'm an idiot.

It's been two hours since she left. Her dad's coming for dinner, so she has to be back by five, but that's still almost three hours from now.

I'm tempted to text her, but what could I say that wouldn't come off as a jealous boyfriend who's imagining Jernigan trying to feel her up? At least I know she can handle herself. And that she doesn't want him feeling her up, meaning there's no way it could ever happen. Yet my mind still won't relax.

Just then, my phone bings. I spring from my chair, launch myself onto the top bunk, and grab my phone that's lying there. It's Noah, not Paige. I sigh in disappointment.

*Needhilp*

And just like that, my disappointment turns to concern.

*What's going on?* I quickly type.

*Com get mee*

What's wrong with him? Why can't he spell anything correctly? *Where are you?*

*1/2way to skool*

*What happened?*

*Im trashed*

Well, that explains his spelling. My phone bings again as another message pops up. *Fell. Ankle messud up. Use Eddies car keys in desk. Door loked*

How am I supposed to get in his room if the door is locked? Before I can ask him, another text appears: *unlocked*

I knead the back of my neck. This is not good. *Where's Eddie?*

*Homefur wekend*

I close my eyes and pinch the bridge of my nose. There are so many issues with his plan. Not only am I not allowed off campus today, but my license is suspended. If I get caught, I'll be screwed.

*I can't. Let me see if I can find someone else.*

I rush up and down the three floors of our dorm, hoping to find anyone who can pick up Noah, but the only ones around are the freshman and sophomores who don't have off-campus privileges or driver's licenses. They're in the same boat as me.

*How bad is your ankle?*

*Bad*

Shit. I run my hand over my practically bald head, and then smack the cinder-block wall with my palm.

*I could ask Paige to pick you up*, I type.

*No! Shell report me Itll tak u 5 min*

He must be on the mountain road leading to Wallingford. I've never seen cops on that road, so it's unlikely I'd have to deal with them. The bigger problem would be another student, although most of them probably wouldn't even know I'm not allowed off campus today. There would only be a few—the highest officers—who would. Realistically, what are the chances I'd pass one of them during my few minutes out there? It has to be low. Most people wait to come back until at least dinnertime, if not later.

*Plz*

*Okay, fine. Be there soon.*

He owes me so big for this. I run across the hall, grab Eddie's keys from his desk, and then race to the parking lot. It's only then I realize I don't even know what car is Eddie's. Luckily, he has an electronic keychain, so I push the unlock button as I walk up and down the mostly empty aisles, looking and listening for the right car.

Make that truck. It's a black Dodge in the third row I check.

I hop inside and put the key in the ignition, then take a deep breath. This is an absolutely half-baked idea. I hear Paige's voice in my head: *Go back to your room and tell Noah to deal with the consequences of his bad decision.* Except I can't. I won't. I never let my friends down.

I put the truck in gear and slowly ease out of the parking lot, checking the side and rearview mirrors every other second to make sure no one's running after me, ready to report me. At the gate, my foot presses the brake, and I pause one last time. This is it. If I roll even two feet farther, then I'm committed. I wipe my sweaty palms on my cammies and wish I had a bottle of water. My throat feels like I haven't had anything to drink in days.

My foot slowly eases off the brake. The truck inches forward. There's no turning back.

I step on the gas and head down the windy road faster than I normally would. The whole time, I curse Noah and whatever his illegal substance of choice was. Once he's sober and his ankle is healed, I'm going to give him hell. For many, many weeks. Maybe months.

I slow down for a curve and then slam on the brakes. He's there, on the virtually nonexistent shoulder, sitting cross-legged like he's a freaking yogi meditating.

I throw open the door and yell his name.

His eyes snap open. "Hey, man," he slurs. "I owe you one."

"No kidding." I bend down, slip my head under his arm, and haul him into a standing position. He hobbles to the truck, and I have to practically lift him inside, where he lies down on the bench seat.

"Don't you dare puke in Eddie's truck," I warn before sliding his feet in and slamming the door.

I sprint around to the driver's side and waste no time doing a three-point turn on the narrow road. Only two miles left. We might actually make it.

I go even faster on the return trip and breathe a sigh of relief when I pass through the gate. I return the truck to its original parking spot and then quickly exit the car and go around to help Noah again.

Except he's asleep.

"Wake up!" I yell, shaking his shoulder. He stirs, then goes limp again.

"Oh my God," I mutter. Noah's taller than me, but not overly muscular. Still he's heavy. And the dorm isn't exactly close. I can either leave him in the truck to sober up or try and carry him back to his room. I'd rather he be in his room, but the chances of someone calling us out on that trek when he's hanging over my shoulder like sack of potatoes are about a million to one.

"Okay, buddy. You take a nap here. I'll be back in an hour to check on you." I start to close the door, when I realize I should probably leave him a note since he didn't hear anything I said and might freak out when he wakes up.

After scrounging around in the glove box, I find a napkin and a pen. I quickly scrawl my plan on there and then put it on the seat, right next to his head.

"Sweet dreams, man," I say before shutting the door. At least we made it this far. I'm in the clear. He may or may not be. It all depends on how quickly he can get that shit out of his system.

I turn around. And run straight into a brick wall.

Make that brick chest.

"What's going on?" Jernigan asks as Paige crawls out of his truck that's parked in the row behind us.

"Nothing, Commander," I say, saluting him with my right hand while my left hand palms the keys and hides them behind my back.

"Whose car is this?"

"Eddie's."

"Were you driving it?"

"No, of course not."

"Hey, Evans," Paige says when she joins us. I salute her, and then she asks, "What are you doing out here?"

Jernigan steps next to me and pushes me to the side with his shoulder as he peers through the window. "What's wrong with Green?"

"He's not feeling very well. Probably the flu or something."

"Why is he here and not with the nurse?"

I shrug. "Dunno. I just got here right before you."

Paige's brow wrinkles, and she steps next to Jernigan to look inside the cab. Jernigan opens the door. When Noah doesn't stir, he shakes his shoulder. Then he leans down to Noah's snoring face and takes a whiff.

"Is he drunk?" he asks.

I shrug again.

"You don't seem to know anything," he notes.

"Nope. Like I said, I just got here."

"Really?"

"Logan," Paige says with a frown. "You need to be honest with us."

I stare into her eyes, hoping she might be able to read my mind and let something go just this once.

She meets my gaze for long seconds, before saying, "Let's get Noah to the nurse. His safety is most important right now."

Jernigan throws Noah over his shoulder like he weighs nothing and starts toward the nurse's office.

"I'll just head back to my room," I say, trying to sneak off.

"No, you're coming with us," Jernigan says, looking back at me. "We're not done yet."

Ten minutes later, Noah, who woke up in the fresh air, has been dropped off with the nurse, who doesn't seem overly concerned by his lack of sobriety. His ankle, on the other hand, has earned him a trip to the nearest urgent care place for an X-ray. Once the nurse has him loaded in her van, I try to run away again, but Jernigan won't have it. The one silver lining is Paige convinces him she should talk to me alone first. So now we're both standing in the hallway, outside the nurse's office.

"What happened?" she asks. She looks concerned, not suspicious.

"I honestly don't know what Noah did. He texted me and said he was trashed, so I went out to help him. That's all." *Mostly.*

"He drove in that state?" she asks, her eyes the widest I've ever seen.

"No," I say, shaking my head.

"So he drove into town, bought some booze, drove back, got wasted in the parking lot, somehow twisted his ankle, then called you for help?"

I shrug.

"Why do I feel like there are a few missing pieces?"

"Look," I say with pleading eyes. "Did you see me do anything wrong?"

"No."

"So let's drop it, okay?"

"Did you do something wrong?"

"Please, Paige," I beg.

She purses her lips and places her hands on her hips. "You did."

"I tried to help a friend. Nothing I did hurt anyone. Sometimes it's okay to look the other way."

She takes a deep breath and shakes her head. I expect her to quote the Wallingford Honor Code. It's not like I don't know the damn code. I have it memorized, too. But, sometimes, the best thing to do isn't the right thing to do.

She's still staring at me as she bites her lip.

What would happen to my pending plea bargain if she found out I drove with a suspended license and then reported me? I'm sure the dean would tell my lawyer, who would have to tell the other lawyer, and then he'd probably never agree to the plea bargain deal we're trying to get. Which means I could be looking at jail.

"Please," I whisper.

She sighs, stares out the window for at least a minute, then faces me again. Despite my crossed fingers and silent begging, I don't have much hope, which is why my mouth drops open and then spreads into a massive grin with her next words.

"You're free to go. I'll deal with Alex."

# CHAPTER 24

# PAIGE

**I watch Logan** through the window as he runs back to his dorm. I could practically feel his relief when I told him he could leave. There's a small part of me worrying I gave him preferential treatment, which we agreed I would not do, but he did have a point. Alex and I didn't actually see him do anything wrong. Had we been five minutes earlier, maybe we would have. Then again, had we been five minutes later, we might have missed everything altogether.

I take a deep breath. This is not how I intended for my afternoon to go. After our group hike, Alex wanted to go to the Dairy Barn to hang out with the other cadets, but I asked him to bring me back to school. Off-campus time isn't as enjoyable as it used to be when I know Logan is back on campus.

"Where's he going?" Alex asks, interrupting my thoughts as he rejoins me in the hallway. He's tilting his head toward Evans's retreating figure.

"Back to his room."

He frowns. "I wanted to talk to him, too."

"Sorry," I say, "but I don't think there's anything else to discuss with him. He says he did nothing wrong, and we didn't see him do anything wrong. Seems cut and dry to me. Green, on the other hand, will have some explaining to do once he's back and sober."

"You believe Evans?"

No. I wish I did, but I don't. "What are you going to tell the dean? You're reporting Evans because you *think* he's lying. Last I checked, we need proof of our accusations."

"You saw the keys he was holding, right? I could lean on him until he confesses."

"You could, if this is really so important to you."

"It is. He went off campus without permission, I know it."

"We don't know for sure."

He continues staring out the window as his jaw tenses.

"If this were any other cadet, would you let it go?" I ask.

He doesn't react to my question. Not a flinch. Not a blink. Not a single movement.

"You would," I say. I know him, and I know he'd drop it at this point in order to focus on Green, who is the more obvious offender. Not to mention, if Logan did go off campus, it was only to help Noah, not to joyride around town. Alex always stresses teamwork and helping each other. If this were someone else, I believe he'd let it slide. "You need to lay off Evans. It's verging on the abuse of power," I quietly add.

This time the muscles in his neck flex.

"It's because of me, isn't it?" I continue.

He chomps on his gum three times, the muscles of his jaw bulging each time his teeth connect. "He's had a cocky attitude from the moment he arrived. He needed to be put in his place."

"All DQs have a cocky attitude."

"His was worse."

"Was. That's the key word." I put my hands on my hips and stare out the window like him. "Evans *was* worse, yet you continue to torment him now, even though he's turned into a respectable cadet. Just admit you're jealous of him."

"He's a goof-off. He doesn't take Wallingford seriously. He doesn't have any military aspirations. Hell, I doubt if he has any aspirations at all." He finally turns his head to look at me. "Why do you like him so much?"

Staring straight ahead, I reply, "There's much more to him than you see."

"He's too short for you."

"He's caring and considerate and intelligent and sweet," I say, turning to look at Alex. "And he would do absolutely anything for those close to him, even if it hurt him personally."

Alex scowls. "Your dad likes me better."

"My dad has been in control of my life for far too long." That's the understatement of the year. With both Logan and the Air Force, it's time for me to finally call the shots in my life. That's one reason I decided to date Logan. Maybe taking such a gigantic leap in the right direction will give me the confidence I need to finally have the Air Force discussion with my dad. The one I've been too scared to have for years.

"Don't you want to . . . maybe give us a chance?" Alex asks, nervousness making a rare appearance on his usually confident face.

I shake my head. "Alex," I say, resting my hand on his shoulder, "you're one of my best friends. You're very important to me, you always will be, but I don't . . ."

"Have boyfriend feelings."

I nod. "I'm sorry. I honestly thought you felt the same until recently."

"Would anything be different if I had told you earlier. Before him?"

I slowly shake my head, feeling bad but wanting Alex to understand there was never going to be anything more between us. "We need to figure out a way to make this work. I don't want the three of us to be miserable until the end of school."

"You want me to give him special treatment?"

"No, of course not. I want you to start treating him like all the other cadets because up until now you've been much, much harder on him."

"What do I get out of this?"

"We stay friends. And maybe you gain a new friend in Evans."

His face twists like the thought of being friendly to Logan makes him feel sick. "Evans and I will never be friends."

"That's fine. As long as you stop torturing him."

He rotates toward the window again and stares out to the gray afternoon. I'm glad this conversation is finally happening. It should have happened weeks ago.

"Don't make me choose between you two," I say.

"Because you'll choose him," he states matter-of-factly.

At least he understands.

The next day, things start off better. At breakfast, Logan asks me what I said to Alex because apparently he raised no issues during morning inspection or formation, something that has never happened before. The only problem is Noah is missing. Logan said he didn't see him in the morning, and his empty spot at the table is painfully obvious. We eat and talk, trying to ignore it, but it's impossible.

"I hope Noah's okay," I finally say.

Logan nods; then his eyes drift over to the door of the mess hall as his whole body tenses.

I follow his gaze. The dean is standing there, perusing the room. He looks in our direction, then starts walking.

My stomach drops.

This can't be happening. Did Alex report Logan? Even after our talk? If so, this is lower than I ever thought he'd go.

"Ms. Durant, Mr. Evans, I would like to see you in my office after breakfast."

"Yes, sir," we say in unison.

I crack my knuckles, my anxiety building with each step the dean takes away from us. But he doesn't leave the room. He goes over to Alex and says something to him. Alex nods, then looks back at me.

Why would Alex do this? Does he hate Logan so much he'd be willing to give up our friendship to land him in suspension? That's shortsighted and not at all consistent with the Alex I know.

Five minutes later, after much stressing, the three of us meet in the hallway as we head for his office.

"What did you do?" I whisper to Alex.

"Nothing."

"What did you tell the dean?"

"I didn't say anything. I'm done messing with him," he says with a scowl in Logan's direction.

"Then why does the dean want to talk to us?"

He shrugs his shoulders. "Hell if I know. Maybe it's about Green."

His words bring a brief sense of relief. He could be right. Maybe it has nothing to do with Logan. Noah is obviously in major trouble. Perhaps the nurse mentioned we all brought him to her yesterday, so he wants to ask us what we know of the situation. If so, this might not be so bad.

We each step through the door and salute the dean before

taking a seat. Noah is already in a chair with his left leg extended, a large black contraption on his foot and most of the way up his lower leg.

He won't make eye contact with me; instead, he stares at a picture of the dean and his wife hanging on the wall. I'm not sure what his behavior means, although that brief sense of relief starts to fade.

"Thanks for joining us," Dean Anderson says. "I understand yesterday afternoon was quite interesting around here." He slowly looks at each of us in turn, holding the gaze until it's uncomfortable.

"I would like all of you to tell me what happened in your own words. Mr. Green, let's start with you."

Noah rubs his temples, then says, "Some friends from home met me in town. They brought beer. We drank it. They tried to bring me back, but I thought I should walk it off. I fell, twisted my ankle, and then passed out. That's all I remember."

"Where did you fall?"

"A couple miles from campus."

The dean nods. "Ms. Durant, your turn."

I nod and gulp against the lump in my throat. I just need to be honest. Nothing I saw will get Noah in any more trouble than what he already admitted, and it should have no effect on Logan.

"Commander Jernigan and I returned to campus and saw Cadet Evans in the parking lot. We went over to say hi and found Cadet Green passed out inside a truck. We then took Cadet Green to the nurse to make sure he was okay."

"Mr. Jernigan," the dean says, "do you have anything to add?"

"No, sir," he says. "That's exactly what happened."

"Well, that leaves you Mr. Evans. Please tell me your side of the story."

"I—" His voice cracks. He clears his throat and starts again. "I got a text from Noah saying he was trashed and had hurt his ankle. He needed help. So I went out to the parking lot to help him and ran into Commander Jernigan and Lieutenant Commander Durant."

The dean slowly sucks in air through closed teeth, as though he's considering everything we've said. After a moment, he says, "Here's the problem. How did Green get from the road to the parking lot? Anyone have any ideas?"

We all shake our heads.

"Whose car was Green found in?"

"Cadet Hahn's," I say.

"How did he get in the car? Who had the keys to the car? Had the car been recently driven? I have all kinds of questions. Surely, Mr. Jernigan and Ms. Durant, you had similar questions for Green and Evans. Jernigan?"

"We did, sir. I let Ms. Durant handle the bulk of the questioning."

He looks to me. "What did you find out?"

"Not much," I say. "Cadet Evans said he didn't know how Cadet Green got to the parking lot."

"Did you believe him?"

Why is he doing this to me? He's putting me on the spot. I either tell the truth and turn Logan against me, or lie, completely turning my back on everything Wallingford stands for. "I felt, because we did not witness any violations with regard to Evans, we should focus on the violations we did witness with Green."

"You're not answering my question. Did you believe Evans?"

I have to fight the urge to slump in my seat. "No, sir," I whisper. Logan's going to kill me. I can't even look at him right now.

"Did you notice anything suspicious about Evans?"

"He"—I gulp—"was holding car keys."

"I see. The security records for our gate show that Cadet Hahn's vehicle left campus at two twenty-three yesterday afternoon and returned exactly four minutes later. What time would you say you found Evans and Green?"

"Around two thirty."

"Was Green in any condition to be driving?"

"No, sir."

"Well, then"—he steeples his fingers—"it seems like there's only one person who could have been driving. Evans, did you borrow Hahn's vehicle, pick up Green, then bring him back to campus?"

"Yes, sir." The defeat in his voice is the worst thing I've heard in years. My throat clenches, and I want to reach out to him, hold his hand, but I can't. It's yet another complication of dating at Wallingford.

"Evans, you will receive a five-day on-campus suspension for going AWOL, starting immediately. Green, you will receive the same for underage drinking. You are all dismissed."

We stand and silently file out into the hallway. As soon as the door to the dean's office is closed, I face Logan. "I'm sorry," I blurt out, placing my hand on his shoulder. "I never would've said anything if I weren't forced into it."

"Right," he replies, rolling his eyes and shrugging away from my touch.

I'm about to say more, but he holds up his hand. "I gotta go, *Lieutenant Commander Durant*."

Suddenly the defeat from a minute ago doesn't seem so bad. Not compared to the vehemence with which he said my name. I understand why he's mad at me, but he has to know I didn't have a choice. I protected him as much as I could.

I'm sure once he calms down he'll realize I did the best I could in an unfortunate situation.

He has to.

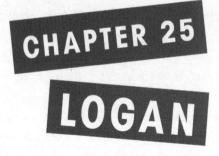

# CHAPTER 25
# LOGAN

**The goal of** suspension is to kill you with boredom, I've realized.

I've never been suspended, and Gordy always said it wasn't so bad, but normal suspension is a day of freedom at home, away from school. Wallingford takes it to the extreme, like they do everything. From right after reveille until right before lights-out, Noah and I are stuck in an empty classroom as teachers and staff rotate through to make sure we stay at our desks, only leaving once every three hours to use the bathroom. They even bring us our meals, and of course, we have no say in what they bring. For lunch yesterday, I got goulash, grapefruit juice, and some sort of sweetly glazed carrots—three things I never would've picked on their own, let alone together. I'm sure that's another one of their torture techniques—serve them the grossest combination of food you can.

The food isn't the worst part, though. Not even an hour after we were dismissed from the dean's office, I got a call from my lawyer. He's coming here Friday to talk to me about what happened. I tried to get him to tell me how bad it is, but he wouldn't give anything anyway. So, now, in addition to being bored, I'm scared out of my mind. The court date is in two weeks. Will they lock me up right after that? Will there be another hearing? I don't even know how any of this shit works.

I may only have two weeks of freedom left and five days of that is spent in freaking suspension. Thanks to Paige.

During my first bathroom break, I forgo peeing in exchange for stopping by my locker to see if my roommate came through. I asked him to get a library book for me—the longer the better—so I'm not forced to stare at the ceiling for twelve hours like yesterday.

As soon as I open the door, I find a nice, thick book, along with about ten folded-up pieces of paper. I grab one and straighten it out. It's a note from Paige, saying she's sorry about what happened. I'm sure she doesn't even realize the full extent of what she's done.

The rest of the notes are similar, except some have a virtual hug or kiss thrown in. Under normal circumstances, I'd love to receive these. Now I toss them in the trash.

One glance at my watch tells me I have twenty seconds before I need to be back in suspension, so I slam my locker shut and race back to the room, carrying the heavy book. I don't even look at the title until I'm at my desk.

*War and Peace.*

For the next thirteen hours, I forget about my doomed future and become consumed by Pierre, Andrei, and Natasha's story. The weird thing is I find eerie similarities to my life here, including competing with a soldier to get the girl. Surprisingly, Wallingford has less drama than St. Petersburg in the early nineteenth century. And, hopefully, the soldier doesn't end up dying and I doubt the girl would ever become frumpy. And, of course, I no longer want to land the girl like Pierre did. A few days ago, I would've. Now, not so much.

"Evans, time to go," the teacher says from the front of the room.

I nod. "Uh-huh, I'm coming," I reply as I stand, still holding the book and reading as I walk toward the door.

"You are such a geek," Noah says, hobbling on his injured leg.

"This is good stuff," I reply, half reading, half paying attention to him. "Duels, affairs, bloody battles, assassinations."

"You haven't looked up from that book in hours."

I finally peel my eyes away. "Did I miss anything?"

"Paige peeking through the window."

"Really?"

He nods. "Do you forgive her?"

"No. Maybe when I get out of jail, I'll see things differently, but I doubt it."

"What?" he asks, stopping and grabbing my arm. "What's going on?"

"I have a feeling my sweet plea bargain is off with me going AWOL and driving with a suspended license."

"You have a suspended license?"

"Yeah. For some reason, they don't want alleged hit-and-run drivers out on the road."

"I didn't realize. Shit," he says, shaking his head. "I feel even worse now. It's my fault, not hers. I never should've called you."

I shrug. He did start a chain reaction that ended in utter badness for me. Still, most of my anger is directed at Paige. Noah was drunk. Drunk people do stupid things. Paige, on the other hand, had her head on straight, like always. And she led me to believe she'd have my back on this, but then caved at the tiniest bit of pressure. She didn't have to admit she didn't believe me or that she saw the keys. We could have all pretended like Noah must walked all the way to the parking lot, found an unlocked car, and decided to take a nap in it.

But no, Miss I-Cannot-Tell-a-Lie had to do me in.

I don't know why I'm so upset. It's not like I'm surprised. She's acting just like she's always acted. I guess I was hoping maybe I meant more to her. Maybe she'd be willing to help me out when push came to shove.

I should've known better.

"How bad is it?" I say on Friday afternoon as soon as I walk into the small office where Mr. Needleham is waiting for me and, of course, holding a Starbucks cup and his notepad.

"Well, things were better before this latest trouble you got yourself into. Do you want to tell me what happened?"

"A friend needed help, so I helped him."

"Did you know you were not only breaking a Wallingford rule but also the law?"

I nod. "But I was only in the car for four minutes. I barely left campus, and I'm not sure I was even on a public road."

"It's not a public road, but that will have little bearing on your case."

"Am I going to prison?"

He taps his notepad with his pen, leaving small dots in the corner. "I don't know. At the pretrial hearing, we're just focused on the plea bargain. As you know, we were shooting for dropping the charges to a Class 1 misdemeanor punishable by community service, a fine, and suspending your license for six months. My concern is the prosecutor might now think a more serious punishment is necessary or even feel as though we should move forward with the trial."

"What are my chances of that happening?"

"I don't know," he says with a shrug. "Maybe fifty-fifty."

"That's not so bad."

"It could be closer to thirty-seventy."

"Seventy I'll get the original plea bargain, or seventy I won't?"

"Won't."

Shit. Those odds aren't nearly as comforting. Which makes me wonder why I'm still covering for Lora. I might end up in jail to keep her from jail for a crime she committed? Wallingford is one thing; jail is something altogether different. Especially for a girl I never even talk to anymore. "What would happen if I tried to take back my confession?" I ask.

His pen tapping stops. "You can't take back a confession," he says. "But . . . we could potentially explore reasons you may have felt compelled to confess. Were you coerced?"

"Maybe."

"Yes or no?"

When I don't answer, he says, "All the charges could potentially be dismissed if we found solid evidence that exonerated you. It would be even better than my proposed plea bargain. You'd have a clean record."

"But the other person would end up in jail?"

"If someone else were responsible for the accident, you mean?"

I nod.

"Possibly. Or maybe they'd get a plea bargain."

Not likely with her outstanding charges. That was the whole reason Lora convinced me to cover for her in the first place. I'd love to get the case dismissed, but not at the expense of ruining her life. Not to mention, what kind of evidence would exonerate me? No one saw what happened. Short of Lora admitting to what she did, I'm not sure there's much hope.

I blow out a long breath and run my hand over my head. I'll just have to get through the next two weeks and see what happens. There's still a chance, albeit a small one, things will work out okay.

"Were you coerced?" he repeats.

"Can I wait to answer until after the hearing?"

He sighs and shakes his head before going back to the tapping. "I don't advise it, but you are free to do whatever you like."

Am I making a mistake? Maybe. Probably. Only time will tell. This whole situation is one freaking huge-ass mess. I'm tired of legal mumbo jumbo. And lawyers. And having no idea what's in store for me.

I just want to go home and have things be like they were over the summer.

No accident.

No Wallingford.

No worries.

Just me and my friends hanging out.

It's all I want, but I don't see it happening again for a long, long time.

# CHAPTER 26
## PAIGE

**"So I heard** Mr. Evans got himself into some trouble last weekend?" Mr. Needleham says.

I nod. I can't believe I have to talk to his lawyer now. Why couldn't this discussion have taken place a week ago? A week ago, I would have had nothing but positive things to say. Now there's this issue obscuring all the good progress he's made.

"Do you know of any other infractions he's had?"

"No, sir. He's been doing great—showing more respect, getting involved in extracurricular activities, following our rules—"

"Except for going AWOL and driving with a suspended license last weekend."

I reluctantly nod again. I'm sure the dean filled him in on everything when they talked.

"Was he aware of the rules when he broke them?"

I bite my lip as I consider saying no. Would that make things better for Logan? Maybe, although I'm sure he knows Logan was aware of the suspended license. I'm sure he told Logan about it himself. Lying about this would likely only make the lawyer realize I'm unreliable, and not help Logan at all.

He's watching me with a patient expression, but his fingers tap the notepad on the desk.

"He was aware," I finally say. Usually when I abide by our Honor Code, I feel a sense of relief, knowing I did the right thing. Now it's more reluctance and less relief I feel.

Hopefully my words don't land him more community service hours or a longer suspended license. Even if they do, he has to realize it's not my fault.

He never should've done what he did.


Later that night, right before lights-out, I wait for Logan near the door of his dorm. It's been five days since we've talked, and I can't stand it anymore. The initial hope I had about him forgiving me has faded little by little as he ignored my notes and never attempted to talk or even smile at me. He's angry, I get that, but there has to be a way for us to move past this. There's no way he'll let one little thing ruin what we have.

Had.

*No*, I think, shaking my head. *Have. We still have it. This is just a minor bump in the road.*

When he reaches for the handle, I take a step away from the building and onto the sidewalk. "Evans, may I speak with you for a moment?"

He goes rigid.

"See ya tomorrow," Noah whispers as he slips past Logan and through the door.

Logan slowly turns around. "What do you want, Paige?" He doesn't bother to salute me or use my title. I bite my lip, briefly considering assigning him laps, but then come to my senses. Punishing him now would not help us move past this.

Instead, I say, "I wanted to see how you're doing since we haven't talked in days."

"Never been better," he replies with a sneer.

"Your lawyer talked to me this afternoon."

"Did you make sure he fully understood how much of a juvenile delinquent I am?"

"No, I made sure he knew how well you were doing here."

"Too little, too late."

My brow furrows at his words. Is he talking about the suspension or something more? "What do you mean?"

He blows out a quick breath, shakes his head, and turns around. "I gotta go."

I quickly grab his arm before he can leave. "Logan," I say softly. "Talk to me."

"I've got nothing to say."

"You're still mad?" He's got to realize I didn't have a choice. I did the best I could in a bad situation.

"Mad? Why would I be mad? It couldn't be because I've got one foot in a prison cell thanks to you running your mouth, could it?"

Prison? My eyes grow wide, and my arms drop to my sides. He's not going to prison. There's no way. He wasn't even involved in the hit and run. And what he did here doesn't warrant a prison sentence. Suspension from school, yes. Prison, never in a million years.

"Yeah, thanks for that," he says. "Your obsession with the Honor Code may get you exactly what you want out of life, but it's ruining mine."

He turns his back on me and throws open the door. I'm left staring into the empty doorway, long after he's gone.

Did I really ruin his life?

# CHAPTER 27

## LOGAN

**"Lo, I heard** the bad news," Gordy says as soon as I answer my phone the next afternoon. It's Saturday and I should be out with Paige, but I obviously opted to skip it. From my desk, I can see the parking lot, and she's out there waiting by her car. It's been twenty minutes so far. Apparently me storming away from her last night wasn't clear enough for her.

"Who told you?" I ask, rubbing the top of my neck, right where it connects to my skull. My head has been killing me since yesterday and no amount of Tylenol seems to make a dent in it.

"Your mom. She asked me to give you a call to see how you're doing."

"I'm fine," I say, rising out of my chair a little to continue watching Paige as a group of guys climb into a car near hers.

"How are things going with Paige?"

The mention of her name causes my headache to spread. It's now working its way up behind my ears. "We're through."

"Why?"

I give him the very long and detailed version, which is probably more than he cares to know, but it's nice to talk to someone, especially someone who will agree with me on everything. The whole time I'm talking, Paige continues to stand outside her car in the freezing cold. Every now and again, she turns toward my window and I feel her eyes on me, but there's no way she can see me in the darkened room.

"Wow," Gordy says when I finally finish. "You really know how to pick them."

"Tell me about it."

"But you do realize you'd never even be in this situation if you weren't such a wuss around Lora last summer, right?"

I roll my eyes at the phone. He's supposed to agree with everything I say, not point out my stupid decisions.

"Hey, does this mean you can come home? Since things are messed up anyway?"

My mouth opens to tell him no; then I close it. He may be right. Why didn't I think to ask Mr. Needleham? It's not like leaving will make anything worse. He wanted me to come here to prove to the prosecutor I was serious about turning my life around. But at this point, the damage is done. In fact, the longer I stay, the more damage I'll probably cause.

"Want to come pick me up tomorrow?" I ask.

"For real?"

"Yeah. I'll have my mom and Mr. Needleham talk to the dean. My trial starts soon anyway. I'm sure I should be in town in case the lawyers need to talk to me. Plus, Thanksgiving is next week. I need to be home for Thanksgiving."

"Okay, sure. What time do you want me there?"

"Whenever."

We finish making our plans, and then I lean back in my chair with my hands behind my head. I know nothing about my long-term future has changed, but the thought of going home makes my head hurt a little less and my desire to hurl something across the room a little more manageable. At least I'll be back with those I can trust—my mom, Gordy, Nate.

Plus, it will be nice to have a little freedom before I'm locked up for good.

During lunch the next day, I receive a text from Gordy telling me he's in the parking lot, meaning he must have left at the crack of dawn since it's almost a five-hour drive. Gordy isn't exactly an early riser, so I owe him big for this.

I still have a handful of fries on my plate, but I'm not about to spend one minute more than I need to spend here.

"Later, man," I say to Noah as I stand.

"You heading out?" he asks.

"Yeah."

He nods, then awkwardly stands with the brace still on his leg. "I'm sorry about what I did. It was a dick move."

I wave him off. "Shit happens."

He nods. "Still, I feel bad. If there's anything I can do . . ."

I nod and offer him a small smile. "Thanks," I say before shaking his outstretched hand, then pulling him in for a hug. "I hope things end better for you than me."

"Don't give up yet. I have a feeling you might be able to charm the judge."

I wish I shared his optimism.

"You've got my number, right?" he asks.

I nod.

"Stay in touch."

I nod again and suddenly realize I'm going to miss Noah. Despite his poor judgment last weekend, he's been a good friend from the moment I arrived and, unlike other people here, would never purposely let me down.

"Thanks," I say, "for making Wallingford a little more bearable."

"You too," he responds with a sad smile.

I slowly turn around and, after tossing my trash and loading the dishes to the conveyer belt, head for the door. At the threshold, I take one last look at the mess hall. It's only half-full since it's a weekend and plenty of students are eating in town. Still, it's loud and full of energy. The posters of Navy submarines and aircraft carriers and old battleships from the turn of the last century give me an unexpected pang in my chest. I frown at myself. There should be no pangs, only elation.

Shaking my head, I start to turn around, but my eyes accidentally clash with someone else's. Paige. She's intense, her face emotionless, her eyes piercing.

I turn around, thankful I'll never have to see her again.

"Evans!" she shouts from across the room.

I keep walking.

Even from the hallway, I can tell the din of the mess hall has quieted. I imagine everyone is whispering about me and Paige. At least I provided some good entertainment for the few months I was here.

Not even ten minutes later, I've got my one small suitcase of belongings and I'm loading it into Gordy's trunk.

"That's all?" he asks, looking around me without even saying hi.

"That's it."

"I take more on vacation. How'd you live out of a tiny bag for months?"

"Standard-issue clothing courtesy of Wallingford."

"Oh, right. Nice hair, by the way." He doesn't even try to hide his grin.

I self-consciously run my hand over my head and wonder how long it will take to grow out. Although, the military look might be good for the hearing. Maybe I should keep it short until at least then.

"Ready to blow this Popsicle stand?" he asks.

"You have no idea."

We climb into the car, and Gordy starts it up. He backs out of his parking spot and then starts to ease forward, when someone jumps out from between two other cars, completely blocking our path and almost getting hit.

"What the hell?!" he yells, slamming on the breaks, then pounding the horn.

I groan.

Paige stands there, hands on hips, refusing to move.

"What's her problem?" Gordy asks. "Is she not quite right in the head or something?"

"That's Paige," I explain.

"Really?" He squints his eyes. "She looks different than in the picture you sent."

"That's because she was smiling then. This is angry Paige, who's about to go on a rampage."

"Want me to back up and go out a different way?"

"No," I reply with a sigh as I open the door and let in a blast of cold air. "I'll take care of this."

As soon as my feet are on the ground, she stomps over to me, her finger jabbing the air between us. "I can't believe you! No good-bye? Seriously? You want to walk away from here and never speak to me again? Like we never shared anything? You can't blame me! It's not my fault. I didn't do anything wrong!"

"Excuse me?" I say, putting my hands on my hips. "You didn't do anything wrong?"

"No!"

"You turned on me in the dean's office!"

"I didn't have a choice!" she yells, raising her hands as if I'm being ridiculous.

"You saw nothing. That's all you had to say!"

"You know it's not that easy. I couldn't lie to the dean. I did the best I could. I've already risked a ton to be with you. It's not fair for you to expect even more from me."

"What exactly have you risked?"

"My future! I agreed to date you when I should be one hundred percent focused on school right now."

"Oh my God," I say in a mocking tone. "Paige dated a boy. Notify the president. She's unfit to be a uniformed officer."

She narrows her eyes at me. "Don't be a jerk."

"There's one person here who's been a jerk this past week, and it's not me. Quit acting like the victim; it's not becoming on you."

I thought it'd be impossible, but her eyes become even narrower slits.

"No," I continue, shaking my head and pointing my finger at her now. "You don't get to turn this around. I've played the game. I've followed ninety-nine percent of the ridiculous Wallingford rules. And you kissed me by the lake, not the other way around. You're the one who said you wanted to date. I never forced anything on you! Yet the first moment you got, you turned on me."

Her fists ball up at her sides, but her eyes drift to the ground.

"See? You know you were wrong!" I yell. "No one at the Air Force Academy would've known if you had withheld information, but now everyone in the courtroom is sure as hell going to know about all my dirty laundry thanks to you! If this is the final nail in my coffin, I will never forgive you!"

"I couldn't lie to the dean!"

"Yep, your guilty conscience is much more important than my entire life."

She takes a deep breath and closes her eyes. Angry puffs of white breath escape my mouth and nose. When her eyes open, she says, "You shouldn't have done it. You never should've gotten behind the wheel. Why would you drive with a suspended license?"

"It's called being a good friend—something you clearly know nothing about."

I start to turn around, but she grabs my shoulder and spins me back. "A good friend would find another way to help him. You could've called me. I would've picked him up."

"And reported him," I say, yanking my shoulder from her grasp.

She's quiet for a few moments. Then her fists uncurl and most of the fire in her eyes burns out. "It was still wrong," she says more quietly.

"At least I tried to help him. That's more than I can say for some people."

She stares at me, unblinking.

"I've gotta go," I say, the fight in me dying out, too.

As I step behind the car door, she asks, "Will you keep in touch?"

I run through a couple answers in my head but don't like the sound of them. In the end, all I say is "I don't know, Paige. I don't know."

# CHAPTER 28

## PAIGE

**"You okay?"** Leah asks from beside me.

"Huh?"

"You were tossing and turning all night. Do you feel okay?"

I roll over to face her. It's Thanksgiving morning, and she's staying with me and my dad since her parents couldn't afford a plane ticket for her.

"My stomach does kind of hurt," I say, stretching my legs out. It's still dark outside, but my dad is already banging around in the kitchen, making coffee and starting breakfast. My stomach growls, and I wonder if hunger's contributing to the pain, although I doubt it. It's been there for a few days now, ever since my fight with Logan. It started out small, like a single match searing the inside of my stomach, but the flame has grown and intensified each day. Now it feels like an entire pack of matches are barbecuing me from the inside.

"Do you need to go to the doctor?" she asks.

I shake my head. A doctor can't fix this. Maybe a psychologist could. Although she'd probably tell me I need to do something to address my guilt. But what can I do? I screwed up Logan's life, and it's not like I can take it back now even if I wanted to. What's done is done. I'll have to figure out a way to live with this pain forever.

"Can I get you some medicine?" she asks.

"No, I'll be fine," I reply, climbing out of bed. "Let's eat."

My dad goes all out for breakfast like he always does on the rare occasions when I'm home. It's as though he tries to make up for all the time I'm absent in one visit.

After a breakfast of scrambled eggs, toast, hash browns, sausage, fruit salad, and my favorite maple-glazed donuts from a local place my mom and I used to go to every Sunday morning, Leah and I get ready for the day. Our neighbors, as well as two of my aunts and uncles, will be coming over this afternoon for dinner.

"You up for making the pies again, like last year?" my dad asks Leah once she joins us in the kitchen after her shower.

"Yes, sir. I'd love to. Pumpkin and apple?"

He nods. "I think I got everything you'll need over on the island. If not, Paige can find it for you."

Leah likes to bake. I don't. So I sit on a stool and keep her company while she gets to work and my dad heads to the gym.

"Feeling better?" she asks as she mixes pumpkin pie mix, eggs, sugar, and a bunch of spices in a bowl.

"No."

"You should probably get that checked out. What if it's something bad?"

"It's not something bad."

"It could be. Like cancer or something." She adds some cinnamon to the mix. "I read an article once about someone thinking they just had a stomachache and, boom, a week later they died from cancer."

I start to roll my eyes but stop myself. How did I ever let his annoying behavior rub off on me? "I don't have cancer."

Leah and I talk about everything, but for some reason, I don't feel like getting into this with her. Maybe it's because I'm worried rehashing it all will only increase the guilt. She knows about the fight—everyone at Wallingford knows about the fight—but she's been a good friend and completely ignored the topic so far.

"How can you be so sure? You suddenly have a medical degree I don't know about?" she asks, pouring the mixture into a store-bought pie shell.

"It's not real pain. It's all in my head, I think."

She pauses, holding the spatula in midair. Slowly, she lowers it and the bowl still containing half of the mix to the counter. "I was wondering when you'd want to talk about it."

Crap. I should've kept my mouth shut. Her thinking it's cancer would be better. "I don't want to talk about it," I say, shaking my head and gathering up some of the dirty dishes. I carry them to the sink and start rinsing them and putting them in the dishwasher.

"If it's making you sick, you should probably talk about it."

"Nope."

She joins me at the sink and puts her arm around my shoulders. "I miss him, too. He was a fun guy to have around."

I nod. He was fun. Until I ruined his life.

Leah goes back to the island and finishes the pumpkin pie, even cutting out little leaves from some extra piecrust and adding them around the edges. After it goes in the oven, she gathers up the supplies for the apple pie.

I grab the bag of apples from the fridge and start peeling. It's the one part of pie making she doesn't like.

"Thanks," she says when she notices what I'm doing. She stands next to me, accepting each apple as I finish and cutting it into slices.

As I mindlessly peel the fruit, Logan's forlorn face from the last moment I saw him keeps popping into my mind like it's been doing the past four days. He felt betrayed by me. The problem is, I didn't hurt him on purpose.

"Leah, I . . . I really messed up," I say, finally putting into words what's been eating me up inside.

"What happened?"

"I said more than I should've to the dean."

"About what?"

"Logan. He was trying to help Noah, which was the decent thing to do. And he barely broke the rules, but now it sounds like he might be going to prison. It's not fair to him. I . . . I feel like the lawyer didn't get the full picture."

"Did you talk to the lawyer?"

"Yeah, but I didn't know he was headed for prison then. If I had, I would've worded things differently."

"Maybe you could call the lawyer and talk to him again?"

Is it really that simple? Could I fix this entire thing so easily? It seems too good to be true, but having a plan does make my stomach feel better. I can't just sit around and wait to see what happens. I need to take action. Logan would do it for me in a heartbeat if the situation were reversed.

The rest of the day drags on, when all I want to do is search for Mr. Needleham's number online and then give him a call. I'm sure he won't be in his office today, but I can at least leave him a message. Instead, I spend hours helping Leah finish the pies, then working with my dad to heat up the premade meal he bought from the grocery store. Before we're even done, our guests arrive and then it's talking to them and dinner and dessert. Finally, at seven, the house is quiet again and I have a moment to myself while Leah calls her parents.

It's surprisingly easy to find a lawyer named Mr. Needleham in Chesapeake, Virginia. He's part of a large law firm that, from the looks of their polished webpage, is quite expensive.

My dad is sitting in the living room, watching a football game, so I take my computer and phone out to the front porch for some privacy. After getting comfortable on the wooden swing, I dial his number.

As soon as his voice mail picks up, I start my message. "Hi, Mr. Needleham. This is Paige Durant. From Wallingford Academy. Logan Evans's peer mentor. I've been thinking since we last talked, and I'm worried you might have not gotten the full picture of how Logan's been doing. He was really excelling at Wallingford, especially academically, but also with adapting to the strict routine and respecting authority. He did make a mistake, but it was to help a friend, just like he helped his girlfriend with the accident." I pause. Did I say too much? Logan should come clean about Lora, but he needs to make the decision, not me.

"Um . . . so, anyway, his heart was in the right place, like it always is. I'd be happy to discuss this with you if you'd like. Please let me know if I can do anything else. I'd hate for him to end up in jail. My number is 540-555-0102 if you have any questions. Thanks."

As soon as I hang up, my stomach feels a hundred times better. The burning from the last four days starts to ease. I take a deep breath and smile as the pain almost completely dissipates.

Next time I have a problem, I'm talking to Leah sooner.


Two days later, I receive the callback from Mr. Needleham. He asks me a few questions and then says he wants me to be a character witness at the hearing. I tell him I'd love to, but I'll have to clear it with my dad and Wallingford. I don't have any tests on the day of the hearing, so it shouldn't be a problem.

"Who was that?" my dad asks with a frown when I hang up.

We're at a Chinese restaurant for lunch and phones at the table are an absolute no with him, but I couldn't miss the call.

"Sorry. It was Logan's lawyer. He wants me to be a character witness at the hearing."

"Why?"

"Because . . . I know his character," I say, not understanding why he'd question it.

Leah squirms in the chair next to me.

"Where is it?" he asks.

"Chesapeake."

"When?"

The waiter approaches our table, so I wait to answer until after he leaves iced tea for me and my dad, water for Leah, and a plate of pot stickers. "Monday."

"I have an important meeting Monday," he says, drawing his glass closer to himself. "I can't take you."

"I'll drive myself."

He runs his tongue over his teeth as he stares at me, and I get a sinking feeling inside. He's never had a problem with me driving back and forth to school. I even drove to Alex's house about an hour and a half away last summer. I'm surprised this is an issue.

He folds his hands together on the black tabletop and says, "You are not driving all the way across the state and back in one day."

"I'll get a hotel room and come back on Tuesday."

"No you will not."

He's treating this like I just want to hang out with some friends. Clearly, he doesn't see the importance. "Dad, I have to. This is very important."

He shakes his head. "The answer is no. End of discussion."

"But—"

"No."

Leah stands and quietly says, "Excuse me."

"May—" I start to say.

"The answer is no, Paige."

I stare at him dumfounded. I assumed my dad would be okay with this. Logan needs my help. Whenever someone needs help, my dad is always first in line to provide it. Why, all of a sudden, is helping a bad thing?

"Ple—" I try once more.

He cuts me off with a single look.

I slump in my chair and fold my arms across my chest as my blood boils in my veins. I cannot believe him. He won't listen to reason right now. He won't listen to me, period. Every time I try, he shuts me down.

I continue sulking and silently stewing in my chair the entire time Leah is gone. When she returns, he smiles at her and asks about her recently received nomination to the Naval Academy. They start talking, but she keeps sending worried glances my way.

Only minutes ago, everything was headed in the right direction. I was going to help Logan. Now, once again, I'm letting him down. What would he do if he were in this situation? That's easy to answer. He'd ignore his dad. The problem is if my dad doesn't give me permission to leave campus, I'll be considered AWOL just like Logan was. And I'll earn a suspension just like he did, too.

A suspension would totally derail my future. My dad would lose it and never let me go anywhere by myself again, especially almost two thousand miles away to Colorado.

Of course, how would I feel if I went there while Logan was stuck in prison? I imagine the burning in my stomach would return with a vengeance and last the entire time he was there. Years and years of guilt.

I bite my lip, not at all comfortable with what I'm considering. But . . . do I really have a choice?

# CHAPTER 29

# LOGAN

**"Thanks for the ride,"** I say to Gordy as we pull up to the curb outside Lora's parents' pristine mansion. My hearing is in two days, and I feel like she and I need to talk.

"Sure thing, man. I'll wait right here."

I exit the car and slowly walk to the front door, suddenly second guessing myself. Do I really want to see her? What will we say to each other? After two unanswered rings of the bell, I let out a relieved sigh and turn around. It's probably for the best.

I'm not even down the first step when the door opens.

Shit.

"Logan, is that you?" Lora's mom says.

I turn around and plaster a smile on my face. "Hi, Mrs. Mitchell."

"When did you get back in town?" she asks, her Botox-laden face emotionless. It used to freak me out. Her face always looks the same, whether she's welcoming you to her home or disapproving of how the yard guy trimmed her azaleas. It's like she's made of plastic or something.

"A few days ago. Is Lora home?"

"You're due in court on Monday." It's not a question. I get the impression she wants to frown at me, but her face is still blank. I think I'd be frustrated, not being able to control my own features.

"Yes, ma'am."

"'Ma'am'?" She's probably wondering what happened to me. I sound like a Goody Two-shoes, just like Jernigan. It's the stupid Wallingford influence.

"May I see Lora?" I ask. "I just want to say hi since it's been a while."

She rests her white-tipped nail against her lips for a few long moments. Finally, she says, "Lora's in the den watching TV." She holds open the door, which I take as my invitation.

"Thank you."

Hopefully this won't be too awkward.

I pass through their double-story foyer, take a left at the marble statue of some Roman God, then slowly open the mostly glass door to the den.

Lora's on the couch with her feet propped up on the coffee table as she rapid-fire types on her phone.

"Hey," I say when she doesn't look up.

My voice causes her to jump. Then she just stares at me like a deer caught in headlights.

"Surprise," I say with a stupid grin.

She doesn't move.

I was kind of expecting her to act a little excited to see me. Maybe not jump off the couch and engulf me in a bear hug, but at least smile. Or ask how I am. Or not appear totally guilty for whatever she's doing on her phone.

"So I was thinking I'd take you up on that offer of dinner," I say, stepping into the room.

"Tonight?"

"Sure, if you want to."

"I've . . . actually got plans." Her eyes dart to her phone. I wonder if it's the guy from the movie theater or someone else. Not that it matters. I was worried, or maybe hopeful, all those old feelings would return the moment I saw her, but they didn't. I feel nothing for her. Not joy. Not anger. I'm absolutely indifferent.

"Oh, okay," I reply with a shrug.

"But maybe we could grab lunch tomorrow?"

"Yeah, maybe." I'm not sure why I even came over here now. It's becoming clear I don't really want to spend time with her. And I'm too much of a wuss to tell her I'm turning her in. This is pointless.

"Do you want to sit down?" She finally lowers her phone and scoots over on the couch a little so there's more space for me. She fiddles with the bottom of her shirt, pulling off nonexistent pieces of lint. "I didn't realize you were home," she says.

I lower myself next to her. "I came back last weekend. For Thanksgiving . . . and the hearing."

"Are you liking your new school better?" She says it like I'm at an ordinary school, not Wallingford. I'd love for her to have to spend a week there. With Paige as her mentor. She wouldn't last half a day.

"Not particularly."

"I'm sorry." She lowers her hand to my knee, like maybe she's feeling a bit of what we used to have. "I really am sorry," she continues. "Thank you for what you're doing." She gives me her big doe eyes. I used to be a sucker for those. Now, not so much.

"Yeah, about that," I say, sliding away from her. "I kind of got in trouble and might not get the plea bargain."

"What?" she asks, her face going slack. "What'd you do?"

"I had to pick up a drunk friend."

"Why's that a problem?"

"No license. No permission to leave campus."

"Oh, right." She starts biting her thumbnail.

"So, um, if I don't get the plea bargain," I say, "I'm looking at jail time."

Her hand falls to her lap. "You can't go to jail!"

"Okay, good," I say with a nod. "I'm glad we agree. So maybe you could admit to what happened?"

"I can't go to jail either!" She jumps up from the couch, wringing her hands in front of herself. "Why did you screw things up at your military school? We had a good plan!"

"I didn't do it on purpose!"

"Oh my God," she says, starting to pace from one end of the room to the other as she holds her head in her hands. "We've got to figure something out. Maybe if we split responsibility. My weed, your accident?"

"That's an idea." Not a great idea, but an idea.

"Or we could say someone else was driving your car."

"I have a feeling no one would believe us."

"This is awful," she says, stopping in front of me.

"No shit."

"We only have two days to figure something out."

I roll my neck. How many lies are we going to tell? I'm already worried I won't remember what I said during my confession the night of the accident. Now she wants to come up with version 2.0?

"I should probably get going," I say, standing.

She nods. "Your lawyer asked me to be a character witness."

"Really?" He didn't tell me he was having any witnesses. I thought it was just me and the two lawyers.

"Yeah, so we should probably get our story straight. Let's figure something out during lunch tomorrow."

"Sure, okay." Now we both have to remember version 2.0? This has the makings of a complete disaster. By the end of it, they may put both of us in jail.

That'd be just my luck—suffer through two months of Wallingford to keep Lora safe, only to have both of us end up in the slammer. The way things are going for me, there's probably a good chance of this actually happening.

Having no more patience for Lora right now, I quickly say bye and escape back to Gordy's car.

"Beach?" he says. He doesn't ask how it went, meaning the answer must be written on my face.

"Yeah," I reply. This may be my last time to go for a while.

Thirty minutes later, we find Nate sitting in our usual place on the boardwalk with three root beer floats by his side. I don't need to see the name on the cups to know where they're from. It seems weird to have an "our" place with two other guys, but we do. Whatever. Swirly's root beer floats and the boardwalk have helped us get through a lot. At least we rely on root beer and not the real thing.

Gordy and I sit next to Nate without a word, and he passes out the drinks.

We're silent, other than the slurping, as we all stare out at the ocean. It's early afternoon, and the bright sun makes the fifty-degree weather feel not quite as cool. Still, I put on my gloves to hold the cold Styrofoam cup.

The waves crash against the mostly empty beach, other than a few people searching for shells or buried treasure with a metal detector. The sound and smell of the water are peaceful and calming, which is why we come here if one of us is in trouble.

When I finish my float, I set the empty cup next to my leg, then draw my feet up on the boardwalk and lean back on my elbows. I bet Paige would like it here.

Shit.

I've been trying to erase her and everything to do with her from my mind and memories, but it's nearly impossible. She'll sneak up on me when I least expect it. Like now. Why would I think about her here? We've never been to the beach together.

We've never even talked about the beach. For all I know, she could hate the beach. Maybe she detests how the wind messes up her hair or how sand finds its way into every body crevice or how you have to dodge the seaweed and jellyfish as you walk along the surf.

Of course, she'd look really, really good in a swimsuit.

I groan at my uncontrollable thoughts and sit back up, swinging my legs over the edge of the wooden footpath. How can my brain be so disloyal to itself?

"Don't worry, we'll visit you every week in the slammer," Nate says, still staring out at the water. He must have misunderstood my current state of annoyance.

"Thanks, you're a true friend," I reply sarcastically.

"Want us to sneak anything in for you? Cigarettes? Porn? A nail file?" Gordy asks, knocking his elbow into me.

I'm about to make a snide reply when I'm interrupted by my phone ringing. I remove it from my pocket and see it's Mr. Needleham.

"Hello?" I answer.

"Logan, how are you doing?"

"Fine. You?"

"Good, good. I just wanted to remind you to get to the courthouse early on Monday. And wear something nice. Do you have your dress uniform from Wallingford?"

"No, I left it there."

"A suit?"

"No, sir."

"Dress shirt and tie?"

"Yes, sir."

"Okay. Wear those and nice pants."

Despite just downing about a liter of soda, my mouth and throat go dry. It's happening. Monday will be here before I know it, and

I'll be one step closer to my fate. At this point, I'm having a hard time imagining anything other than badness being thrown at me.

"When you're addressing anyone, make sure you say 'sir' or 'ma'am' a lot. We want everyone to see you as polite."

"Yes, sir."

"Yes, just like that. And we're going to focus on how you were helping your friend at Wallingford. You were very concerned about his safety and didn't see any other way to help him."

"That's true."

"Good. Okay, we're in the best shape we can be in right now. If you have any questions . . . or want to tell me anything about your confession . . ." He pauses, a nice long pause, waiting for me. When I don't take the bait, despite desperately wanting to, he continues. "Give me a call if you need to talk, okay?"

"Yes, sir. I will."

We say goodbye, and then I stare out at the water again. I should've asked him about the witnesses. Is anyone else coming besides Lora?

"Hey," I say, looking at the guys on either side of me, "did my lawyer ask you to be a witness at the hearing?"

Both Gordy and Nate shake their heads.

Why would he ask Lora but not them? They're much closer to me. I wonder if my parents will have to say anything. I know my mom's going, but I don't have a clue about my dad. I haven't talked to him since my birthday.

"I should get going," I say, standing. Thinking of my mom makes me realize I need to spend a little time with her before everything has the potential of crashing down. "Can I bum a ride off of one of you?"

"I got you covered," Gordy says, reaching for the railing and hauling himself up. Nate joins us, and as we're walking to the cars, says, "Maybe it won't be so bad. Maybe Lora will decide to come clean."

"Doubtful," I reply.

"Maybe the plea bargain will work after all."

"Unlikely."

"Maybe they found a surprise eyewitness who will say it was Lora without you having to be the bad guy."

"You're grasping for straws."

"Maybe Paige will show up and change her story," Gordy says.

"Never in a million years."

She acted exactly how she's been brainwashed to act. The last time we talked, she made it absolutely clear she had no second thoughts about anything.

When this is finally over and I can start my life for real, I'm no longer trusting my instincts with girls. Hell, I may turn to a life of celibacy. Maybe I could join a monastery or something.

It'd be painful, but not nearly as painful as what I've already endured, especially with Paige. I get what Lora was doing, trying to protect herself because of her other trouble. But Paige? All it would've taken was a couple white lies that no one would have ever been able to call her out on. After everything we went through, I had put my faith in her. She talked to Jernigan and seemed like she was going to protect me. I was beginning to think our relationship was real and genuine.

To trust someone . . . and to start feeling something for someone, only to have them turn on you when you need them the most . . . it's like being blindsided by a freaking tsunami and swept away from everything you thought you knew.

And then you're left alone to pick up the pieces of your damaged life.

And your damaged heart.

# CHAPTER 30

# PAIGE

**Saturday evening,** after the awful lunch with my dad and an afternoon of me finding every excuse possible to avoid him, I'm sitting on the front porch again, calling Logan's lawyer.

"Hello, this is Arthur Needleham," he says when he answers.

"Hi, Mr. Needleham. This is Paige Durant."

"Hi there. Is everything set? Will you be able to come to the hearing on Monday?"

This is it. I truly am risking it all to try and save him. "Yes, sir," I reply, ignoring the queasiness in my stomach.

"Okay, good. You mentioned in your original message that Logan was trying to help his girlfriend the night of the accident. You meant Lora Mitchell, right?"

"I'm not sure what her last name is. Her first name is Lora."

"Can you tell me more about what happened?"

"Um . . ." What am I supposed to do? His lawyer needs to know, but I don't want to betray Logan's trust again. After a long pause, I say, "I'm not sure he'd want me to talk about it. Maybe you can ask him?"

"I have. He's being evasive. He wants to wait and see how the pretrial hearing goes before deciding whether to admit he was coerced into confessing, which I fully believe he was."

"As his lawyer, can't you force him to admit he was coerced?"

"No, but I can present evidence to clear him." He pauses, and I hear the distinct crackle and distorted voice of someone talking on a drive-thru speaker. "Give me a minute, please," he says; then there's a rustling like he's covering the speaker with his hand. While I wait, I use my feet to push the swing back and forth as I watch my dad through the window. He's in front of the TV with Leah and keeps changing the channel from football, his choice, to the Food Network, her choice. Under normal circumstances, I'd assume I only have a few more minutes before he'll come looking for me, but with how angry I've been today, he's kept his distance. I'm sure he figures I'll eventually get over it, not that I'm planning my first teenage rebellious act, in epic fashion.

"Sorry about that," Mr. Needleham says returning to our call. "Like I said, I'm trying to find evidence. The problem is I've had only a few days since realizing he was likely coerced. Every piece of evidence I've reviewed—traffic cams, witness statements, and the like—are all inconclusive. Did he tell you anything else about that night?"

"I—I don't want to betray his confidence."

"Do you want him to end up with, at best, a Class 1 misdemeanor on his permanent record? At worst it could be a felony conviction."

"No."

"I know it's a long shot, but if I find exculpatory evidence between now and Monday, the case could be dismissed. It would be like this never happened."

That's what needs to occur. He needs to be done with this, and Lora needs to deal with it instead of him.

When I don't say anything, he continues, "I'll clear anything you tell me with Mr. Evans before I use it at the hearing."

"You promise?"

"Yes."

I take a deep breath. I don't want Logan to think I stabbed him in the back, but I also don't want Mr. Needleham to miss an opportunity to potentially gather evidence. What if Logan changes his mind at the hearing, but it's too late? It'd be better for Mr. Needleham to have the evidence ready in case Logan comes to his senses. Surely, he would realize I'm doing this to help him, not hurt him.

"He told me he let Lora borrow his car," I say with conviction. Someone needs to stand up for him and if he won't do it himself, it'll have to be me and his lawyer. "He was playing video games with his friend Gordy all night. When Gordy dropped him off at home, the cops were waiting. He was arrested on the spot and spent the rest of the night at the police station."

"Did he talk to Ms. Mitchell between the time of the accident and when he was arrested?"

"I'm not sure, sir."

"Do you know Gordy's last name?"

"No, I don't. He's Logan's best friend."

"Okay, thanks. I've got a couple leads here. There's not much time, but maybe I can turn something up."

I'm not a superstitious person, but I cross my fingers anyway. At this point, Logan needs all the help he can get.


The next morning, Leah and I decide to leave my house earlier than we had planned. I'm still furious with my dad, and he knows it.

We're sitting in my car as he leans against the driver's side door. "If you talk to Evans, let him know I hope his court case turns out okay," he says at my open window.

"It'd turn out better if you'd let me go," I mutter through gritted teeth.

"Paige," he warns, giving me his serious dad look.

Once again, he's shutting me down. Controlling my life. Making me do whatever he says without any input from me. I'm almost eighteen, and he's still doing it.

"I'm going to the Air Force Academy," I blurt out, tightly gripping the steering wheel and staring straight into his eyes.

My plan was to tell him while I was home, but not under these circumstances. My grandpa had given me some pointers, and none of those were to blurt it out in the middle of an argument.

My dad doesn't blink or look away. His jaw doesn't even tense. Instead, he just stares back with absolutely no emotion. It's almost like he didn't hear me.

"I applied and got in," I continue. "I'm going. There's nothing you can say to stop me." I might as well get it all out now.

I hear Leah drop something next to me and imagine she'd rather be anywhere but here. So would I.

"What about the Naval Academy?" he asks in a low, steady voice, despite the anger I know is brewing under the surface.

"I got in—the letter came two days ago—but I will be declining."

"You've been lying to me? What has gotten into you? Is it Evans's influence?"

"No," I reply, shaking my head. "I've never lied. I've always said the academy. You were the one who assumed I meant the Naval Academy."

"Lying by omission is still lying, Paige." The thick vein in his neck is now pulsing. He's getting angrier and angrier, though he's an expert at hiding it.

"I'm joining the Air Force," I say again, so he knows I'm serious. Of course, he may lock me in my childhood bedroom after tomorrow. I may not have another day of freedom for years and years to come.

"We'll see about that," he replies, narrowing his eyes at me in a way that finally shuts me up. I've never talked to him like this. I've never been even close to this disrespectful to anyone. I know it's wrong, but I don't regret it. I can't regret fighting for what I want.

He steps away from the car, crosses his arms over his chest, and glares at me as I turn the key in the ignition. We don't even say bye. Instead, I ease off the brake and start rolling down our driveway. I glance in the rearview mirror and find him standing perfectly still. He stays that way until I turn onto the road and can no longer see him.

Having him out of sight cools my temper a little, but not enough to make me change my mind. I have to help Logan, and it's beyond time to follow my own dreams.

No doubts. I need to commit to everything with absolutely no doubts.

"Um . . . on the one hand I'm proud of you for finally telling him," Leah says. "But on the other hand, I think you maybe could've eased into it a little better?"

I blow out a long breath. "I know. I . . . I let my anger get the best of me."

"It was bound to happen sometime. I'm sure he'll come around."

It'd be nice, but I don't see it happening, especially with what I've got planned for tomorrow.

After a mostly silent ride, we make it back to an empty campus around lunchtime. There's not even a real lunch prepared for us—just some sandwiches and bags of chips. We consider going for a hike afterward, but it's cold and drizzling outside, which matches my mood to a tee. We end up heading to the rec hall, where we play a couple of games of pool before settling onto the couches. Leah reads a book; I stare into space, still wondering if I'll be able to leave campus in the morning.

After a few hours, students start to return and fill the rec hall.

It's not until four thirty when the person I want to see comes strolling in. I jump up and rush to his side.

"Alex, can I talk to you for a second?"

"Sure," he replies with a smile. "How was your Thanksgiving?"

"Awful."

"What's wrong?" His face hardens as he studies me.

I motion for him to join me in an adjacent room that's used for various club activities but is empty now.

He closes the door behind himself and then watches me wringing my hands.

"You're making me nervous," he says with a forced laugh.

"I need your help."

"Okay."

I focus on the wood-paneled wall behind him as I try to determine the best way to say what I need to say. I thought I had it worked out from thinking about it for the past twenty-two hours, but now that the time is here, I'm feeling less confident.

"Just spit it out," he says.

"I need to go AWOL tomorrow."

He laughs, a real laugh, obviously thinking I'm joking.

"I'm serious."

His laughter dies on his lips, and then sadness fills his eyes. "It's for him, isn't it?"

I nod.

He shakes his head and presses his mouth into a tight line. After a long pause, he says, "Don't do it. Why would you put a black mark on your permanent record for a guy? That's not you."

I crack my knuckles. "Right now, his entire future is on the line."

"Because of the bad decisions he made. No one forced him to crash into a building or flee the scene of a crime or drive without a license."

My arms drop to my sides. After two months, Alex knows Logan pretty well. I understand he doesn't like him, but he should still have a good idea of what he's capable of. "Other than drive a couple miles with a suspended license to pick up his drunk friend, do you really think he would do any of those things?"

His nose wrinkles, and he looks to the side with disgust. He doesn't want to admit it, but he knows it, too.

"He's innocent," I say. "Your gut has to be telling you that. The only bad decision he made was trying to protect his ex-girlfriend. He's always trying to help his friends, yet there's a good chance he's going to end up in prison for it."

"What?" he asks, surprise now clouding his disdain. "I thought he was getting community service or something?"

I shake my head.

"He doesn't belong in prison."

"Exactly."

He blows out a long breath and massages the back of his neck.

"Come on, Alex. You always stress the importance of teamwork. A member of your battalion desperately needs our help right now. We can't abandon him."

He winces.

"Would you be able to live with yourself if he's sent to prison for years when you might have been able to prevent it?"

He closes his eyes for a long moment. When they finally open, he says, "What do you want from me?"

"I need to go down for the hearing. I'll leave tomorrow morning. Just cover for me as long as you can and then make sure everyone knows I'm safe. I don't want my dad worrying I'm lying dead in a ditch somewhere."

"Why doesn't he just give you permission to leave campus?"

"He doesn't want me going that far by myself."

"He's going to kill me," Alex says, shaking his head and starting to knead his neck again.

"He'll get over it eventually," I assure him. It may take a while, but it won't be nearly as long as with me. He may not speak to me for years.

"I'll keep my phone on me during classes," he finally says, placing his hands on his hips and straightening his spine. "You need to text me every hour so I know you're okay." His steely gaze meets my eyes like they always do when he provides an order to a cadet.

"I will."

"Do you think this will work? Your testimony. Will it convince the judge to be lenient?"

"I sure hope so."

# CHAPTER 31

# PAIGE

**The next morning,** at exactly five past five, I sneak out of bed, grab the bag I packed last night, and head for the door. After Leah fell asleep, I also changed into jeans and a sweater, figuring the less noise I made in the morning, the better.

"Where you going?" Leah asks in a singsongy voice, still lying in bed. So much for being stealthy.

"Nowhere. Pretend you didn't see me," I whisper.

"Okay. Be safe."

"I will."

As I'm about to close the door, I hear her whisper, "Tell Logan I say hi."

Am I that obvious? Apparently so.

I tiptoe down the hallway and ease open the door to the stairwell. After stepping inside, I try to close it without making a sound. I'm not quite successful, and the small thud makes me jump.

"Calm down," I whisper to myself. If I ever want to be part of secret military missions, I need to be able to handle nerves like this. With my heart pounding in my ears, I sneak out to the parking lot, hiding behind trees and shrubs as much as possible, though it's probably not necessary. The only person up right now is the security guard, and I haven't seen his truck yet.

As soon as I reach the pavement of the parking lot, I sprint to my car, quickly unlock the door, throw my bag in the back, and crawl inside. I allow myself two deep breaths to slow my racing heart; then I inch down in my seat so only my eyes are above the window. Then I wait. The guard opens the gates at 5:15 every morning.

Like clockwork, his white truck appears right on time. He frees the padlock, then swings the gates open. I wait until he gets back in his truck and continues following the road behind the boys' dorm before I start up my car and ease out of the parking lot, trying to balance getting out quickly with not making too much noise.

The whole time, my eyes keep darting to the rearview mirror, positive I'll see headlights or an administrator shaking his fist at me, but it never happens. I pass through the gates with no problem. A small wave of relief washes over me, but I know I'm not in the clear yet. Any of the instructors or staff could be coming up this road and spot me. I won't feel safe until I'm in town or, even better, on the highway.

My fingers clench the steering wheel, getting tighter with every hairpin turn down the mountain. I've driven this road hundreds of times and know it like the back of my hand, yet I feel as though I'm seeing it for the first time. Every branch that sways or dead leaf that blows into view has my heart rising into my throat.

"Seriously, pull it together, Paige," I whisper. It's not like someone's waiting in the woods to catch me sneaking off campus.

Just then, a loud beeping sounds from my phone, scaring the crap out of me and sending my heart beating even faster in my chest.

"Oh man," I whisper to myself. "You can't act like this all day."

I'm tempted to look at my phone, but it's too dangerous on this road. Besides, I'm sure it's just Alex.

I take a few more deep breaths as I start to approach town. It's even quieter than normal at this hour, and all the businesses are dark. I pull into one of the empty parking lots and unlock my phone. I have a voice message from Alex. Rather than listen to it, I call him back.

"Did you get out?" he whispers.

"Yeah. I'm in town," I whisper back, though I have no reason to be so quiet.

"Good. Don't forget to text me every hour and let me know where you are."

"I won't."

"Drive carefully."

"I will."

We hang up without saying goodbye, and I realize my nerves are a little more relaxed after talking to him. I turn on my music and switch it to the album Logan loaded on my phone a while back. The strong, fast beat gives me something else to focus on, and soon I'm merging onto the highway with other rural commuters.

Each hour, I stop at a gas station or restaurant or bank and text Alex. I half expect to get a reply from the dean at some point, saying he confiscated Alex's phone, but it doesn't happen by the time I reach Chesapeake.

I'm much earlier than I need to be for the hearing, so I wander around town a bit. It is bigger than Roanoke, but not intimidatingly so. It's not like New York City or even Washington, DC. My dad was being ridiculous.

Around eleven, I stop at a McDonald's for lunch and wonder how I can occupy the next two hours. The beach isn't too far away, which is tempting, but I'm worried I'd lose track of time or get lost and miss the hearing.

In the end, I take my time eating lunch and changing into my dress blues before heading over to the courthouse early. It only takes me a few minutes to pass through security and check the docket for the correct room.

I climb the stairs, turn right, and find the room at the end of the hall. The lights are off inside, so I sit on a bench in front of a window. The view is nice—some government buildings with plenty of greenery beyond and even a river. I alternate my gaze between outside and to the people wandering the halls. It's a mix of four types—professionals in suits, prisoners in orange jumpsuits and handcuffs, unkempt individuals who look like they've been through the roughest of times, and clean and put-together individuals who look like they're going to work in an office park, not facing criminal charges. That'll be Logan. Of course, he truly doesn't belong here. His ex-girlfriend does.

Finally, after thirty-two minutes, people start to file into the courtroom. I stand and follow a woman with blond hair inside. She sits in the first row. I take the second so I can be on the aisle and put my cover on the bench beside me. A woman with a bulging briefcase, thick-framed glasses, and three-inch heels marches in as she barks orders on her phone. I had to leave my phone in the car, so she must be someone important. When she passes through the gate at the front of the room, I realize she's the prosecuting attorney. I know nothing about this woman, but I immediately hate her. The fact that she has the power to ruin Logan's life is enough of a reason.

While I'm focused on her, more people pass through the door, and two of them head to the front of the room.

Mr. Needleham and Logan.

Their heads are close together. Mr. Needleham says something, and Logan nods multiple times. Then he takes a seat and stares straight ahead.

It's been only eight days since I last saw him, but he looks different. Part of it is the dressy civilian clothes, but it goes beyond what he's wearing. He looks older. Tired. Anxious.

Seeing him like this makes my fists curl at my side. I glance around the room, searching for his ex-girlfriend, but I don't know who I'm looking for. If she's here, how can she live with herself, knowing the pain she's causing him?

The woman I followed in slides to the middle of her bench, leans forward, and says, "Hey, honey."

Logan turns around and gives her a small, sad smile. It must be his mom. They talk in hushed whispers for only a few seconds before she sits back and he starts to turn around.

But his eyes land on me. His gaze shifts up to meet my eyes, and I offer him a subdued, half smile. He doesn't return it. He simply twists back around in his chair. I deserve it, but it still hurts. He really may never forgive me for what I did. Even if Mr. Needleham is able to get the case dismissed, Logan may never speak to me again.

That thought causes my anger to morph into something I'm not nearly as familiar with. Really, the only time I've felt something similar was eight years ago, when my mom died. It's an uncomfortable feeling, which makes me uneasy. I'd rather be angry. At least anger I know how to deal with.

With a sigh, I bury my feelings. Being emotional right now will solve nothing. Logan needs me to have a clear head when I take the stand.

His shoulders are back and his spine is straight with his hands folded on the tabletop. It's exactly how I taught him to sit in class months ago. He may not realize it, but I'm certain his posture will earn him a few points with the judge. This is much better than the lazy, slouching Logan I first met.

Over the next five minutes, the number of people entering the room slows and then the bailiff asks us all to rise as the judge enters.

The Honorable Melissa Carrizosa. She's older, probably in her fifties, with graying hair and a friendly face. She reminds me of a young grandmother, not a judge. It immediately makes me feel more at ease. She radiates an air of baking cookies and bandaging scraped knees, not sentencing innocent guys to decades of jail time.

She and the lawyers talk, using legal terms I don't understand. Then she focuses on Logan. "The charges against you are felony hit and run and Class 1 misdemeanor for possession of marijuana. Do you understand these charges?"

"Yes, ma'am."

She nods. "The purpose of today's hearing is to consider and potentially negotiate a plea bargain. Am I correct, Mr. Needleham and Ms. Aronson?"

"Yes, Your Honor," the say in unison.

"Very well. Mr. Needleham, the floor is yours."

"Thank you, Your Honor. The terms Ms. Aronson and I originally discussed were dropping the felony hit and run charges to a Class 1 misdemeanor, punishable by suspension of Mr. Evans's driver's license for one year, six months of community service, a thousand-dollar fine, and finishing his high school education at a military boarding school."

"Are these the terms you're still seeking?"

Mr. Needleham leans down and whispers something in Logan's ear. Logan rotates in his seat, scans the benches behind us, focuses on a blond girl with too much makeup in the row behind me, and seems to share unspoken words with her. After a few seconds, he turns back around and nods to his lawyer.

"Yes, Your Honor," he replies with a sigh.

"Ms. Aronson, are these terms agreeable to you?"

The prosecutor is scanning a print out, marked with yellow highlights. She holds up a finger, flips the page, continues reading, then says, "No, they are not. Mr. Evans has gotten himself into more trouble. Two weeks ago, he was found by the dean of his boarding school while driving with a suspended license."

My stomach instantly tightens up. It feels like before Thanksgiving all over again.

"Actually, Your Honor," Mr. Needleham says, "he was not found. No one witnessed this alleged behavior."

"He admitted to it!"

"Will you be filing a formal charge?"

She huffs. "No, of course not. Law enforcement was not involved in the incident, but it does show how nothing has changed during his time at Wallingford."

"Do you have alternative terms to offer?" the judge asks the prosecutor.

"Six months incarceration and a twenty-five-hundred-dollar fine."

"That's excessive!" Mr. Needleham says. "Mr. Evans has no prior record. He's still in high school. He needs to graduate, not be locked up!"

"He's eighteen. He understood the severity of his original offense, yet he committed another major driving violation. I believe it's in society's best interest to ensure he's kept off the roads over the next six months."

"Allegedly committed," Mr. Needleham says, raising a finger. "Your Honor, may I call a witness to the stand?"

"We're not at trial," Ms. Aronson says, lowering her glasses as she focuses on Mr. Needleham.

"Given the terms you're proposing, I have a few witnesses the court needs to hear from. They will attest to what is in *society's* best interest."

"We don't have all day," the judge says. "I'll give you ten minutes."

Looking at his watch, he nods and stands. "Ms. Durant, please come forward."

Finally. I've been looking forward to this moment for four days.

I walk through the gate, and the judge motions for me to take the chair to her left. A woman who has been sitting next to the judge hands me a Bible and asks me to put my left hand on it while she swears me in.

"You may be seated," the judge says with a warm smile when I'm done.

"Please state your name and relationship to Mr. Evans for the court," Mr. Needleham says.

"Paige Durant. I'm Mr. Evans's peer mentor at Wallingford Academy."

"What is a peer mentor?"

"I served as a positive role model and helped him learn the rules of Wallingford."

"How would you say he performed at Wallingford Academy?"

"Exceptionally well. It's a very strict school, and those who are not there by choice often struggle. From an academic perspective, Mr. Evans shined from day one."

"Would you say you saw changes in his personality while he was there?"

"Yes, sir. Initially, he was argumentative and lacked motivation. In a matter of weeks, he began to respect authority and set goals for himself, including deciding to run a half marathon in April. And he's been tutoring a sophomore in algebra. That student's grade has gone from a C to an A-minus. He also joined the Wallingford jazz band. He's an amazing guitar player. And he was volunteering at local charities for two hours every Saturday."

"Do you feel he's a risk to society?"

"No, sir."

"Wh—"

He's interrupted by the door swinging opening. It draws everyone's attention to the back of the room where Alex marches in.

I blink my eyes a couple of times, sure I'm hallucinating.

But no matter how many times I blink, Alex is still there, looking deadly serious and commanding as usual in his uniform.

I stand at attention.

Then Noah enters. And Leah. And Richard. And Jason. And Sydney. Soon, the room is overflowing with Wallingford uniforms. The last person to walk through the door is the dean. They all take a seat in the back row.

"What's going on?" the judge says as her eyes drift over at least a third of the Alpha Battalion.

Alex stands. "We learned one of our cadets was being treated unfairly and felt we needed to set the record straight."

"Mr. Needleham," she says, "surely you don't plan on calling each of these students up as a witness?"

"No, Your Honor, but I thought the court should understand how well-respected Mr. Evans is at Wallingford Academy. This is a world-renowned boarding school where over half of the students go on to attend prestigious universities. Not one of these students believes Mr. Evans is a risk to society."

She nods. "Very well. Do you have any further questions for the current witness?"

"No, Your Honor."

"Ms. Aronson, would you like to cross-examine the witness?"

She shakes her head.

"You may step down," she says to me with her grandmother smile again.

I return to my seat, wishing I could have said more about Logan. I've been thinking about my testimony for the past four days. I had example after example prepared to show how well he's been doing, but then again, having a large contingent of his battalion show up on his behalf may be equally persuasive.

I still can't believe Alex. I look in his direction and smile at him. He gives me a subtle nod. When push came to shove, he did the right thing, even more than I was hoping for. This, right here, is my best friend Alex, not the guy from the last few months.

"With all due respect," Ms. Aronson says, "I appreciate what you're trying here, but I have serious reservations about letting Mr. Evans off so easily after what he did two weeks ago. No one is denying he drove with a suspended license, are they?" She looks to the sea of Wallingford uniforms, but each cadet remains still. We can't deny what he's already admitted.

"I'd be willing to drop it to ninety days of jail time after graduation," she continues. "Along with the twenty-five-hundred-dollar fine."

I can't believe it. Even after everything I've done, and Alex has done, it still might not be enough.

Mr. Needleham checks his watch once more before whispering something in Logan's ear. Logan stares straight ahead for a moment before slowly nodding. Mr. Needleham says, "May I call one more witness to the stand?"

The judge reluctantly agrees, and then Lora Mitchell shuffles her way to the seat I was just occupying. It's the blond girl Logan focused on a few minutes ago. My earlier hatred for the prosecutor pales in comparison to what I'm feeling right now. Lora needs to fix this. She's the only one who can.

She keeps her eyes down the entire way, even while being sworn in.

"Please state your name for the court."

"Lora Mitchell," she whispers.

"A little louder, please."

She clears her throat and repeats herself.

"What's your relationship to Mr. Evans?"

"F-friend."

"What about at the time of the accident? What was your relationship then?"

"Girlfriend."

"In all the time you've known Mr. Evans, had he ever gotten into a car accident before the night in question?"

She shakes her head.

"Had he ever used marijuana?"

She shakes her head again.

"You must have been surprised when you heard of the accident, then."

She nods.

"What was your first thought after you heard?"

"I—I hoped everyone was okay."

My Needleham fiddles with his watch as he glances toward the door. After a moment, he says, "When did he tell you about the accident? That night? The next day?"

"Um . . . I'm not sure. That night, I think."

"How did he tell you? In person? Phone call? Text?"

"Um . . . t—actually in person, I think."

"Do you remember what time it was?"

She gulps and licks her lips. "It was late. Maybe three or four in the morning."

"Okay, I'm just trying to get the timeline straight," he says slowly. "The accident occurred at eleven thirty-four. His abandoned car was found at"—he checks a piece of paper in his hands—"eleven fifty-two. At twelve ten, police went to his home, but he wasn't there. At two thirty, he returned home and was arrested. Then you're claiming h—"

"Is there a point to this?" the judge asks.

"Yes, I—"

Just then, the door opens again and a younger man in a suit along with a sweaty teenager in ripped jeans and a hooded sweatshirt rush through. The man is holding a small manila envelope.

"What now?" the judge asks as they go straight to Mr. Needleham.

"Give me one more minute, please," he says with a smile.

The two newcomers huddle around Mr. Needleham and Logan. The teenager is animated and whatever he says causes Logan's whole body to relax.

The guy in a suit sits next to Mr. Needleham while the teenager comes back to the benches. He squeezes past me and practically plops himself on my cover. I glare at him as I draw it onto my lap.

He says, "I can't believe you're here, Paige. I'll bet you ten bucks he's already forgiven you."

I give him another glare. It's not appropriate to be talking in a courtroom. Plus, how does he know who I am? But does he really think Logan's forgiven me? He won't hate me forever? I want to ask him about it, but I bite my tongue. I will not be as disrespectful as he is.

"I have no further questions for the witness," Mr. Needleham says.

"Ms. Aronson?" the judge asks.

She shakes her head.

As soon as Lora clears the gate, Mr. Needleham holds up the manila envelope. "I'm sorry for the intrusion, Your Honor, but this envelope contains exculpatory evidence for Mr. Evans. It clearly proves he could not have been the driver of his vehicle at the time of the accident."

Ms. Aronson throws her hands up. "He confessed!"

"He was coerced."

"In my chambers, both of you."

The lawyers stand and follow the judge through a door at the back of the courtroom. It's initially silent; then everyone starts murmuring at once.

"What's in the envelope?" I ask the guy next to me.

"A flash drive showing my live stream of *Overwatch* the night of the accident. I focused the webcam on Logan a few times. The ladies like when I include him. Anyway, it shows him playing both right before and after the time of the accident."

"What's *Overwatch*?"

His mouth drops open. "Do you live in a cave or something? *Overwatch* is only the best hero shooter game out there."

"A video game?"

"Yeah.

"You're serious?"

"Yeah. Why?"

It's truly laughable. Video games, the biggest waste of time there is, might save him? It almost makes me think I should reconsider my stance on video games. Almost.

"I'm Paige," I say, holding out my hand. He stares at me like I've lost my mind.

"Yeah, I know."

This guy has got the manners of a cockroach. "And you are?"

"Gordy."

Oh. "Logan's best friend," I say.

"Yeah. So I know *all* about you. He gave met the full rundown on our way back from Wallingford. You need to loosen up."

"You need to gain some manners," I mutter.

With a grin, he says, "We're going to get along great." Then he puts his sweaty arm over my shoulder. A perfectly placed squeeze at his elbow makes him rethink his decision. He winces, then laughs. "You'll be a lot more fun to have around than Lora."

# CHAPTER 32

## LOGAN

**Five minutes.**

They've already been in the judge's chambers for five freaking minutes. What's taking them so long? Mr. Needleham said the evidence was foolproof. If it were foolproof, wouldn't they be done already?

I stare at the tabletop, wringing my hands together. Every couple of minutes, I have to wipe my sweaty palms on my khakis.

I'm still shocked Mr. Needleham was able to find evidence. Apparently a junior lawyer from his firm worked with Gordy to get video footage from Twitch, the online streaming service Gordy is convinced is his path to fame. I'm not sure who came up with the idea—Mr. Needleham, the junior lawyer, or Gordy—but I'm impressed. It never crossed my mind.

Still, I wasn't going to use the evidence if I got a good plea bargain. As long as my punishment was limited to something reasonable, I was willing to continue covering for Lora. Jail, not so much. She's going to kill me. I glance behind me, and she looks even more nervous than I feel.

I quickly rise from my seat and join her on the bench.

"Hey," I whisper, then bite my lip.

There's wetness in the corner of her eyes, and a single tear drips down her cheek. I wipe it away for her. "I'm sorry," I say. "I tried to help you, I did. But I can't go to jail."

She nods. "I know."

"If anyone asks, I'll tell them I let you borrow my car, but I don't know what happened. You can make up whatever story you want."

She nods again.

"It might not turn out so bad."

Another tear rolls down her cheek.

Just then, the door at the front of the room opens. "I'm sorry, Lora," I say before hugging her and quickly taking my place again.

The lawyers and judge sit down. Mr. Needleham gives me a subtle thumbs-up as the judge says, "Mr. Evans, we have just been shown evidence proving you could not have been driving your car at the time of the accident. As a result, the commonwealth's attorney's office has no choice but to dismiss all charges against you."

My mom sobs behind me, and I'm on the verge of doing the same. It's over. It's finally over.

I don't think I fully realized the amount of stress I was under until just this moment. With one big sigh, my muscles relax, my head stops throbbing, and my anger at the world fades away.

"Next time, if I were you," the judge continues, "I'd think twice before confessing to a crime you did not commit."

"Yes, ma'am. I won't do it again." There's no way in hell I'd do it again. In fact, I may never let anyone borrow my car again. Or anything else that could potentially cause some sort of damage.

After she dismisses everyone, I stand and give Mr. Needleham a hug.

I owe him. If it hadn't been for him pushing me on the coercion, things would've turned out much different. "Thank you," I say. "I'm glad you looked for evidence, even though I wasn't sure what I wanted."

"You need to thank Ms. Durant. She's the one who provided the lead."

"Paige?"

He nods, and I turn to watch her.

She's talking to Gordy. He's all smiles and laughs while she's got her typical attitude. For some reason, her frown makes me smile.

I start to head in her direction when the door slams open, and Mr. Durant, red-faced, storms into the room. That's enough to make me take two steps backward to hide behind Mr. Needleham. I don't know what happened, but I have a feeling Mr. Durant was not on board with Paige coming here.

Peeking around Mr. Needleham's shoulder, I see Paige spot her dad. She jumps to her feet, rushes to him, grabs his elbow, and pulls him through the door. What I wouldn't give to be a fly on the wall of the hallway right now.

Gordy looks at me and mouths, "Wow."

I nod and race to the door. Sticking just my head out, I try to listen to what is probably World War III based on their matching glares. But it's silent—eerily silent, as if every single person in the hallway zipped their lips the minute they saw the pissed-off Navy SEAL and his equally pissed-off daughter pass by them.

"Want me to see what happens?" Gordy asks.

I nod as my mom and dad surround Mr. Needleham. "Yeah, I've got to finish up things here." When I join them, my dad tries to give me a hug but settles for the "hey" I offer. It's more than he usually gets, probably because my life is in the best place it's been in months.

"This calls for a celebration," my mom says, hugging me.

"Dinner?" my dad asks.

Despite being over-the-moon thrilled with what the last five minutes mean to my life, I still give him the evil eye. The three of us haven't had dinner together in over four years.

Before I can answer him, I see all the cadets start to file out to the hallway. "Actually," I say, "dinner sounds good *if* I can bring a few friends."

"Of course!" my dad says, beaming. He probably thinks this whole ordeal has brought us closer. It hasn't. By now he should realize I'll never forgive him, although I do, begrudgingly, appreciate him showing up today.

"How about GameWorks?" I ask. It's an awesome restaurant/arcade we used to go to a lot. My battalion will love it.

In my mom's car, I try calling Paige, but it goes straight to voice mail. Gordy never found her and her dad, so they must have made a quick exit. I try texting her, too. *We need to talk. Can you come to dinner at Gameworks?*

She doesn't reply by the time we make it there. The Wallingford bus is already in the parking lot, so I'm hopeful she and her dad have finished their fight and she's inside. Unfortunately, it doesn't take long to realize she's not.

"Do you know where Paige is?" I ask Jernigan as we shoot baskets side by side. I'm up by two, not that I'm keeping score or anything.

"She had to go back to school for suspension. Plus, her dad will ground her for months or years. I have a feeling her dreams of the Air Force Academy may be over."

"Wait, what?" I ask, placing the ball on my hip and facing him. There's no way she put herself at such risk to help me. She wouldn't do it. Never in a million years.

"She went AWOL."

"Everyone went AWOL for me?"

"No, only her. After she told me what she was doing, I figured you could use a little more help, so I told the dean what was going on and he got permission for a bunch of us to come down here. She should've waited, but . . . well, love makes you do stupid shit," he says.

He makes a basket, and I quickly face forward and start shooting again. "Sorry for being an asshole," he says.

"Me too. Thanks for . . . you know."

"Yeah."

That's the extent of our conversation and all we will probably ever say about our contentious past. It's enough. Guy relationships are a hell of a lot easier than girlfriend relationships.

# CHAPTER 33

## PAIGE

**In about three minutes**, I'll have to face my dad. He wouldn't talk to me at the courthouse, other than order me to drive straight to school. He's been following me the whole way, and I'm sure his silent treatment will end as soon as we park. Then I'm in for the reaming of my life.

After today, there's no way he'll let me move all the way to Colorado. I destroyed seventeen and a half years of trust in a matter of hours. He may not even let me go to the Naval Academy. I may have to go to Roanoke College so I can live at home and he can always keep an eye on me.

I won't let that happen.

I made the best decision I could given the difficult situation *he* put me in. If he doesn't like the outcome, he needs to consider how he could have handled the situation better. As horrible as it will be, I need to tell him. He needs to understand he can't continue to control my life.

After parking my car, I take a deep breath and slowly look through the window at my dad, who's sitting in his SUV right next to me. He motions with his hand for me to join him.

This is it. The epic showdown that was bound to happen eventually.

If my mom were here right now, she'd give me a big hug and smile, before shoving me out the door to finally put him in his place. She was always good at finding some choice words for him that would leave him hanging his head and mumbling an apology. I need to draw on my memory of her now. I need to find the strength she always had.

With another determined deep breath, I ease open the door and march to his vehicle. Sliding inside, I keep my eyes straight ahead and fight the urge to crack my knuckles. I can't show any sign of weakness.

"I've never been more scared than I was this morning," he says in a soft voice I'm not used to hearing. "Not during SEAL training, not even in enemy territory. Do you have any idea what it's like to not know where your daughter is and if she's dead or alive?"

"No, sir," I say, "but Alex was supposed to tell you I was okay."

"Hearing from someone who's covering for you is not the same as hearing from you."

"I understand, but—"

"You are never to pull something like this again. Do you understand?"

"Yes, sir." Crap. He cut me off and got the upper hand again. I can't keep letting him do this. I need to stand up for myself. "You gave me no other option. I had to do the right thing and was willing to face the consequences of my actions," I say quickly so he can't interrupt.

"He means a lot to you, huh?"

"What? Who?" I ask, slowly turning my head toward him. He's staring at the steering wheel where his hands are resting casually. I'd expect them to be gripping it with white knuckles, but he doesn't appear angry at all. He seems . . . sad.

"Evans. You like him. Love him?" he asks, meeting my eyes.

"Oh, um . . . yes, I guess so. Like. I—I don't know about love,"

I say, my cheeks heating up. How did we get here? We're supposed to be talking about my future at the Air Force Academy, not my relationship with Logan. "Love's a strong word," I add. And not something I've given any thought to. Can you love someone after only a few months?

"I'm sorry I didn't see it earlier. I should've been more . . . open during our discussion at lunch."

My jaw drops. He's never admitted he's been wrong to me. My mom, yes. Me, no. This is what I wanted, but I guess, deep down, I didn't expect it.

With a chuckle, he adds, "I know, I know." He rubs his palm down his face. "You're getting older and I'm not adjusting well, okay? I'm used to my little girl who needs me to tell her what to do. Not"—he waves his hand in my direction—"a practically grown woman who is capable of making her own decisions. I don't like it."

"I'm sorry," I say automatically, and then want to kick myself. I have nothing to apologize for.

He chuckles again and, as if reading my mind, says, "I'm the one who needs to apologize. Even though I don't like it, I've got to let you go. I've got to trust I've given you everything you need to make the right decisions."

"You have."

He nods again and sighs. "So, Air Force Academy?"

"Yes, sir."

"Colorado Springs is a long ways from here."

"I know. I'm s—" I'm about to say "sorry" again, but I catch myself this time. "It's only four years. I'll request a base closer to home once I'm done. And I'll email every day. And call every weekend. And come home every break. And maybe you can come visit once a month?"

"I'd like that."

We both stare straight ahead again, at the stone archway leading to the quad, as my muscles relax and the stress from the last few days escapes little by little with my even breaths.

Logan's life is back to normal. My dad has forgiven me for what I've done and accepted my plan for the future. The only thing that would make this day even better is if Logan and I could return to the way things were, but I'll take what I can get. This is still pretty good.

"Thank you," I say, reaching over and wrapping my arms around my dad's shoulders.

He kisses the top of my head. "You'll be a damn good Air Force pilot."

# CHAPTER 34
# LOGAN

**Over the next** few days, I obsess over what to say to Paige. I write and rewrite text after text. At least I know she won't get it until the weekend anyway, so I have plenty of time to perfect it.

In the end, I go with something simple: *Thanks. Jernigan told me what you did. I know how hard it had to be for you. I appreciate it and hope all your dreams don't fall through. You deserve to be a pilot. Would love to stay in touch, if you want to.*

Not even a minute after sending it, my phone rings. One look at the caller ID and my heart thumps a little faster.

"I thought you'd text me," I say.

"I hate texting."

"Good to know."

"Do you plan on communicating a lot?" she asks.

"Yeah. Someone's got to make sure you don't revert back to your old stickler ways."

"I've already reverted back."

"Noooooo! Seriously?"

"Yeah, I had to."

"Why?"

"My dad. I need to prove to him he can trust me again. He came around on everything, and I don't want him to regret it."

"That's good."

"Yeah."

"Thanks, by the way."

"You're welcome."

"And sorry I got so angry with you. I never should've blamed you for everything. That wasn't fair."

"It's okay. We both could've done things differently."

"Yeah."

"Logan, honey," my mom yells from downstairs, "lunch is ready."

"Sorry, I gotta go," I say to Paige. "Can we talk tomorrow? Or tonight? Or in like twenty minutes?"

She laughs. "Yeah, I'd like that."

"Which one?"

"All of them."


"We really need to consider getting a winter drink," I say, lowering my Swirly's root beer float to the boardwalk. Even with gloves, my fingers are turning into icicles.

"I thought Wallingford was supposed to make you stronger," Gordy says, holding his cup with his bare hands. "You can't handle a little cold? What a wuss."

"You've got like thirty pounds of insulation on me."

He and Nate both laugh. Before Wallingford, this would've been great. Me and my best friends hanging out on the boardwalk and messing with each other. Now something feels missing. Yes, one missing piece is Paige, but she's not all.

School is boring and annoying with all the troublemaking pricks constantly causing a scene. And my days seem to drag on and on. I used to be able to sit my ass on the couch and not move for eight hours. Now I grow fidgety after thirty minutes.

Nate and Gordy think I've lost it, I'm sure. I still hang out with them, but I end up doing lunges in the back of Gordy's basement or going out for a ten-mile run or researching colleges or playing the guitar while they're virtually chasing each other around digital mazes.

It's . . . not what I expected. The whole time I was at Wallingford, I just wanted to get back to this. Now that I'm back, I'm not exactly loving it like I thought I would.

"How's Paige doing?" Nate asks.

"Good. She decided she needs to add even more extracurricular activities, so she joined the drill team, which takes up whatever little free time she used to have."

"Is she ever going to come visit us?" he asks.

"I don't know."

Honestly, I haven't invited her. I'd love to see her, but it'd be weird outside of Wallingford. Not to mention, it'd probably cause an argument between her and her dad. She said they've come to some sort of agreement, but I find it hard to believe that agreement would include driving five hours to stay at a boy's house. We do have a guest room, but still.

"Oh," Nate says, lightly punching me in the shoulder. "Did you hear about Lora? Her dad offered to build a new vet clinic for the place she crashed into and suddenly most of her legal troubles disappeared."

"Really?"

"That's what my brother said." His brother is dating a girl who started working at the clinic a few months ago, so she's probably heard rumors.

Gordy shakes his head. "They could've done that back in September and saved you from all the shit—the hearings, Wallingford. If I were you, I'd let her have it. Maybe her dad will throw a few bucks your way," he says, rocking his shoulder into me.

"You know, it wasn't so bad. I actually think it might have been . . . good for me." It's true. It was the kick in the pants I needed. I won't tell Nate and Gordy this because they might think I'm insulting them, but my life was headed nowhere. Maybe I would've been content having a job that put a roof over my head and food in my stomach, like I told Paige, but who wants to only be content? I want to be happy. More than happy. I want to be excited about my future.

"Uh-oh," Nate says. "Sounds like someone's getting nostalgic."

I chuckle and try to play it off like he's being ridiculous, but he's right. I am feeling a little nostalgic for Wallingford.

What in the hell has gotten into me?

# CHAPTER 35

# PAIGE

**My head bobs** along with the music as I half-heartedly read ahead for my Intro to Business class. It's Sunday evening, which means Logan should be calling soon. He mentioned he had to do something with his mom, so it might be a little later than usual, but he promised we'd talk before lights-out.

This has become our routine—talking Saturday afternoon as soon as my personal time starts and again Sunday evening after yearbook and before my phone gets locked up for the week. In between those times, we exchange numerous texts. In general, I hate texting, but it's different with him. A lot of things are different with him.

Still, talking and texting are not as good as having him here, but I am grateful we've continued to keep in touch over the past six weeks. And he's still doing the half marathon, which means I'll get to see him in April.

My phone finally lights up and vibrates against my desk.

"It's about time," I say after answering it. "I was starting to worry."

"You must really like me, then."

"Hmm . . . maybe a little," I reply with a grin. "How'd your thing with your mom go?" He was vague when he told me about it, so I have no idea what it was or even if it was a thing for him or her.

"Good. Did you know there's a supermoon tonight?"

"What's a supermoon?"

"A big moon."

"The moon is always the same size."

"Well, duh. It just looks bigger because it's closer to the Earth. Go to your window and look outside. It's pretty cool."

I stand up and push my curtains aside. The moon is full and bright but doesn't necessarily look bigger to me. "I don't see it," I reply. "It's pretty but not excessively large. Maybe it's different here compared to Chesapeake."

"No, I'm definitely seeing the same moon as you. Take another look."

"I am. It looks like every other full moon."

"It's brighter, right?"

"I don't know . . . maybe."

"Does it light up the quad more than usual?"

I scan the grassy area between the two dorms that's covered in a light coat of snow. It's still dark other than where the lights illuminate the pathways. "Not really," I reply.

"Oh my God. You're killing me, Paige."

Why is he acting so bizarre? He's never shown any interest in astronomy before, but this is critical to him for some reason? "Fine. It's huge and bright. Happy?"

"No. Really look at the quad."

"I am. It's the same as always."

"Tell me what you see."

He must either miss this place or is starting to lose his mind. "It's dark other than the areas lit up by the overhead lights. A few people are walking around with backpacks. Someone's trying to make a snow angel, but there's not nearly enough snow. A guy is tossing a snowball at her. I think they're flirting. He might like her."

"Really? Who are they?"

"Um," I squint, "Jillian and Justin, maybe. They're far away, so I'm not positive."

"Okay, not the point anyway. Look closer to you."

My eyes drift downward to scan the sidewalk directly beneath my dorm. There, under the light, is a crazy man waving his hands overhead with a large duffel bag at his feet. My heart momentarily stops and then starts beating a mile a minute.

"Paige?"

I sprint out of my room and down the stairs.

"Paige, you there?"

I fling open the door and stand on the steps as our eyes lock and my heart now threatens to beat out of my chest.

"I see the best-looking cadet to ever walk the halls of Wallingford," I whisper, still holding the phone to my ear.

"That's not possible, because I'm staring at the best-looking cadet," he replies with a grin. He's wearing civilian clothes, and his hair has grown out significantly. It now hangs over his forehead a bit.

"Are you just going to stand there?"

I'm not sure I could move even if I wanted to. Shock and amazement have my feet firmly planted to the cement. "I'm taking it all in," I say to buy myself a little time.

"The supermoon is pretty awesome, right?"

"No."

He laughs and closes the distance between us so I don't have to. After disconnecting our call, he pockets his phone and says, "I'm back." When he steps directly in front of me, he reaches for my hand and gives it a squeeze.

"For good?"

He nods. "Until graduation."

"Why?" He made it clear time and time again Wallingford was not for him. What happened in the last six weeks to change his mind? And why didn't he tell me he was considering it? We talked every weekend so there were plenty of opportunities. Unless this was a recent, spur-of-the-moment decision.

"Turns out life on the outside wasn't quite as good as I remembered."

I chuckle at his realization. It's the same one I had after my freshman year. "Video games and TV and going to the mall didn't cut it anymore?"

He shakes his head. "Weird, right? Plus, I found myself waking up at six A.M., waiting for the damn bugle, and being strangely disappointed by the silence."

"It does have a pretty sound."

He nods. "I used to be able to sleep twelve hours a day, no problem. Now my body forces me out of bed after eight, but I had nothing to do at home. I'd end up jogging around my neighborhood for hours just to kill time."

"And to think you used to hate running."

"I know! Wallingford has ruined lazy Logan," he says, shaking his head, trying to look disgusted with himself, but the glint in his eye reveals pride, not loathing.

I smile, happy to see him embrace his motivated, eager, and industrious side again. Based on what he's told me, I know this is the real Logan despite years of him suppressing it. It's a shame he let his dad affect him like he did.

"I also might have missed a few of the people," he continues.

"Alex?" I ask.

He rolls his eyes. "No, definitely not. Maybe a certain lieutenant commander, though. And her roommate. And Noah. And some of the teachers. It's funny how you don't appreciate what you have until it's gone."

"I appreciated what I had," I say with a frown. He should never think I took him for granted.

"That's not what I meant. Don't get me wrong—I appreciated you. I was thinking more about the classes here and how they're small and the teachers take an interest in each of the students. It used to seem intrusive, but . . ."

"Now you realize they really want us to succeed?"

He nods. "Yeah. It's like we're all in this together."

"All for one, one for all."

"Exactly. I've always had that with Gordy and Nate, but not everyone in my school, including the adults. It's kind of . . . nice."

"Did you just call Wallingford nice?"

He makes an exaggerated gagging gesture. "I can't believe it myself. Apparently, structure and order and rules are actually good for me."

I want to engulf him in a hug, but I can't. "You have no idea how happy you've made me tonight. I . . . I still can't believe it. If I could, I'd hug you."

He smiles and passes me a note. "Luckily, I came prepared." He reaches into his pocket and pulls out a small piece of folded paper. It's a virtual kiss. I accept it from him and smile. "So I take it you want to try the girlfriend-boyfriend thing?" he says.

He can't be serious. I was ready to call him my boyfriend after our first kiss. "Was there any doubt?"

He shrugs. "I don't know. Maybe you finally gave Jernigan the time of day with me out of the picture."

I wrinkle my nose and say, "No."

"Or maybe your dad has forbidden you from dating me."

"No."

"Or maybe you figure there's no sense with graduation looming." He's wearing a casual expression, but it doesn't hide the seriousness underneath. I understand this concern. What's the point of five months together only to end up thousands of miles apart?

To enjoy life. That's the reason. And it's a very good reason.

"We can't predict what's ahead," I say. "Let's enjoy the now and deal with the future when it comes."

"You sound wise beyond your years."

"Or like a teenager with a bad case of the jumblies," I say, checking my watch. We still have thirty minutes until we have to be back on campus. "Come on." I grab his hand and lead him across the quad, down the path to the parking lot, and through the gates. We don't stop running until we're standing on the grassy patch in front of the Wallingford sign just off campus. Tiny snowflakes land on our hair and clothes. I engulf him in a hug and press my lips against his. He squeezes me tight.

After a moment, I say, "I see us running this path many, many times."

"You know, I'm realizing I just might be willing to run to the ends of the Earth for you."

Smiling against his lips, I reply, "The Earth is round; there is no end."

"It's figurative. I'd run forever for you."

My smile grows even larger. "That's sweet."

"Yeah, every now and again my romantic side likes to make an appearance."

I take a step back and stare deep into his eyes. "I know I'm not romantic or great with words, but I feel very fortunate to have met you. You've taught me how to relax. You've given me the strength to fight for what I want. You've . . ."

"Removed the stick from your ass?"

I playfully smack his arm, but I don't disagree, even though it wasn't a stick, more like a small twig.

"I love you, Lieutenant Commander Durant," he says. "Sticks and all."

I've never been in love before, but there's no doubt in my mind about what I'm feeling right now. He makes me happy by simply standing next to me. He brings out a playful side of me I didn't know existed. And he supports me in all my dreams, even when it may mean never seeing each other again.

It reminds me of my mom and dad when I was young. Sure, they argued occasionally, but they were always there for each other. No matter what. I know Logan will always be here for me, and I hope he feels the same now. After everything we've gone through, he has to realize I'd do anything for him.

"I love you, too."

It's short and sweet and to the point. No need to be flowery when simple will do. I love him. He loves me. And despite Wallingford's aversion to love and the couples before us who have failed, there's no doubt in my mind we'll make it work.

After all, failure is never an option.

# ACKNOWLEDGMENTS

This book would not have been possible without my military family and friends who answered all my questions, from the ridiculously basic to the most complex. Thank you to my dad, Floyd (Marines); father-in-law, Dick (Army); family friend Pete (Navy); and fellow MWADVM Deborah.

I also greatly appreciate the guidance I received from Jason, Chris, and Pat on the legal aspects within this book.

And, of course, I cannot forget the friends and colleagues who helped me iron out all the kinks, especially with Paige's story. Thanks to my beta readers Melissa, Stacy, Kristin, Amanda, Nathalie, Jennifer, Catherine, Jillian, and Rachel; my editors Kat and Lauren; and my indispensable brainstorming buddy Sara.

Finally, a very special thank-you goes out to Melissa for coming up with the title *Risking It All*!